VOICE OF VIRACOCHA

TETRASPHERE - BOOK 3

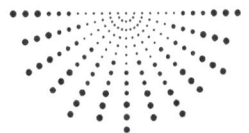

P.T.L. PERRIN

VOICE OF VIRACOCHA

TetraSphere
Book Three

P.T.L. Perrin

Voice of Viracocha – Tetrasphere Book Three

By P.T.L. Perrin

Cover by: Ewald Sutter, Azar, Trostberg, Germany

Cover Photos: Sky: © William Moss | Dreamstime.com

Background: © Pavalache Stelian | Dreamstime.com

Edited by Lydia Moore and Mary Vallale

Copyright © 2017 by Patricia T.L. Perrin

Published in the United States of America

Worldwide Electronic & Digital Rights

Worldwide English Language Print Rights

Print ISBN-13: 978-1-950940-05-9

SeaQuill Press

Jupiter, FL 33458

❀ Formatted with Vellum

For my family and friends, whose enthusiastic support uplifts me and whose dynamic and varied personalities inspire me, and for my Creator, who so graciously gives me ideas and helps me explore them.

VOICE OF VIRACOCHA

~

"He takes one look at earth and triggers an earthquake, points a finger at the mountains, and volcanoes erupt." Psalm 104:32 (The Message)

~

"Earth wobbled and lurched; the very heavens shook like leaves, quaked like aspen leaves because of his rage. His nostrils flared, billowing smoke; his mouth spit fire." 2 Samuel 22:8-9 (The Message)

~

"Tongues of fire dart in and out; he lowers the sky. He steps down; under his feet an abyss opens up. He's riding a winged creature, swift on wind-wings." Psalm 18: 8b-10 (The Message)

1
JEWEL AMARYLLIS ADAMS

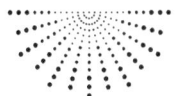

The problem with the ancient Cherokee prophecy isn't that it foretold my friends and I were chosen to save the world. No. The problem is, it didn't predict whether we'd succeed or not.

What if we fail? What if two planets die and it's our fault?

My eyes follow a shaft of moonlight creeping across the ceiling, casting soft rainbows, each one an endless blend of subtle hues. Even the return of my enhanced vision doesn't soothe the jumbled nerves tying knots in my gut. I can't shake the idea something is terribly wrong. It's been with me, a constant gnawing presence, since we returned from the Bahamas.

A strange vibration in the bed quickly grows into a ground-shaking earthquake, rattling the pictures on the wall. I hold tightly to the bed frame with one hand while I reach out to save the lamp on my nightstand from crashing to the floor. It isn't as strong as the earthquakes last fall, caused by Dracans digging tunnels, but someone will undoubtedly report it.

The Dracans have kept their promise. They've returned the artifact and sealed the passageway. It should give me some measure of peace. It doesn't. I watch the light for a while longer, then get up and dress to greet the dawn, grabbing my favorite blanket on the way out.

~

SPRING COMES EARLY in the North Carolina mountains. It's only the beginning of March and already warming up. I sit on the porch swing, wrap my blanket around me and glance up at two alien discs reflecting the colors of the rising sun. Allaran ships. Invisible to everyone else, they're a common sight to me, the only human who can see through their cloaking ability. Before I met my three friends, I only saw one and called it my Sentinel. As a child I thought it was my guardian angel. Not anymore. Now I know we each have one assigned to us, and the aliens occupying them are not angels.

The Allarans have as much to lose as we do if we fail. More. They'll lose our planet and theirs, too. The wormholes they created to travel between the planets have formed a permanent connection, giving Terran artifacts a direct link to the ones on Allara. The artifacts, tetra-hedron in shape, act as planetary organs, keeping it in balance. If ours die, so will theirs. You'd think they'd be more helpful.

I turn away to watch two does and their tiny fawns at the edge of the forest, each one outlined by bright light in the early morning dark. One fawn frantically butts his mother's tummy then stills as he nurses. The other stays close to her mother, investigating the busy forest floor nearby. Although I can't tell their gender from here, my imagination takes over and gives them identity.

"The Dracans returned the artifact this morning. Did you feel the quake?" My best friend Sky pushes the door open with her hip, care-fully holding a mug of steaming coffee in each hand. She settles next to me on the porch swing and hands me one, prepared just the way I like it, with cream and plenty of sugar.

"Is it glad to be back home?" It's still chilly out and she isn't wearing a jacket, so I offer to share my blanket.

"Very much," she answers, pulling her corner over her shoulders. "I felt its joy before they closed the tunnel." We discovered the artifacts are sentient when we fixed this one last fall.

"Sky, do you think we'll find them all?"

"I wish I knew," she replies, taking a sip of her coffee. "While you were living it up in Atlantis with your Dracan friends," she teases, "and the rest of us frantically searched for you, we all wondered what would happen if we fail. Will we end our planet? Would it be our fault? Anyone could break under that weight of responsibility. The stress is getting to all of us." The concern in her eyes is something I've seen far too often lately.

I jab her with my elbow, and she yelps when hot coffee sloshes out of her mug. I'd been abducted by the reptilian Dracans, imprisoned, half-blinded when they blocked my ability, and was cut off from communicating with my friends and family. Their frantic search included diving the stunning barrier reef and exploring underwater caverns. Most importantly, they had each other and could use their gifts freely.

Not that living with the Dracans was awful. I learned to care deeply for them and their hybrids, especially Marla Snow. As much as I didn't like her during my short stint in high school, she proved to be a great friend when I needed one.

In the end, we fixed the second artifact. It was the first time I'd been able to see normally in months and the colors in my friends' auras fed my starving soul.

I force back tears. They come too easily these days. Sky is as puzzled as I am, and we're not the only ones. My mother took several vials of my blood to identify what might be causing my emotional roller-coaster ride. She does genetic research in her lab below our house. If anyone can spot an anomaly, it's my mom.

Sky nudges the porch with her toe, and the motion of the swing soothes me as we stare out at the field. "Do you believe everything the watchers told us?" she asks.

"Not really. They were mistaken about the Dracans' motives for wanting the artifact. They could have been wrong about other things, too."

We grow quiet, remembering the little aliens who'd died leading us to the tetrahedron under Clingman's Dome. If not for them, we would have been killed, too.

Sky breaks the silence. "We almost died getting to the first two artifacts. How often can we do that? How long can we keep it up? It's crazy we're the only four people on Earth who can save the entire planet."

2

JEWEL

A n eagle leaps off a high branch, spreads its wings and begins its search for breakfast in the meadow, now alive with little critters hunting their own food. The sky lightens with pastel rays piercing the air, masking the fading stars. The sun's rim edges over mountaintops, and clouds reflect the shades of dawn in millions of colors. My heart fills and overflows, thankful my full range of vision has been restored.

Are you up? Pax's voice is clear and strong in my head.

Yes. I couldn't sleep. Why are you up so early? Before he answers, I know he couldn't sleep either.

When Dad designed our wristbands to enable us to communicate telepathically, he didn't know our connection would grow beyond simple intentional speech. While I was held captive, unable to use my gift or the wristband, the others learned to increase the depth of their link. I wasn't a part of that, but they brought me up to speed quickly.

You know why, he answers. *I'm up because you're awake. Are you on the porch? I'm on my way.*

I'm here with your sister. I tap once on my wristband, opening the link to both Sky and Storm, but he doesn't respond. He must still be asleep.

I smile and again set the swing in a gentle motion with my foot.

Sky and I are wrapped in a soft blanket a Cherokee neighbor gave me. Geometric patterns around the edge, woven in red, white and black, frame waves in colors of the sea. The sea part matches the aqua of my eyes. I love living on the reservation among such generous people.

My heart speeds up when I spot Pax's car turning into our long driveway. He parks, hops out, and strides toward us on the porch swing. A breeze ruffles his shaggy hair, highlighting the contrast between its sun-bleached blond streaks and his tanned skin. Heat flows through me and creeps up my face in a blush. He notices and grins, and I want to kiss his perfect mouth. I could watch him day and night. My cheeks grow warm with another blush.

Sky gets up, hugs her brother, and says to me, "I'll go help your mom fix breakfast. It smells delicious." She winks and heads inside. He takes her place under the blanket.

"Nice. Warm," he murmurs, pressing close to me. It's jacket-cool out here, but he's only wearing a cotton tee shirt, worn blue jeans, and sandals.

"Really, Pax? Do you think you're still in the Bahamas? Where are your shoes?" His face lights up with his irresistible grin. I love the way his eyes crinkle at the corners when he smiles.

"Takes too long to lace them up," he says, pulling me close under the blanket. He leans over and kisses me, reaching for my hand. I snuggle into his chest.

"Dad wants us on a regular training schedule," he says. "Juliana learned some moves from Max, but Dad and Storm can teach the two of you so much more. Come over this afternoon. Mom's making stew for supper."

Storm, Pax, and Sky have their black belts in karate and mixed martial arts. The boys passed their fourth degree tests a week after we returned, but Sky hasn't advanced from first degree. Her dad, our sensei, is a sixth-degree master.

Juliana and I are both new at it. Max, the sheriff's son who was also in Atlantis while I was there, trained with Storm under Hunter Smith, the Cherokee sensei. He held classes in Atlantis for humans and the few Dracans who were interested.

"I'll be there if Sky will." Like me, she hates to sweat, and will avoid it if she can.

"She will. Storm's coming. Watching her pine for that idiot makes me want to deck him. I hate how he's hurting her."

"How can I help?" I ask. What is wrong with him? Sky is beautiful and as vivacious as her wild red hair. Everyone who gets near her knows she's in love with Storm. She can't help projecting how she feels. He loves her, too, but he fights it, pretending he doesn't care for her at all, which usually means she needs her brother to calm her down. I want to stuff his head in a bucket.

When he was ten, a Dracan craft attacked his parents' car, killing them. Everyone believed it. Storm escaped using his telekinesis, but he couldn't get his parents out. Rage still eats at him, even after he discovered they're still alive.

A time warp in Atlantis meant his parents lived twenty years to his eight, which is why his sister Juliana is only one year younger than he is. Storm would have had his parents back, along with his sister, if Shaula, one of the scariest Dracans I've met, hadn't taken them through a disappearing wormhole. Where do we begin searching for them?

Pax squeezes my shoulder, drawing my attention back to himself. "Why don't you and Juliana go car shopping with Sky tomorrow? She wants another red Mini Cooper." He sniffs my hair and plays with a strand. If I were a cat, I'd purr. "I'm not too thrilled about it. It'll remind me of the Dracan attack that could have killed her."

"Isn't it more important how she feels about it? She lived through the trauma, and knows not all Dracans are enemies, and not all red Minis are death traps."

"I guess so," he says. "The fact is, we may need the Dracans' help to find Storm's parents. You'd think knowing they're alive would lift his mood."

"He could be afraid we won't find them," I say. "There's no telling where they ended up. All we know is Shaula has them and wouldn't hesitate to kill them. What if Storm loses them again, knowing they're still alive? I'd be afraid to hope if it were me. My heart aches for him."

"Juliana, too. It's the first time she's lost them," Pax reminds me. "More reason to take my sister shopping. Don't you women focus on the hunt when you shop? Keeps your mind off other things."

I shrug out of the blanket and Pax's warm embrace and head into the house. "Let's get some breakfast before we go to your place. The coffee is calling me."

"You do realize your mom's cooking is the only reason I came over this early, don't you?" he says, patting his flat belly. He follows me in and makes himself at home at the table.

"Hey, kids," Mom says, flipping an egg from the pan to a plate. "How would you like to take a trip to South America?"

Since we got home, I've suspected we'll be going to the Ring of Fire, a hotbed of volcanic activity and earthquakes circling the Pacific Ocean. If we're heading to South America, my guess is we'll go somewhere along the west coast.

"Is there any chance we can wait until after our birthday party?" I ask, knowing what her answer will be. The four of us were born within minutes of each other, during an alignment of planets called the Grand Stellium. I still don't understand the significance, other than it convinced the Cherokee we were the ones their prophecy spoke about. Sky, Pax, and Storm were born on May second, and, due to different time zones, my birthday is May third. We'd planned to celebrate all our birthdays on the second.

"I doubt it. Northern Chile had another major earthquake last night, at the same time another formerly extinct volcano erupted. The upheavals are stronger and more frequent. There's a very good probability we'll find an artifact there, and it needs you."

"Maybe we'll be done by then, Jewel," Sky says, hoping to soothe Mom. She isn't fooling me. She's as disappointed as I am. Turning eighteen may not be as big a deal as turning twenty-one, but it does make us legally adults in some ways.

We may not live to see twenty-one.

3
CAROLINA SKY FLETCHER

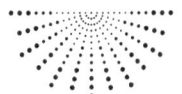

S torm's eyes stare at me from his impassive granite face. His right fist rests in his open left hand, and he bows slightly. I mirror him and bow when he does. A rush of adrenaline accelerates my heart. He's fast, and I'm ready.

He strikes first. I block and spin, bringing my leg up in a round-house kick. He blocks the kick, holds my leg, drops, and flips me on my back on the mat. He's up in a flash, and I'm right behind him. Despite my racing heart, stillness fills my core. We circle each other, eyes focused on eyes, hands ready for the next blow. I anticipate his strike and counter with a punch to his midsection, spinning out of danger. He blocks it and follows my spin. His leg shoots out, trips me, and lands me on my back.

Ooof! My breath rushes out, and I can't draw it back. Pax senses my distress and sends peace. A thin cushion of air lifts me just above the mat, a little gift from Storm's telekinesis. I gasp until I can breathe again. I push off the mat with shaking arms. Neither of the boys has moved or changed their stony expressions. Then Pax winks and spoils the gravity of the moment.

I bow to the victor and gratefully accept the towel and bottle of water Jewel offers me.

"I hate sparring," I mumble through the towel as I dry my face and hair. I hate sweating, but I secretly enjoyed the match.

"I know, but Sensei is only watching out for your good. There's no point in getting rusty. What if you need to fight?"

I nod. She's right, of course. I relax and watch the match between Storm and my brother. It's an intricate dance, a graceful, dangerous back and forth of movement, often so fast the human eye can't follow it. I pity any creature that goes up against either of them.

Juliana joins us on the pile of mats we've claimed as our vantage point.

"You did great, Sky. I can't last two seconds against my brother."

I share her admiration for Storm. Juliana's telekinesis is as strong as his. She can certainly hold her own against any human attacker. Could she use it against the Dracans, if necessary? She was raised among them in Atlantis, and she cares for Murphy, who has a human mother and a Dracan father.

"Where's Murphy?" I ask her. The two are usually together.

"Jewel's dad took him to the observatory. He's getting along with the astronomers, and the telescopic view into the universe fascinates him."

I don't correct her. Charles Adams is an astrophysicist, but some of the other scientists are astronomers. I wonder what they'd think of Murphy in his Dracan form. He's maintained his movie-star-handsome human persona since he left Thuban's ship and landed on the research vessel Proteus. He's also a genius, and if he's let loose in public, no doubt he'd be swamped by people who find him irresistible. If my feelings for Storm hadn't spoiled me, I'd be one of them.

It's Jewel and Juliana's turn to spar, and I'm impressed with the progress they've made. Dad has them run through a series of katas to warm up. Both are about to test for the next level. The sparring isn't nearly as quick and agile as the boys', but they manage to toss each other to the ground and both land and block each other's punches. I send them strong approval, and Jewel grins at me before turning her face to stone for the final bow.

Mom's hearty stew with home-made bread is the perfect meal for us after we've showered and changed. One of the best things about training is our need for extra calories.

Dad finishes his stew and reaches for a slice of warm bread from the basket in the middle of the table. Before he takes a bite, he says, "The arrangements have been finalized. We're going to Peru next week."

He delivers his announcement in a tone of voice he'd use to announce we're going to the movies after lunch. I choke on a mouthful of food, while Jewel's anxiety spikes. Pax's eyes widen as his gaze shoots to Jewel, while I send calm to both. We probably all thought we'd have more time to prepare.

Storm keeps chewing, as if he hadn't heard a word. I get a sense of excitement from Juliana and wonder if she and Murphy are coming along on this trip. I hope so. We might need their help.

I guess we'll miss out on a birthday party, after all, unless we get our task done quickly. What are the chances? I know I'm projecting my aggravation when I notice everyone staring at me and frowning.

I try to cool down but can't quite pull it off. What will we find in Peru? How will Jewel handle it? I'm worried about my friend and her volatile emotions. She tries to control it, but I've caught her crying at the oddest times. If I didn't know better, I'd say she's going through adolescence all over again. I don't know how it was for her, but I made my family miserable as changing hormones sent me skyrocketing, only to crash and burn every few minutes. Maybe it wasn't so dramatic, but it's how I remember it.

Pax is worried, too. She's different.

Storm finishes his stew, wipes his mouth on a napkin and asks my dad. "Where, exactly, are we going in Peru? Why there? What do you know?"

"I'll be happy to answer your questions, but your folks are headed over here, and so are Jewel's. It's best if we discuss it together, in person. Murphy and Juliana are coming along, and we need to iron out some logistics." Juliana tries to hide her elation, but her joy is infectious.

The front door opens, and Murphy strides in, dressed in a blue plaid shirt, jeans, and worn work boots. He looks more like a lumber-jack than a scientist, with his powerful build and short sandy hair. A day's growth of beard shadows the strong lines of his face. He tosses a brown leather jacket on the coat rack and beams his perfect smile at us. His brown eyes sparkle as he stares at Juliana, whose shy smile is a dead giveaway. She's crazy about him, and I don't blame her. He's easy on the eyes.

4
SKY

"Y ou must be starved," Mom says as she leads Murphy to a seat next to Juliana and places a bowl of stew in front of him. He nods at the rest of us and digs in. Charles takes a seat next to Dad. It's odd I didn't notice him come in. Murphy can be distracting.

A flash of annoyance from Storm lifts my spirits. He doesn't like me admiring Murphy. My grin is lost on him.

Wolf and Sequoia have come in, and Storm rushes to help his aunt with her coat. A loose yellow tunic covers her baby bump. I send joy to the baby and receive her contentment in turn. She's on the verge of waking up after the car ride soothed her to sleep, safe in her snug womb. Sequoia smiles at me. She and her baby are empaths, like me. The baby's gift might be even stronger than mine. I can hardly wait to meet my little friend, my sister empath.

Analiese is the last to arrive. Charles takes a container from her and helps her with her coat. She's brought dessert. Mom serves tea and coffee, and Dad hands out slices of Analiese's cake. We eat while settling down to our discussion, just like old times, before the aliens abducted Jewel.

Wolf says, "We'll start our search at Nazca. I'm sure you've heard about the geoglyphs you can only see from the air. There's no telling how ancient they are, but the natives claim they predate the Inca. They were drawn for, or by, our alien friends, and we hope to find out exactly what they mean and why they're there. If nothing else, we should find something to lead us to the next artifact."

Pax's eyes light up. He's wanted to see the geoglyphs since he first read about them. Still, he asks, "What makes you think Nazca is a good starting point?"

Charles replies, "It's fairly close to the epicenter of Chile's quake last night, and people have reported hearing strange sounds in the region."

"Stranger than the ones they've been reporting for years, along with their many sightings of UFOs?" Storm asks. He may be projecting indifference, but he's been researching the area.

Charles nods. "Many of the locals believe their gods are about to return. One report I read says they believe the sounds are the voice of their deity Viracocha."

Analiese breaks in, "The mountains are also in the Ring of Fire, where volcanic activity and earthquakes are increasing at an alarming rate. Between the sounds and the location, we have a pretty good idea an artifact is in that region. There may be more than one. The Ring of Fire circles all of the Pacific Ocean."

"Would the Dracans be willing to help us find it?" I ask. "Or the Allarans? They have a stake in this, too. Wouldn't the ones living in the Pacific area know more about where the artifacts might be?"

"If Max were still here, we could have asked him to call Marla. Maybe the Allarans can contact their allies," Jewel suggests.

"Where did he go?" Storm asks. He and Max were never friends, but they did train together, and Max helped Jewel escape Atlantis. I share Storm's grudging respect for him.

I can tell Jewel is reluctant to share her thoughts. Something about the Dracans bothers her deeply. When she talks about them, it's with fondness, but she isn't willing to contact them. I wonder what's holding her back.

"Max only came back home to say goodbye to his father," Jewel explains. "He's in love with Marla and won't leave her. The Dracans planned to take him back to Atlantis when they brought the artifact back. They returned it and filled in the tunnel last night."

"The earth shook," Sequoia says. "I'm glad it was nothing more serious." Her baby moves a lot at night, which keeps her awake. I hope she's getting enough rest.

Jewel smiles at her. "There's a good chance they might go through another time warp. If he does return here, he might be much older or much younger than the rest of us."

"I'm a good example," Juliana pipes in. "If I had been born here, I'd be seven years old."

"You're pretty mature for a seven-year-old," Murphy answers, winking at her while a pink blush creeps up her cheeks. Why can't Storm relax enough to tease me? I send him a flash of annoyance and enjoy the way his brows furrow.

What was that for? His voice in my head sounds annoyed. I ignore him and quickly break the connection he'd opened.

"We can expect it to be hot during the day and cool at night in Nazca," Dad says. "If we don't find what we're looking for there, we're going to Lake Titicaca, which is at a much higher elevation. We'll start on the Peruvian side of the lake, and will probably get to the Bolivian side, as well. We'll have to pack for both summer and winter, but pack lightly. There's been a lot of UFO activity reported around there. It's likely the Dracans have a base under the lake."

Pax adds, "I read they've discovered an actual star gate near there, in the region of Hayu Marca. It does sound promising."

"There's a sun gate on the Bolivian side, in Tiahuanaco," Storm says. "They could be related."

"It has some interesting carvings," Pax notes. "The deity Viracocha is the central figure carved above the door. Legend has it he created humanity right there, at the lake. I wonder if any of our alien friends are monitoring it."

"It's possible," Dad says. "We may have to explore both gates to find the artifact."

Wolf says, "The Allarans will pick us up in five days. They'll get us there, but the local travel will be up to us. Our wives will stay here with Sequoia."

"I understood we'd be going with you," Mom says, sounding annoyed.

"Our baby is due in June." Wolf's face is apologetic. "We could run into danger, or our quest might take longer than we hope. In either case, Sequoia needs to be here, and we'd hoped you and Analiese would keep her company."

"It's up to you, Coral," Sequoia says softly. "I'd understand if you'd rather be with your children, but when it's close to my time, I'm going back to Andros, and I'd hoped you and Analiese would go with me."

Mom nods and hugs her friend. Analiese isn't happy, but she also hugs Sequoia. It will be harder for her. Jewel was lost for nearly five months. Since she's been home, her mother has hardly left her side. I send her assurance and love, and she turns and smiles at me.

Wolf says, "The Cherokee Council has agreed to fund all our travel expenses until you kids have fulfilled the prophecy and saved Terra, or until they run out of money. Let's hope we find a way to speed up the process."

I hope so, too. With so much at stake, I'm willing to do whatever is necessary, but I don't relish the idea of spending the rest of my life searching for sick artifacts.

A flash of fear reaches me from Jewel. Underneath it, a deep well of sorrow. What is wrong with my friend?

5

PAXTON HUNTER FLETCHER

The folks are still talking in the dining room, but I need some fresh air and alone time. Evenings are crisp in March, and I'm glad for my jacket. I shove my hands in the pockets and wander around the side of the house to Mom's vegetable garden.

She's surrounded it with a mesh fence to keep the deer and rabbits out, and Dad built her a tool shed and a canopy-covered bench in the shade of an oak tree. The canopy has come in handy during acorn season. A big wind can shoot those nuts like bullets. They hurt when they land on your head. I would know.

Other than to see the Nazca lines, Peru is not one of the places I've dreamed of visiting, but any trip with Jewel is better than going anywhere without her. I haven't told her what I promised myself I would when we found her. My stupid nose won't let me. I can smell her subtle fragrance of citrus, spice and a hint of honeysuckle, pure and uniquely hers. She still carries it, but there's something else. Something reminds me of the thing in the cul-de-sac in California, and of Marla and now Murphy. She smells of Dracan, and not only because she was in Atlantis surrounded by them. This is deeper, as if coming from her pores. What happened to her?

I love her more than ever, but I can't bring myself to tell her. I've got to get to the bottom of this.

"Pax?" Sky's voice carries over the garden. She knows I like to come here and opens our private link when she spots me. We each have one, in case we don't want everyone listening in.

Are you okay? What's wrong? I can't hide anything from my sister.

Do you sense something's off with Jewel? She'd know better than anyone.

Her emotions are all over the place. Why?

This might sound weird, but she doesn't smell the same. I'm picking up a trace of Dracan, and I know she's no hybrid. I scoop up a couple twigs and twist them together.

Sky watches me and finds her own twigs. I think we both need to keep our hands busy to expend a little nervous energy. *I wish I knew what's going on,* she says. *Let's give it a little time. Maybe she's still recovering from her captivity.*

How much time? We're leaving in a few days. If she isn't better by then, will she be up to what needs to be done? I'm worried about her.

Sky's twigs disintegrate. She drops them and picks up a small stick. *I'll talk to her before we leave. She's confused, and I doubt she knows anything. Juliana was there with her. Maybe she can shed some light on this. Do you smell anything like it from Juliana? She's not a hybrid, either.* She stands, dusts her hands off and reaches for mine, helping me up, as if I need it. She's ready to go back in.

I haven't checked, but I will now, I say, determined to figure out what's wrong with my girl.

We don't have to go far. Murphy and Juliana stroll around the corner of the house, holding hands. I drop my scent guard for a quick sniff, but Murphy's alien odor overpowers Juliana's human scent. I'll have to wait until she's nowhere near him before I can determine whether she has the same combination of human and Dracan smells Jewel has.

"It's a beautiful evening," Murphy says with his usual cheerfulness. Does anything get this guy down?

"Yep," I answer. "Enjoy it while you can. Nazca is pretty barren and won't smell nearly as sweet."

Sky slugs my shoulder. *Be nice*, she insists.

What? I am being nice. Let's go get Jewel and bring her out here, too. She would love this. The thought makes me grin. Then I remember that jerk Storm. I won't invite him.

He and Jewel are deep in conversation in the family room, and all thoughts of a garden walk disappear. Light from the window slants over her black hair, glinting blue and purple like raven feathers. His head, with hair nearly the same color, is too close to hers. Sky should be sitting next to him. I hate this anger every time I see him, and my sister knows it. She settles a blanket of peace over me. It's hard to describe, even for us, but we've settled on calling it "sending calm."

Stay out of my business. Storm will come around in his own time.

I turn on the charm for her sake and sit on the couch, scooting close to Jewel.

"I'm so sorry," she says. "I wish I could tell you more. If I had any idea where Shaula might be holding your parents, I would certainly have told you and everyone else. He's cunning, and whatever his plans are, I'm confident they include keeping your parents alive for now. We'll find them in time. We have to."

Sky hands Jewel a tissue from a box on the table next to her recliner. She's crying. Again.

"Leave her alone, Ryder. You're upsetting her." I can't help the threat in my voice and don't care. I'm sick of him hurting the girls, whether he intends to or not. He needs to back off.

He glares at me and stands up. "I'm leaving. Once I find my parents, I won't bother any of you again."

Sky's alarm is evident as he strides to the door, grabs his coat and slams it behind him. She hits me with sharp annoyance and starts to run after him.

"Don't," Jewel calls out. "He's hurting, Sky. He needs some space."

My sister comes back, sits down and resumes glaring at me,

projecting the heat of her anger. I don't try to explain. I deserve it. The sound of his dirt bike firing up breaks the silence.

Jewel squeezes my hand. Even with my guard up, her subtle fragrance blends with a thread of something alien and wrong.

6
STORM DARROCK RYDER

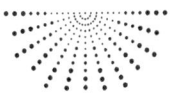

The shed door doesn't want to shut, so I kick it and hear something splinter. Too bad. Just another broken thing I'll have to fix.

Her brother is one more reason I can't let myself fall for Sky. They come as a package, and I can't stand him. The artifacts are more important to him—to all of them—than my parents' lives. If not for Wolf and Sequoia, I'd be entirely alone. They'll be hurt when I leave, but they'll understand.

I grab an apple from the kitchen and go to my room, slamming the door shut. My shoes and socks hit the floor as I stretch out on the bed with my back propped against the headboard and stare at my poster. A solitary Indian in a feathered headdress, holding a spear in one hand, sits on his horse with his head bowed. They're in silhouette with the setting sun behind them. I picture myself in his place.

Juliana has the guest room across the hall. Resentment keeps me from warming up to her, and even though I recognize it, I can't help it. She's had our parents to herself for the last eight years, which was nearly seventeen years in Atlantis because of some time warp. For eight years, I believed them dead, killed by Dracans.

It turns out the same Dracan who abducted them before is the one keeping them prisoner now. If the wormhole Shaula's craft disappeared into was unstable, they could have ended up anywhere on our planet or any other. Finding artifacts is child's play compared to finding my parents.

The monster inside me dreams of tearing that lizard limb from limb. I've gotten good at keeping it caged most of the time, but it's getting stronger, and I hardly care anymore. I'm itching to let it loose on Shaula. I hope no one else is around when it happens. Especially Sky.

"Storm?" Sequoia's voice soothes me, as usual. My aunt is a healer, intuitive and brilliant with herbs and natural medicine. Her husband Wolf has taught me everything I know about the ways of the Cherokee.

"In here, Auntie," I answer.

She comes in and sits on the bed near my feet. I draw my legs up to make room for her and toss her my pillows. She throws me a smile, scoots to the wall with the pillows behind her and sits cross-legged.

"Where's Wolf?" I ask.

"He stayed at the Fletchers' to work out some travel details. Since I tire easily these days, Analiese drove me home." She turns slightly to face me, and her expression grows sad.

"Please understand, when we speak of finding the next artifact, your parents are foremost on our minds," she says. I'm convinced she can read my mind even without using the wristbands.

Sequoia swipes a tear from her face. "My heart yearns to see my sister Salali again. I ache to hold her in my arms and tell her how much I've missed her all these years. Your father, too. I clearly remember the day she came home from college with him in tow. Tom took to our ways as if he'd been born Cherokee. Their wedding was a celebration of great joy, and our clan was blessed to have him."

Tears start to burn, and I blink them away. The rage helps to keep me impassive most of the time, but never around Sequoia. My throat tightens, forcing back my emotions.

I get up and reach out to help her off the bed. She's still graceful and beautiful, but her pregnancy has made it harder for her to get up. Her baby girl is due in a little less than two months. I won't leave them until I've met my cousin and Sequoia has named her. I imagine holding and playing with the little one as she grows, and I know when I leave, it won't be forever.

I help her settle in the family room and turn on the news while I pull dishes out of the cupboards and sandwich fixings out of the fridge, all before I get to the kitchen. Sequoia laughs and I'm glad my gift makes her happy. She's eating for two, and I can always eat. Telekinesis burns a lot of energy.

The news isn't good.

"BREAKING NEWS: A minor earthquake last night shook some residents awake and filled many with fear we might be about to experience a repeat of the quakes resulting in the worst mountain slide in the history of our nation. Seismologists urge everyone to remain calm and assure us it was an isolated incident."

"IN OTHER NEWS, a long-dormant volcano roared to life in a remote location in northern Chile yesterday morning, accompanied by a magnitude 5.8 earthquake. This is the latest in a string of recent new volcanic activity around the Ring of Fire, which covers all the west coast of the United States. Scientists are closely watching these incidents."

"THE SEARCH CONTINUES for an island that mysteriously disappeared last month from the Tierra del Fuego archipelago on the southern tip of South America. Residents of Ushuaia claim they see lights where it once stood and hear loud sounds as if the island itself is groaning. Ushuaia is commonly considered the southernmost city in the world. Kyle Johnson reporting for Cherokee Nation News."

~

SEQUOIA STIFFENS and I wonder what she knows about Tierra del Fuego. Before I can ask her, the door opens and Wolf comes in, followed by Juliana. They hang their jackets on the coatrack by the door and Juliana waves and heads to her room.

Wolf pulls his boots off and sighs. He makes a beeline for his wife and bends to kiss her. I'm glad I ended up with these two. My own parents couldn't have been better role models.

"What is it, Sequoia?" he asks. He always knows when something is off with either of us.

"I'm afraid of what you'll find at the end of the world."

"Peru and Bolivia aren't exactly at the world's end," he says. He hugs her from behind and nuzzles her neck.

"No, but your journey will lead you there and to the missing island. I'm sure of it."

Sequoia's eyes darken and her haunted face makes me shudder.

When I get to bed, I stare at the ceiling wondering why she's so disturbed before I drop off to sleep.

7
STORM

Something startles me awake. Without moving a muscle, I listen intently. There. Juliana's door opens with a tiny squeak. It's a good thing I haven't gotten around to oiling the hinge. I ease out of bed and listen to her soft footfalls heading down the hall. A muffled yelp tells me she's bumped into the step leading up to the front door. I open my door just as she slips outside.

Years spent hunting with Wolf have taught me to move virtually silently, which makes it easy to follow her undetected. We're on a path leading to a meadow ringed with trees. A stream runs along the edge, and I watch her balance on the log Wolf placed over it when I was younger. I never needed it. It was a simple matter to float over the stream, even when it was swollen with rain.

The object blends so well with the dark trees, I don't see it until a portal opens on the bottom, casting dim light over a small patch of ground underneath. A gigantic Dracan descends from the craft and waits. Is Juliana walking towards a trap? I fight the urge to call out a warning, thinking I can lift her away if she's in danger. Heck, she can lift herself away. What is she doing here?

The gurgling stream nearly drowns out their voices, but I catch a few words in their odd language. I recognize one of them, the name Shaula.

This probably isn't Shaula, but just in case it is, I pull a small boulder from the stream bed and prepare to hurl it at him. When he extends his hand toward her, I throw the boulder. It glances harmlessly off the skin of the ship above him, but he ducks, and I hope some of the debris got him.

Juliana whirls toward me, and the reptilian scurries toward the beam of light, but not before handing her something she slips into a pocket. He rises into the ship and the portal closes behind him.

"Quit it! He's a friend," she shouts, and gestures toward the ground in front of me, blocking me with a wall of grassy dirt. Lights appear at the edge of the triangular ship, and for a second, it's outlined against the stars as it lifts and accelerates out of sight.

"I was worried about you," I yell back, pushing the earth back into place. I'm much angrier than worried, but it doesn't pay to let her know. I need to find out what she was doing with the lizard, and what it was he gave her. My rage would only shut her up. She walks past me to the log, and I turn and follow her.

"Who was that?" I ask, keeping my tone even.

"No one," she says, tossing her head.

I throw up my hand and block her with a wall of solid air. She shoots straight up and hovers above my head, a trick she pulled in Triton's cave when we first met.

"It's none of your business. I have friends in Atlantis, remember? I know and trust them a lot more than I know or trust you."

"It became my business when it said Shaula's name. He took my parents, so what were you talking about?"

"They're my parents, too. I'm going to rescue them whether you and your friends plan to help or not. All you talk about are the artifacts. When I told you about my parents—your parents—you just got angry. Aren't you glad they're alive? I'm your sister. Don't you care? I hate being around you."

She's right. I resent her and it must have been obvious to her from the start. She learns quickly and does everything I ask her to during training, but it isn't because I've been nice. I'm becoming the monster in the cage.

"I'm sorry," I concede. "I can't explain it, and I can't excuse my behavior. I promise to try to do better. I'm more concerned about finding Mom and Dad than you know. When we find Shaula, we'll find them, too."

She floats back to the ground and faces me. "In that case, the Dracan I met is a friend of Murphy's. Thuban sent him to give me a locator locked onto Shaula's ship."

She digs into her pocket and hands me an egg-shaped object.

"How does it work?" As far as I can tell, it's completely solid and seamless, with no lights or depressions and no way to open it.

"Murphy's friend told me it will only open for Jewel. He didn't have time to explain why." She frowns at me.

"I'm sorry," I apologize again. "I blew it and I'll find a way to make it up to you. To all of us. We'll find Shaula and our parents, but for now, our goal is to find the next artifact and fix it. That takes priority or our world will end, and it won't matter whether we find our parents or not. We'll all die."

8
JEWEL

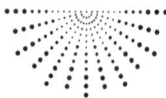

*W*hat's wrong? Sky's voice in my head startles me out of my near doze. Sleep is better than worrying while we wait for the Allaran ship in our meadow. I can tell she's on our private link.

I wish I knew. Is it obvious? I answer, hugging my knees tighter to my body and burying my face in my arms. It's cold tonight. I hope we've packed the right clothing for the trip. Will our jackets be too bulky?

Your emotions haven't exactly been stable since you've come home. What happened in Atlantis that has you so worked up? I glance up, and her concerned expression makes me want to cry. This is too weird.

I honestly don't know. At first, I thought these weird feelings had something to do with grieving my losses, but they haven't improved since I've been home. Any suggestions?

Pax is afraid for you. Something is different about your scent.

Great. I hope I don't stink.

Sky laughs. *Have you noticed him avoiding you? My brother's crazy about you.*

Warmth spreads through me. I know he likes me. His kisses tell me that much, but this takes it a step farther. I wonder why he hasn't said anything.

My moment of pleasurable reverie is rudely interrupted by the appearance of the Allaran ship. Vega's voice booms out from the open portal.

"This transport is for you and your families, Star Children. Please proceed to the portal."

The others open their links.

Will we all fit in there? There are nine of us with Juliana and Murphy. Pax sounds worried.

If Vega says we'll fit, we will, Sky answers.

What happened to the other ships? Pax and I have the same thought at the same time. When we left Andros, we came home in three ships.

It'll be tight. I hear the annoyance in Storm's thought.

He's right. The observation room on Vega's ship is just large enough for the nine of us to squeeze together, each in our own bubble seat. For some reason, I don't want to be near Juliana and sit between Pax and Sky, instead. Something about her is making me sad. I wonder why?

Allaran ships travel at unimaginable speeds because their skin offers no resistance to air or water. Within moments, we're transfixed by the view of Nazca below. Vega recounts the true history of the Nazca people, pausing to remark on each of the geoglyphs we glide over. Lines, triangles, spirals, and geometric patterns crisscross the landscape.

The Allaran isn't in the room with us, but his voice is clear over a hidden speaker, and I realize we aren't reacting to his disembodied voice like we do in person. Women are unusually attracted to the Allaran males, while men become aggressive and struggle to keep from fighting them. Allaran females produce the opposite response. Women want to kill them while men fawn all over them.

"Our offspring lived among the Nazca," Vega was saying, "By the time the civilization disappeared, most of the Nazca were descendants of our children who took human mates. Your archeologists date their civilization to between the years one hundred B.C. and around A.D. five hundred. They are, in fact, tens of thousands of years old.

Earlier signs of their culture have long been buried deep underground.

"When Creator banished our race from Terra's surface, we left them behind with everyone who was not pure Allaran. We also left tools, plans, and portable energy sources to ensure their survival. We were forbidden to do more and forbidden to interact further with them. It was devastating for those of us ripped from our families.

"We watched from our cloaked ships as they used the tools, not to build solid shelters and restore their lost technology, but to clear the iron-oxide-rich pebbles from the underlying layer of limestone in lines of geometric and mathematical shapes to communicate with us and draw us back. We grieved for them and with them.

"Some of us, whose ties were particularly strong, defied Creator and took small transports back to the surface, where they were swallowed by the earth. The consequence of disobedience was grave."

"Did they disappear into wormholes?" my dad asks. "Could they have returned to Allara?"

"We thought so, at first, until it happened just below us. A mound of earth rose to meet the craft, and a hole opened, filled with sharp boulders like the teeth of a shark. It surrounded the craft, closed around it and literally swallowed it. The hole snapped shut and sank back to the earth, leaving no sign of our craft. We never heard from our people again."

A sob closes my throat, and my eyes burn. The Nazca people have been gone for centuries, at least, but the sorrow in Vega's voice touches me. I wonder how long the Allarans live, and whether he was one who lost his family here.

"The humans lost their knowledge of mathematics and engineering and began to draw plants and animals. The monkey below us was carved after many generations, when trade among scattered cultures was restored, and they were once again exposed to such things. We believe they continued creating the geoglyphs in the fashion of their ancestors, large enough to be seen in their entirety only from the air, but their reason for doing so had changed. They had forgotten us."

We glide over the figure of a man with his hand raised in greeting or perhaps waving goodbye. His bulbous head and the lines of his clothing remind me of the spacesuits our astronauts wear when they work outside the orbiting space station.

"Was that one done before or after they stopped drawing lines and shapes?" I ask.

I detect a deeper note of sadness in his voice when he answers. "It was the last."

"Someone remembered," Sky says, sniffing and wiping at her eyes.

"What about the geoglyphs in the Atacama Desert in Chile?" Wolf asks. "Like the Atacama Giant. Did you leave offspring there, too?"

"There, and in Tiahuanaco, and in nearly every place where evidence of lost civilization has been found. We were not alone in leaving mankind to its own devices. The Dracans were also forbidden to interact with humans after the great war, and they, too, left children behind. It was a time of great sorrow for all creation."

He pauses, and we watch as form after form passes below us. I wonder about the meaning of the killer whale we glide over.

Vega continues. "Archeologists have unearthed gravesites where the bodies of our offspring were preserved through mummification. They are puzzled by the elongated skulls, a genetic anomaly that often occurred when we mixed with humans. Dracan-human offspring tended to be much larger in stature than their parents, giving rise to legends of colossal demigods. You must remember, our war ended around twelve thousand years back. We did not manipulate DNA the same way we do now, in our laboratories. Modern hybrids are close in size to most humans."

"When was the ban lifted?" Pax asks.

"Creator allowed us to interact with humans once again when it became evident our planets, linked as they are by ancient wormholes, would die without the four of you. You were not the first genetically enhanced humans. You were the only four who were born during the Grand Stellium, an auspicious alignment of the planets. You are the chosen ones, and we have been watching over you since your birth."

I glance at Murphy, who hasn't spoken a word since we entered the Allaran ship. His scales gleam in shades of green and orange, darker than his usual yellows and pale blues. Yellow reptilian eyes stare, and he bares his sharp, gleaming teeth at me. I smile back. When nothing is blocking my gift, like now, I can only see him in his Dracan form.

"The Dracans have been interacting with humans all along, haven't they?" I ask.

"We cannot answer for them. Creator's plan may be different for them," he answers. Murphy winks at me, and I chuckle.

"We have arrived, Star Children. You and your families will join with Dr. Jack Austin's team."

"The noted archeologist?" Dylan asks.

"Yes. He is in Nazca investigating a possible link between the spiral geoglyph and the Stargate of Hayu Marca. There have been rumors the Stargate may be operational. It could lead to an underground Dracan city, or to the location of another artifact. Our instruments cannot determine what is below the gate."

The door to the entry bay opens and Murphy leads the way out. We don't see Vega as we drop, one by one to the barren desert floor.

9
JEWEL

I t's too late to build shelters for the night, but we settle in small groups in a series of depressions between boulders. I share a hollow with Sky and Juliana. We shake off our backpacks, sip a little water from our canteens, and settle back to wait and, hopefully, sleep. I fight off a heavy dread of impending doom. This is not like me. Sky sends me peace, while her face remains troubled.

"How does this Jack guy know to find us here?" I wonder aloud.

"Maybe the Allarans are in contact with someone in his camp," Juliana answers. "Other people know about them, don't they?"

"I hadn't thought about it," Sky says. "I hear plenty of talk about aliens, but I haven't heard of anyone who knows them personally, other than us and some of the Cherokee from the reservation. I guess it's possible."

"I've never seen stars like these," Juliana says, changing the subject. I share her awe at the inky sky filled with trillions of points of light, mostly concentrated in a wide path I recognize as the Milky Way, one of the spiral arms of our own galaxy. A sliver of moon rides just above the outlines of dark mountains to the east.

"You hadn't seen stars at all until a month ago," I remind her.

"They're never like this in North Carolina," Sky's voice is full of wonder. "How insignificant, how tiny our planet is in comparison to just this visible part of the universe. It makes our problems seem so small."

"I wouldn't say saving a planet teeming with life is a small problem, Sky," Juliana says.

The colors of my friends' auras are muted in the dark, but their life forces glow brightly. The soft murmuring of the men's voices comforts me. The thought of those beautiful lights going dark makes my heart ache.

The desert is not as silent as I'd imagined. Diminutive insects jump through branches of dry brush and set them scraping together in a brittle dance. Desert critters glow as they skitter along the ground, dislodging bits of sand and tiny pebbles. I marvel at the night music, until a larger scrape jars me. I stiffen when I spot a life force slinking low to the ground, heading toward the guys. It's bigger than a human. Could it be a cougar or a bear?

If I shout, will it run away or attack? There's only one way to find out.

I stand up, wave my hands and yell as loudly as I can. "Watch out! Animal attack!"

Dylan, Pax, and Storm immediately leap to their feet and assume a fighting stance. Wolf and Dad turn on flashlights, playing them over the ground around our makeshift camp. Wolf pulls a pistol out of his pack and aims it at the desert.

I've lost sight of it in the light of the flashlights, but I spot it again as it whirls to run away. My voice catches in my throat as I'm about to point it out. It's a humanoid, with bright red hair. And it's gigantic. Before I find my voice again, it's gone.

"Are you out of your mind?" Storm yells. "You woke us up for nothing."

"Hold on," Wolf says, his voice quiet and even. "Jewel wouldn't have warned us about nothing. Remember her gift."

He turns to me and asks, "What did you see?"

Everyone is tense. I wonder if there's another way I could have handled this.

"I thought a large animal was creeping toward you. I was afraid it would attack, so I yelled. It worked. The thing is gone."

Dad comes over and hugs me. "You did the right thing. You might have saved our lives."

"What was it?" Dylan asks.

"I glimpsed its back when it ran away," I say, reluctant to continue. I lower my voice to just above a whisper. "It was a giant. With red hair."

Storm snorts, and Pax punches his arm.

"We'll check the area in the morning," Wolf says. "If it left a trail, I'll find it. We'll get to the bottom of this." Wolf is a master tracker in the North Carolina woods, but here in the desert...? We'll find out.

"I can see clearly in the dark," Murphy reminds us. "If I hadn't been asleep, I would have spotted it before Jewel. I'm sorry I didn't."

"No worries, Murph," Dad says, draping an arm across the Dracan's shoulders.

"The point is," Murphy says, "I can follow its trail tonight and report back in the morning. It will save time. What if Jack comes early? You might not have time to search."

"I'll go with you," Juliana says. "You shouldn't be in the desert alone."

"You're right," Dylan says. "Charles and I will go along. Juliana, you stay with the girls."

I watch as Dad reaches into his backpack and puts a pistol in his pocket. He hefts the pack up and joins Dylan and Murphy. Storm, Pax, and Wolf stay behind to protect us. They'll take up the search at first light.

We settle back into our depressions, but I'm guessing no one will get any sleep.

As soon as the sky lightens enough to see the desert floor, Storm and Wolf hunt for traces of our visitor. We help as best we can but find nothing.

The hard-baked ground yields no clues, other than a small patch of disturbed gravel. The creature left no footprint or any other indication it had been there. I sit on a small boulder and take a sip of water. Dad,

Dylan, and Murphy crest the hill, and I gather from their expressions they didn't find a trail.

"Whatever that thing was," Dad says, "it's disappeared. Let's hope it doesn't show up again."

We grow silent as the heat rises and we wait for Dr. Jack Austin to arrive. I doze off.

"Over there," Wolf calls out, and I rub my eyes and yawn loudly. He's pointing toward the west. A cloud of dust nearly obscures the glint of metal from a line of vehicles. In a moment, we hear laboring engines as they navigate the rough terrain.

Three Hummers pull up and park side-by-side in a flat area between boulders. The drivers get out, stretch, and take long drinks from water bottles. We grab our packs and go down to the cars.

I recognize Dr. Austin immediately, with his brush of brown hair, highlighted with glints of gold and pale yellow, falling artlessly over a colorful woven headband. He swipes at rainbow drops of sweat trickling down his face, and grins, revealing a row of slightly crooked teeth. I wonder if he bleaches them. He's handsome in an Indiana Jones way, with a deeply tanned, weathered face. His series on the History Channel, "Mysteries of the Ancients" is one of the programs I try to keep up with.

"Call me Jack," he says, holding his hand out to Dylan, who shakes it heartily, then to Wolf and my dad.

He grabs the hand of an exotic Asian woman, with classic high cheekbones and straight black hair tied in a ponytail, and pulls her forward. "This is my assistant and chief camera woman, Jaina Chen," he says, giving her a quick side-hug.

She's dressed in jeans tucked into calf-high hiking boots and a loose brown shirt. I spot a holster hanging from her right hip. She's staring at Murphy, her obsidian eyes drinking him in. A swirl of dust kicks up at her feet, and as I watch, her ponytail rises and her head yanks back. She spins, drawing her revolver, but no one is there. She turns back, frowning, and holsters her weapon.

Juliana's narrow-eyed glare makes it obvious she doesn't like the attention Jaina is paying Murphy. It was fun watching her use her gift on Ms. Chen, and I'm almost sorry for the woman, until she turns her attention to Pax.

We'll have to keep an eye on this one, Sky says, after tapping my code on her wristband. *There's something strange about her, and I don't like how she's checking out our men.*

At least she's human, I answer. *She has an angry aura, like Storm's but with different colors. Do you sense anything?*

It's odd. Most people have something going on, but either she has iron control, or she has no feelings. Storm's anger comes across loud and clear, and yet I don't get any emotion from her at all.

We glance at each other then back at her. Who is she?

10

PAX

I don't like the way the Chen woman is watching us. The dry desert
air interferes with my ability, and I don't expect the strange hint of
unfamiliar pheromones from her when I drop my guard. Her perfume,
heavy with musk and sandalwood, nearly covers it, but it's there, and
it's coming in thin waves, as if the air is undulating. I've never smelled
anything like it before. I have the strongest urge to stay away from her.

Dad, Wolf, and Charles climb into the lead vehicle with Jack. The
three girls ride in the second, driven by Jaina Chen. I'm relieved to join
Storm and Murphy in the third Hummer, where I tap my code for Sky
on the wristband.

Are you picking up any strange vibes from the Chen woman? I ask.

*She doesn't project emotions. The hair on my arms stands up when
I'm near her, like right now,* Sky says with a slight shudder.

*Like static electricity? I'm picking up an odd scent undulating
through the air.*

Yeah. Like that. I don't like her. Should we warn the others?

Later. Meanwhile, let's see if we notice anything else.

I break the connection and pay attention to the driver next to me.
He appears to be in his mid- to late-forties. A jagged scar runs down
his sun-wrinkled face, from below his eye, down his cheek to his chin.

A deep groove between bushy eyebrows makes me think the frown he's wearing is permanent. He's big, muscle-bound, and appears dangerous, especially after he tosses his hat to the console between us to reveal a shiny bowling-ball of a head. Bodyguard, no doubt.

I drop my guard for a second and wish I hadn't. No wonder Ms. Chen wears so much perfume. Showers must be scarce out here.

"So," Storm asks him, "What do you know about red-headed giants roaming the desert?" If he weren't in the back seat, I'd elbow him. What a way to start a conversation with Ivan the Terrible.

The man's steely eyes glance at the rearview mirror. "What about them?" he asks. His voice matches his appearance, rough and gritty.

"Have you seen them? Do you know who or what they are?" Storm is relentless. I guess he figures it would be no problem to take the guy down if he becomes belligerent.

"Yes, and yes," he answers. His mouth twitches in an almost-smile. A sense of humor is a good sign. "So, what are your names, and why are you here? I'm Alexander Loren. You can call me Mr. Loren."

"I'm Storm Ryder." I'm no empath, but I can sense his irritation. "You can call me Mr. Ryder."

Mr. Loren's belly laugh is as unexpected as the giant's visit was last night. I stare at him. He glances at me and laughs harder.

"I know who you are," he says when he finally catches his breath. "I don't know why you're here or what you hope to find, but please, call me Al. I was just messing with you."

"Messing with?" Murphy asks. I sometimes forget he isn't completely familiar with our idioms.

"Joking," I tell him. "Al was joking."

He settles back in his seat, muttering, "Messing with means joking. I understand."

Al looks at me curiously. "Is he a foreigner? He doesn't have an accent."

"So to speak," I answer. "He's been sheltered all his life. Can you tell us about the giants?"

"They're Indians," he says. "Been around for centuries, at least. Elusive creatures. I'm surprised one of them let you see it."

"We didn't. Not really. One of our friends spotted its back as it retreated, and only caught a glimpse of the red hair and human shape. We don't know if it was male or female."

"Female, no doubt," Al says. "They're a matriarchal society and the females are the hunters and warriors. As far as we know, they live underground and only come out at night."

"How do you know what kind of society they have?" I ask. "Have you had contact with them?"

"Jack found a wounded male a couple years ago in Tierra del Fuego. He gave him the medical attention he needed, and they spoke, using Henry as an interpreter. His language was similar to the Ona's, a recently extinct tribe.

"Henry?" Murphy asks.

"The name we call our native friend from Puno," Al replies. "He didn't want us to know his real name.

"The giants are all over South America, but, as I said, they're elusive. We don't know their origins or how they've survived. Most mainstream archeologists still insist they're myths, and Jack prefers to leave them in the dark. He doesn't want a bunch of skeptics messing with our digs."

"He doesn't want them joking with your digs?" Murphy asks. I turn to see his eyes crinkle at the corners. It's his turn to mess with Al.

"Where are we going?" I ask, changing the subject before Al asks too many questions about Murphy.

"Nazca, for now," he answers. "Jack heard they've found something new in the Sun Star mandala. It could be a link to the Stargate in the mountains."

"The Sun Star is a distance from most of the geoglyphs, isn't it?" I ask. I remember reading about it and its uncanny similarity to many of the mandalas found in India and to some of the more recent crop circles. Some say the Temple on the Mount in Jerusalem is designed the same way.

"It's more remote than the others. The good news is most tourists spend their time snapping pictures while they fly over the animals. We probably won't be bothered."

"What do you mean by link?" Storm asks. "Do they connect?"

"Now that would be something, wouldn't it? No, I'm pretty sure they've found some artifact that connects the two historically."

"How far is it from Nazca to the Stargate?"

"About six hundred miles, or a fifteen-hour drive," Al says. "If we drive it. Lucky for us, Jack has a cargo plane and all our vehicles fit in the bay. Not sure if we can squeeze all of you and your packs in, though."

"You're messing with us, right?" Murphy pipes up.

Al's big laugh puts us at ease.

"So," he says when his laughter trails off. "How did you end up way out here in the middle of nowhere?'

"We were dropped off," Storm says, without further explanation. We have no idea how much Jack and his team know about the aliens.

"Sorry," Al says with a note of sympathy in his voice. "People don't usually get dumped out here. Pirates? Robbers? Aliens?"

"Yes, yes, and yes," Murphy says, and I suddenly have a new appreciation for the half-Dracan. Al simply laughs.

11

PAX

Our vehicles labor up a trail to the top of a high plateau where we park by a corner of the mandala, near a line of rocks piled in straight lines going off in two directions.

I wondered if we passed some of the figures Vega flew us over, but we're nowhere near the geoglyphs. We wouldn't have recognized them from the ground, in any case.

Jewel emerges from the back of Jaina Chen's hummer, yawning and stretching. I walk over and hand her a fresh bottle of water. I love her smile and the way the sun sparks off her eyes, like it does off the turquoise ocean in the Bahamas. I grab her hand and we walk toward the men gathered around Dr. Austin.

"The Sun Star glyph is, in my opinion, the most interesting of all the geoglyphs," he says. "We believe it was created by someone other than the people who drew the Nazca lines by sweeping away stones and the top layer of the ground, leaving lighter tones to make the lines. Their designs have been preserved all these centuries by the windless air in one of the driest deserts in the world. This was built by piling stones into lines."

Dry is right. I fight the urge to pour every drop from my water bottle down my throat, while the air sucks every bit of moisture out of my body. I take a sip.

"It's also known as the Mandala because of its similarity to the mandalas of India, which usually represent the universe. This one was laid out with mathematical precision, measuring one hundred-eighty feet across with an inner circle of the same diameter. Several smaller circles, measuring twenty feet across, are in the landscape around it."

He hands a photograph to Wolf, who passes it to Charles. Murphy, Juliana and Jewel crowd around me when I get it. Dark lines outline the actual geoglyph in the photograph, forming two large squares at right-angles to each other, connected in the center. The corners of the squares form an eight-pointed star. Small squares, each with an "x" through them, fill each corner of the inner square. Three concentric circles lead toward the center, starting from the perimeter of the inner square, each smaller than the one closer to the outside. In the center, a sun symbol of sixteen rays, or spokes, is surrounded by more small squares forming a cross.

I ask Murphy, "What's the significance of this mandala? Do you know?"

"Yes," he says. "It's a mathematical template which was used in astronomy and other disciplines. This is the first one I've seen outside a book or diagram." His infectious grin lightens my spirit. Or maybe it's Sky sharing her approval. Murphy pulls Juliana close to his side.

Storm seems disinterested until Jack says, "Some of my colleagues found a strange object in the middle of the central sun symbol. They've unsuccessfully tried to excavate it without doing damage to the glyph, and it remains where they found it. Perhaps you might be able to shed some light as to its origins and purpose."

Dylan replies, "We'll do our best. Lead on."

"Let's go," Jack says, and strides through the point and toward the middle, careful not to disturb the rock lines.

Murphy and Charles form a line behind Jack, and the rest of us follow, walking single file. The girls are in front of me, with Juliana far enough away from Murphy for me to get her scent. I draw closer and sniff. This is the first opportunity I've had to tell if she has the same trace of Dracan that Jewel does. She does, but it doesn't tell me anything. She and Murphy have been holding hands. Jewel's has nothing to do with proximity to a Dracan.

We step over both straight and curved lines until we get to the spokes, where we gather around the center. An egg-shaped object lies half-buried in a hole, leaving about six inches visible above ground.

"Juliana," Storm says. "Do you recognize this thing?"

What is he talking about? Why would she know anything about it? I watch as Juliana concentrates on it, using telekinesis to wriggle it out of the hole and lift it so it's floating at eye level.

"What the...?" Al grunts. Jaina gasps but says nothing, and Jack remains silent. He must know about our gifts.

"It's a Dracan tracking device," Murphy says. "Who would have left it here, and why?"

Storm glares at Juliana, who remains silent. Jewel is close to tears. I hope Sky can find out what's wrong with her. I hate she's in pain. I hate feeling so helpless

I open our communal link. *What do you know about it, Storm?*

Juliana has one, too. One of her Atlantis friends give it to her a few nights before we left.

And you didn't think it was important enough to tell us about? Sky aims a shaft of annoyance at him, but it hits us all through the link.

He replies, *I forgot about it while we were getting ready to come here. I wish she had a wristband. It would be better if she explained it. We can't ask her about it with Jack and his team here.*

Dad is working on one for her, Jewel says. It's news to me, but it's probably the smart thing to do. She is Storm's family, and if things progress between her and Murphy, he might become part of the family, too. I wonder if Charles can make one for Murphy bypassing the Dracan technology that blocked Jewel from using hers in Atlantis. If he can, maybe he can also find a way for us to use our gifts in blocked areas.

Jack turns to my father and says, "Mind explaining to everyone what a Dracan is? Maybe you should also tell my colleagues what you told me about these kids and their abilities."

"Of course," Dad replies. "But not here." He turns to Storm, "Why don't you float that thing back to the cars and we'll decide what to do with it after we've had some water and can relax in the shade for a bit. This heat is getting to me."

Everyone mumbles their approval and we walk back the way we came, the object floating along in front of Storm. I wonder if we're asking for trouble by bringing it along with us. If it's a tracking device, won't whoever is using it be tracking us, now?

12
SKY

Dr. Austin's crew drive us to the airport just southwest of Nazca, where his cargo plane is fueled and ready to go. A hydraulic ramp lowers from the back of the wide-bodied aircraft, and Jaina skillfully maneuvers the Hummer, with us inside, to its spot behind Jack's car, where crew members quickly secure and strap the wheels to the floor of the plane. When all three cars are in place, we follow her forward to a passenger cabin and find seats.

Jewel lets me have the window. "You're shorter. I can lean over you to look outside if I want to." We settle in and stow our packs.

I imagine Storm has the egg-shaped object stowed in his backpack.

No one talks while the engines rev up or during take-off. As soon as we level off, Jack stands and faces the rest of us. The flight isn't as quiet as a passenger airliner, and it's much louder than the silent Allaran ships. He raises his voice to be heard over the engine noise.

"It'll take about two hours to get to Lake Titicaca. Our compound will be our base of operations. Before I commit my team to your quest, Al and Jaina need to know what you're searching for and why."

"I want to know how that object floated out of the hole when none of the other archeologists were able to move it," Al says, his gravelly voice blending with the engine roar.

"I can answer," Storm says, nearly shouting. "My sister and I are telekinetic. We move things with our minds." To illustrate, Al's pack eases out from under the seat in front of him and flies over to Storm, who's sitting by the window across the aisle.

"I know what telekinetic means," Al replies. He scowls at him, his expression masking his excitement.

"I can track like a bloodhound," my brother says. He leans across the aisle toward the big man and takes an exaggerated sniff. "And I'm regretting it right now."

Al reaches over and smacks him on the head, and Pax grabs his head and moans loudly. I know he isn't hurt. In fact, he's enjoying this.

"Children, behave." Dr. Austin pinches his lips together and peers down his nose, like a caricature of a stern principal. His annoyance surprises me. I send him calmness and he looks at me sharply. He felt it and knows where it came from.

"Sky, please share with Al and Jaina what your ability is."

"I'm an empath," I say. Jaina, who's sitting two rows ahead and across the aisle, leans over and stares back at me. The air crackles between us and I wonder if she knows I'm not able to read her. How does she do it? Is she a stronger empath than I am, or is there something alien about her?

Jewel grabs my hand and shakes her head slightly. She speaks up, "I can see colors no one else can. I also see life forces, auras, and through disguises."

Jaina's eyes narrow and she turns her stare to Jewel. Her body language tells me something Jewel just said had disturbed her. She disturbs me. Doesn't she ever blink?

"I understand you can see the alien ships when they're cloaked, and you've met one species and lived with another." Dr. Austin is intensely curious, with a hint of jealousy, as he addresses Jewel. I tap her code on my wristband.

He's jealous of us, Jewel. Can you tell?

Yeah. His aura is streaked with brown. There's something strange about Jaina's aura, too. She's exuding a metallic gray, a color I've never witnessed around anyone else.

She makes my skin crawl. Why can you see her aura, but I can't sense her emotions? Who, or what, is she?

Jewel shrugs and closes the connection. She gives me a little shove and shakes her head when I begin tapping on the band again. When she points toward Jaina's head in the front row, now facing forward, and her long-nailed hand on the armrest, I guess Jewel has figured something out. I'm curious but trust my friend to tell me about it when she can.

"Our kids have been given a task no one else can accomplish," Dad says, standing in the front when Jack takes his seat. "We've learned the strange weather patterns and environmental anomalies, including the increased seismic and volcanic activity in this region, are caused by Earth's failing organs, which we call artifacts."

As I watch, Jaina's hand clenches then relaxes, as if she's forcing herself to appear composed. I wish I could read her.

Dad continues. "Apparently, only the combination of their particular gifts can repair them. If they aren't all fixed in time, Earth will destroy itself. You can understand why we're eager to find them."

"How do you propose to do that?" Jack asks.

"They emit a sound when they're in distress. It's unmistakable and can be heard for miles," Charles says.

"Yeah," Al interjects. "It hurts, too." He smacks his ear and grimaces. He's right. I wish there were some other way for them to signal their location.

"We've heard it a few times near the lake," Jack says. "After the last one left people in town writhing on the ground, we set up instruments to try to pinpoint the source. It's been silent since then, but we've picked up some other sounds from underneath the Stargate."

Our folks are surprised. "Underneath?" Wolf asks.

Jaina stands up and turns to us. "Normal instruments haven't been able to detect anything but solid rock under the gate. However, a vast underground labyrinth of tunnels and caves exists, cleverly hidden by a race that wishes to remain unknown."

I hear the murmurs of everyone talking at once, but Jaina's stare is fixed on me. I turn to Jewel, who is staring at Jaina. Her fear hits me as she shudders. Fear from Jewel, who survived months imprisoned by the Dracans, is not a good sign.

13
SKY

A fter our uneventful landing, the flight crew works quickly to unload the vehicles and equipment. All I can think about is getting into a shower. There's nothing we can do about what's under the Stargate tonight, and there's no imminent threat to any of us. I could sleep for a week.

"We have to talk." I jump at Jewel's voice. I didn't hear her come up behind me.

"Can't we talk in the morning?" My voice sounds whiny, even to me.

"No. Tonight. We're sharing a room with Juliana, and she needs to hear it, too."

I've had enough mystery for one day, but mystery isn't through with me, yet.

"Okay," I answer, sending her a little annoyance to punctuate how begrudgingly I'm giving in.

Jewel pokes me in the side with her elbow. "I wouldn't insist if it weren't important."

"After our showers." I wonder how tired my voice sounds. I send her some love and walk away, eager to get in the Hummer and get going.

When we finally stop, our headlights illuminate an ornate iron gate in a thick adobe wall at least fifteen feet tall. Surveillance cameras face us from their perches on the corners. When the gate swings open, we drive into a barn-like building and park. Six men, some no taller than me, rush to help unload the cars.

The one-story house doesn't appear big enough for all of us. Once we're inside, though, it reminds me of our own place in North Carolina. The bulk of it is underground.

The men remain with Jack and his crew while they bring the gear into the house. Jaina leads us girls down a set of stairs to lower level.

"You girls will stay here," she says.

The room is fine, even without windows. A fan turns lazily in the middle of the ceiling, and single beds line three of the walls, each spread with a colorful quilt and topped with fluffy pillows. Folded towels and washcloths lie at the foot of each bed.

"The bathroom is there." Jaina points to a white door on the left. An armoire stands against the wall on the right, flanked by a micro-fridge under a cabinet topped with a microwave.

"You'll find water and snacks in the fridge and cabinet. Breakfast is upstairs at six a.m. Someone will come get you. If you need anything, use the phone next to the bed against the far wall. It connects directly with the house staff." She turns and walks out, closing the door behind her.

"How do you read her, Sky?" Juliana asks.

"She doesn't," Jewel answers for me. "Sky can't feel her emotions, but she has an aura, which means she's neither Dracan nor Allaran. She isn't human, either."

"What do you mean?" Juliana asks.

"An odd metallic color in her aura suddenly flared when we were using the wristbands. I think she knows something about them. Juliana, Dad is working on yours, and when he's done, you'll be able to communicate telepathically with the rest of us."

Juliana abruptly sits on the bed farthest from the bathroom. Good. I want the closest one. Jewel can have the house phone next to her bed.

"I knew you could speak with your minds, but never dreamed I'd be a part of it." She stretches and yawns, starting a chain reaction. Her wide grin radiates the joy flowing off her. It energizes me enough to grab my towel and make a beeline for the bathroom.

"Anybody need to use it before I shower?" I ask politely. Any further conversation about Jaina can wait.

14
STORM

"Hey! Wake up!" Strong hands pin my arms flat on the bed, and I buck, trying to dislodge the heavy body sitting on my stomach. I shove with my mind, but it doesn't budge. Is this part of the nightmare?

"Wake up, Ryder. It's just us. Calm down." Pax's voice breaks through the fog and when I open my eyes, Murphy gets up, still holding my arms down.

The room is in shambles. I don't remember throwing anything around, but the dream sent me into a panic.

"You can let go. I'm alright." Murphy releases me and I sit up and start putting things back. It's a good thing there's nothing breakable in the room.

"What happened?" Pax asks.

I don't answer right away because I honestly don't know. I've never had a dream before, or if I have, I don't remember it. Once, when I talked to Sequoia about it, she thought my mind must go into a state of sleep beyond dreams, to protect me and others from my gift. It's probably genetic. I believed her and didn't worry about it anymore, until now. This was a nightmare.

"I don't want to talk about it," I say. Talking about it might make it real. I can't risk it.

Murphy shrugs, his expression odd, as if he can tell what I'm thinking. "Do you dream often, Storm?"

I shake my head and say, "Go back to bed. We all need the sleep."

"In my culture," Murphy says, "when a dream causes the body to physically engage, then it carries an important message. Perhaps yours is a message, too?"

"No!" Oh, God. I don't want it to be.

"You were shouting my sister's name," Pax says. "After you shouted, 'let her go' several times, things started flying around the room. If it was a message, maybe we can help you protect her."

Pax Fletcher, the voice of reason. Telling them about it won't make it any more real than it already is. If someone planted it in my head, as Murphy thinks, then he's right. I'll need help to keep her out of danger.

"Fine. I'll tell you. I saw a group of ugly female giants in a cave, with long noses and teeth filed to sharp points. No offense, Murphy."

"None taken," he replies. Dracans have crocodile teeth. These were longer and as sharp as stilettos.

"They all had red hair, but much duller than Sky's. Stringy. Thin. Their fingernails, filthy things, were pointed and sharp, like their teeth. I don't scare easily, but they terrified me."

"You must have dreamt about the same thing Jewel saw in the desert two nights ago," Murphy says. "Al told us about them, too, although he's never seen a female. What did they want with Sky?"

"I don't know. The tallest one poked her in the back with one of her nails, and Sky went with them."

"Was she alone?" Pax asks. "Were the other girls with her?"

"Only Sky. When she didn't see me or hear me call out to her, I knew it was a dream. It felt real." My freezing gut hasn't stopped shuddering since I came out of it. The same icy fear and terrible helplessness had overwhelmed me when the lizards took my parents.

I'm about to ask what time it is when the ground starts vibrating. Pax's eyes grow wide and Murphy runs for his bed.

"Cover your ears," Pax yells, grabbing a pillow and diving to the mattress. He scrambles for his bed and I cover my head with a pillow just as the sound hits and everything is lost in a blur of pain.

Agony rips through my head and spreads like molten fire through my bones. I know I'm screaming but can't hear it over the pulsating boom of sound about to rip me apart. I welcome the blackness as I lose consciousness.

Waking up to silence, I'm afraid I'm alone in the room, until I spot the lumps under the covers on my friends' beds. They're moving. We're alive. Once again, I'm surprised we survived it.

I tap my wristband and open the communal link to my friends, and the one to Wolf and Sequoia. She's a continent away but the bands work with Earth's magnetic grid, and only Dracan technology can interfere with their connection. Charles is working on a way to get around their tech.

Who's awake? I ask, relieved when they all answer. I hear my aunt question her husband, but there are too many voices in my head, and I break the link and take deep breaths. Hearing should come back soon.

As soon as we can stand on our rubbery legs, we make our way to the girls' room down the hall and enter without knocking. They wouldn't have heard us, anyway. Juliana has lifted the three of them in a bubble of air. It's a tactic she used to keep us off the burning sand in the dragon's lair under Andros. They smile at us while she lowers them. Has she discovered a way to insulate them from the sound of the artifact? It's a sure bet one of the artifacts is very close by.

Sky opens the link. *Your sister is amazing. She figured out how to block most of the sound waves.*

I can't help the surge of jealousy, but I tamp it down and throw it into the rage cage. Sky should get a kick out of it. Instead, she sends love and comfort. Pax is right. I'm an idiot.

The girls drop to the floor, and together we float up the stairs. At least I'm good for something.

Wolf, Charles, and Dylan have a room in the main house with Jack and his team.

Our view is better than yours, I imagine, Wolf says. I hear the smile in his thought, and I'm glad we have the wristbands.

Jack leads us to a dining room, where a huge bowl of scrambled eggs with peppers and onions sits in the middle of a sideboard, surrounded by freshly baked rolls and fruit. My stomach rumbles in anticipation and I grab a blue dish off a stack of multi-colored plates.

I sit at one of four square tables scattered through the room and dig in. Sky sits next to me. I have no objection. She's become my priority after the dream. We'll find the artifact. Heck, we're probably sitting right on top of it, judging by the intensity of the sound. If all goes well, we'll also find my parents. Though with our luck, what are the chances of it happening?

The rage rattles in my chest, and I force it to be still. I'll need a cool head to handle the coming challenges.

"I don't think we should split up," Dylan says. My hearing is gradually coming back, but did I hear him correctly?

"We have to," Wolf replies. "Sequoia says there's another artifact near or on the island that disappeared in Tierra del Fuego. She thinks Storm's parents may be there, and we're running out of time."

I remember the tracking device. I have the one we found yesterday, and Juliana has the one the Dracan gave to her. Does Jewel know she's the only one who can open it?

15

JEWEL

I'm amazed at Juliana's quick thinking. When she surrounded us with the bubble of air and lifted us off the ground, it muted the sound waves. How did air become a sound barrier? Rather than twisting us up into blubbering masses of pain, the call was no louder than the music I listened to during my early teen rebellion, when I turned the volume all the way up. I knew my parents hated it. It was too loud for me too, but I did it to annoy them. We're all glad that phase is over.

Sky worries me though. We go back to our room after breakfast to gather our gear, and I open our connection.

What's bothering you? Her eyes widen, her fear battering me. Or is it my fear for her?

Do you believe in premonitions?

Do you need to ask? We're the answer to a hundreds-of-years-old prophecy. I'd call it the mother of premonitions. Why? Have you had one? If something is scaring her, I'm not sure I want to know what it is, but it probably involves the rest of us.

I still remember each detail of the vivid dream I had last night. Most dreams fade as soon as I wake up.

Do you want to tell me about it? Part of me hopes she doesn't.

Juliana comes in and picks up her backpack. "Time to go," she says, waiting for us to walk out with her.

Later, Sky says, closing the link.

I follow Juliana upstairs and again sense impending danger. Grief hits me in the pit of my stomach, and I need to stop for a moment. I motion for Sky to pass me. She pats my shoulder and sends me peace, trying to alleviate my pain. I send a quick "thank you" to God for her. She makes a good buffer between Juliana and me. I hate this. Juliana and I have been friends since Atlantis. Her aura hasn't changed since Triton's cave. So why are my emotions going haywire?

When we get to the garage, Jaina is in her car, drumming on the steering wheel with long, red-tipped nails. Pax and Murphy lean against Al's Hummer, laughing at something he said. Storm's aura is darker than usual. He's standing by himself, lost in thought with a deep line between his eyebrows, worried about something.

Dr. Austin marches in and announces, "Hop in. We're going to the Puerta de Hayu Marca, or the gateway to the City of Gods."

"Is it the same as the Stargate?" Juliana asks.

"One and the same," he replies with a grin. "It has several names, and I'll tell you about them when we get there." Dad, Dylan, and Wolf pile into his vehicle.

The road is in bad shape, with plenty of small stones making the ride bumpy. We hang on to the frame, wherever we can get a good grip, and duck every time we hit one of the frequent bumps and potholes. I'm exhausted by the time we pull up to a parking area. A line of identical green jeeps is already there, with a logo of a sun surrounded by the words "Isla del Sol Aventuras" emblazoned on the doors.

"The tourists trickle in all morning," Jaina explains. "They don't stay long, and during the heat of midday, none of the tour guides will come out here. They'll return in the afternoon, but by evening we'll have it all to ourselves."

"Why are we here so early, then?" Sky asks. "What do you hope to accomplish with other people around?"

"Jack wants to fill you in on the history of the place, and why we're so interested," Jaina answers. "Keep in mind, he didn't know about you or the artifacts when we started excavating in this region. We're after entirely different things."

I notice she said, "he didn't know," and not "we." I remember how she tensed up in their cargo plane when Dylan explained about the artifacts. She's hiding something.

Jaina opens the hatch and pulls out woven drawstring bags, one for each of us. I admire the colorful patterns on the bags. Whoever created these must also have made Jack's sweatband.

"This is food and water for the day," she explains. "We won't be coming back to the cars until we're finished at the gate."

Two stone pillars mark a gravel path leading toward jagged cliffs rising out of the desert. At first, there's room enough for me to walk between Juliana and Sky. Juliana frowns when I tap on my wristband to open my link to Sky. I grab her hand and squeeze it in apology. She shrugs and moves ahead to walk next to Murphy. She asks him something and they're quickly engaged in an animated conversation. I wonder why my mood lifted as soon as she walked away.

Tell me about the dream, Sky.

I'm sorry. Sharing it makes it real, somehow.

If it's a true premonition, then not sharing it won't make it any less real. Maybe I can help. In fact, we all need to hear it.

She swipes at a tear rolling down her cheek, struggling to control her emotions. The link to the others opens, and Pax sounds alarmed. *What's wrong?* He's particularly sensitive to his sister's moods.

Sky is about to tell us about a disturbing dream she had before the artifact's cry woke us up. Storm's back stiffens, and a small dust devil kicks up and swirls a few feet to his right, keeping up with him as he walks. Pax shoots him a concerned glance.

What is that about?

I'm sure it was nothing, Sky says. I know she's lying. *Between what Jewel saw in the desert and all the talk of giants, my imagination probably painted a weird scenario.*

Giants? Storm's tiny whirlwind grows larger, picking up small rocks and tearing some dry grasses out of the dusty ground. *How many?* His voice in my head sounds strained.

I'm not sure. We were in a dimly lit cavern, and only the one who spoke to me was visible.

Describe her, Pax says. His aura has grown dark with streaks of black, very much like Storm's. This means something to them. My gut is jittery, both with my own worry and with the increasing fear Sky's projecting.

Enormous, with red hair and teeth filed to sharp points. Her fingernails must have been three inches long and sharp as knives. She was grimy as if she hadn't bathed in a long time, and her clothing stank like uncured animal skin. Her boots covered her knees. The boots were as tall as I am.

What did she say to you? The anger in Storm's mental voice pierces the peace Pax is trying to project to his sister.

She said, "You belong with us. We claim you." When she turned to leave, something nudged me from behind and I was compelled to follow them. I woke up and felt the vibration of the artifact just before it sounded off.

God, please let this be nothing more than a bad dream. My gut tells me it isn't, especially when Pax's horrified face turns to Storm. The dust devil is now a whirlwind, racing off to the cliffs, ripping up the ground behind it. Pax breaks the link and rushes to catch up with him.

16
JEWEL

I trudge along in silence, with my gut clenching and thoughts racing. What's going on with those two? They're planning something, but they must be using their private link. Storm nods and glances back at Sky. Pax grabs his arm for a second and lets it go. The swirls of red and black in their auras remind me of rain-dark clouds scudding across the sky as a thunderstorm rushes in.

Since there's nothing I can do, and worry won't help anything, I turn my focus to the men leading the way and concentrate on listening to Dr. Austin as he points out some landmarks. I know he wants us to call him Jack, but it's hard getting used to thinking of him so informally. He's quite a character on the television program he hosts. He entertains as he leads the audience through some fascinating, mysterious locations. I wish I could tell him about some of the places I've visited, like deep in the sacred rock of Uluru in Australia, or the city beneath Superstition Mountain in Arizona. How would he react to learning Atlantis sank in the Bahamas and still exists under the ocean?

It probably wouldn't do to broadcast the confirmed existence of two alien species sharing our planet Terra. Most people would consider it fiction, I suppose, unless they see them in person. I hope they'll reveal themselves once we've saved the planet. If we do.

The cliffs are red granite rock formations jutting out of the land-scape like rows of uneven teeth. They're free-standing, unlike our North Carolina cliffs carved by nature on the sides of our mountains. Some branch off others and some have sloping sides. The area is known as Stone Forest or City of the Gods, with shapes including the forms of animals and men, bridges to nowhere and strange grottoes.

The Puerta de Hayu Marca is nothing more than a flat rectangle carved on one side of a cliff, with a squared-off keyhole-shaped depression cut into the center at ground level. I watch as a woman takes a picture of a young man standing in the shallow opening, his head touching the top and arms stretched out to the sides. It's hard for me to imagine this small, unremarkable indentation leading anywhere.

A formation of boulders slants across the top, like the figure of a semi-reclining woman gazing up at the sky. It makes me think of a lounge chair at the beach, with pillows propping her up as she star-gazes. Is she supposed to be one of the giants, or one of the gods?

Jack leads us off to the right, where we find rocks to sit on in a bit of shade. Jaina opens her drawstring bag and pulls out a sandwich and a bottle of water. It's our cue to do the same, and as we eat, he talks.

"As soon as the tourists clear out, we'll examine the inside of the door," he says. "You'll see a small circular depression in the middle. Legend has it, when a golden sun disk is placed in the depression, the gate will open, much larger than it appears on this side, to allow the gods to return to Earth in their sun ships."

"It sounds like it could have been a wormhole at one time," Wolf notes.

"It's possible," Jack says. "The locals believe Star People came through this gate to Earth, and earth people traveled through it to visit the worlds of the gods. They say it closed for good after the last of the Inca priests of the Star People walked through it into a blue light, and it won't open again until the earth is about to end."

"Unless these young people find and fix the artifacts, we could be there now," Wolf says.

"I'm not sure I'd take that part of the legend seriously. The gate appears to be operational at times and has been for years. We've heard stories of people disappearing and even returning. When it happens, a blue light appears where the small door is now. Could it be the gateway to another dimension, another planet, or perhaps, to another world inside this planet?"

He could be right on all counts. If the wormhole opens occasionally, it's probably one of the unstable ones the Allarans told us about. If so, it's unlikely it will lead to Storm's parents, but we can't discount the slim possibility. What if it does?

Jack continues. "I had the pleasure of interviewing a man who claimed he went through the portal to a series of tunnels and caverns deep below us. He was guided by what he called "spirit beings" to a cave filled with golden objects which he claimed were from the City of Gold. The city is thought to have been lost after the Conquistadors conquered these lands.

"Shortly after our interview, he was found dead here, at the threshold of the gate, gripping a necklace with a small replica of a golden sun disk."

"Did he take his own life, or was he murdered?" Dad asks.

"There was no investigation. The natives are rather superstitious and didn't allow anyone to touch the body. Their priests buried the man in a location known only to them," Jack replies.

"The gate is also known as Aramu Muru, named after a priest who saved one of three golden sun disks from the Conquistadores. Incan priests performed a secret ritual here, and the portal opened. He entered and was never seen nor heard from again."

"Is this related in any way to the Gate of the Sun found in Tiahuanaco, on the other side of the lake?" Pax asks.

Jack nods. "Many people believe they're related in appearance and aligned with five other archeological sites in the region. I'm sure you've heard of ley lines or lines of power. You'll find this and the Gate of the Sun are both at junctures of these lines."

"What's your interest in this location?" Storm asks. "We're searching for the artifact that made the noise last night. Do you suspect we might find it here?"

Jack takes a swig of water, wipes his mouth with the back of his hand and bends to wipe his forehead with the hem of his shirt. "Where is the object we found at the mandala? Do you have it with you?"

"What does that have to do with anything?" Storm sounds defensive, and his aura turns darker.

Pax steps in to say, "There's a chance it might trigger the Stargate. Isn't that what you were thinking, Dr. Austin?"

"Exactly," Jack says with enthusiasm. "On our way here, Wolf filled me in about the Dracans and those other aliens, the Allarans. I've long suspected they were here among us but had no proof. I believe the object might belong to them. If so, maybe it'll activate the wormhole. If the gate leads to an underground city, I'd like nothing better than to explore and, perhaps, find the cache of golden treasure."

I suppose it will make a great episode on his program. Is he taking this whole "find the artifact and save the earth" thing seriously, or is his focus on treasure hunting? If we don't find the artifact, no amount of treasure or television ratings will be worth a hill of beans.

17
STORM

"When the tourists leave, we'll see if the locator beacon does anything other than pinpoint our location to the ones who planted it in the mandala. We could be the bullseye in an alien target with this thing," I say.

I refuse to take it out of my pack until then. I don't trust Jack and his crew, and there's something off about Jaina Chen. After the dream Sky and I shared last night, I'm not eager to open any portals that might lead to tunnels. It's irrational, of course. The artifact could be down in some cave below us.

"How do you know it's a locator beacon?" Jaina asks. The beast inside rattles the cage. I don't answer.

"It's Dracan technology," Juliana says. I wish she'd keep her mouth shut. No, I wish I'd kept my own mouth shut.

"I know," she says, "because I can use my telekinesis to move it, but I can't use it to open the thing, and only the Dracans can block our gifts."

"So we know it's Dracan, but how do you know what it's used for?" Jack asks. How much does he know about Juliana and Murphy?

"I'm familiar with some of their equipment," Charles answers. He and Murphy have been working together, both in his home lab and at the observatory. I should have realized Murphy would share some of his knowledge with Jewel's father. Is he covering for us, or does he know how this thing works?

His answer satisfies Jack, but Jaina's glare reveals her suspicion. A snort, followed by a steady rhythm of snores, draws my attention to Al, comfortably stretched out on the uneven ground with his hat covering his face. I take his cue and stretch out, too, using my pack as a pillow, and drift off.

My sleeping brain is hyper alert to the faintest breath out of the ordinary, like now.

My backpack moves a whisper under my head, and I'm alert and ready to fight. Whoever owns the hand making its way into the pack must be a skilled pickpocket.

In an instant, I toss the thief into the air and hold him there while I get up and dust myself off. I hear the others stirring around me and let the thief stew in his bubble over our heads, refusing to acknowledge him. Al is the first to spot him.

"What the heck are you doing up there, Jaina?" he shouts. Jaina? When I finally look up, there she is, sitting cross-legged and serene, like a floating Buddha. She shrugs and smiles. Smiles?

"What were you doing in my backpack?" I ask her, bouncing the bubble enough to make her reach out to the sides for balance.

A deep scowl replaces her stupid smile when she glares at me. "Put me down, child."

"Child?" I shout, and she shoots off toward the flat wall of the Stargate. I stop her just before she hits. "Now, tell us what you were doing rummaging around in my pack, or I'll..."

"Stop!" I vaguely hear everyone shouting, but Wolf's voice penetrates the rage. "Storm, you can't hurt her. Put her down. Gently."

I draw her back toward us and say, "I'll put her down when she explains. Not before. And whether I drop her hard or ease her down will depend on her answer."

"I was simply adjusting your pillow," she says. Her voice sounds oily in my ears, and I'm not buying it.

"You lie," Jewel says, glaring at Jaina. At least she agrees with me.

"Tell us what you were doing, Miss Chen," Sky says, sending bullets of rage toward the woman.

Pax takes a deep sniff and says, "We don't know who or what you are, Miss Chen, but we know you're up to something."

Wolf, Charles and Dylan stare at her silently, presenting a united front with us, even though they don't understand why we're being obstinate about this. I'm proud of them and make a silent promise to communicate more with them from now on. I believe we're all going to need each other more than ever.

"That's enough, kids. If you want our help, you'll let her down this instant." Jack Austin's angry voice cuts through our wall of solidarity, and Wolf opens our link.

Go ahead, son, let her down. We'll get to the bottom of this another way.

I drop her to the ground without warning, and she lands the way she's sitting. I take her glare as a warning to watch my back from now on. The fact is, she'd better watch hers.

"What's that?" While our attention has been on Jaina, Jack has been watching the wall, and now he's pointing at the Stargate behind us. I turn to see what he's excited about.

A blue glow fills the small doorway, growing both in size and intensity as we watch. I hear Jewel gasp behind me and turn back. She's staring at Jaina, who's as transfixed by the light as everyone else. I turn my attention back to the wall, and there they are, just like in my dream.

The one in the lead steps out of the glow into ordinary daylight. We're standing in the nighttime darkness of the surrounding desert. Is she in another dimension?

She's as tall as I remember, with wildly stringy red hair and wearing the animal skins Sky had described. When she opens her mouth to call out in a strange language, I see her pointed teeth.

Sky finds her voice and calls back, "Do you speak English?"

"You," she says, her voice booming with power. "Fire Hair. You come."

"No," Sky says, sending a shaft of power. The woman staggers from the emotional blow. I step up to Sky and grab her hand, tapping our private code on my wristband.

Don't go with them.

I have no intention of going with them. Besides, this isn't the scenario in my dream. We were in a cavern, remember? You had it, too. If we find ourselves in that place, then I'll count on you to help keep me away from them.

"You come," the giant says again just before the blue light fades, taking her and the others along with it.

Our stunned silence is broken by a loud whoop, as Jack starts doing something resembling a rain dance. "Did you see that? Did you see that?" he repeats, obviously overjoyed.

"The Stargate came to life, and the gods actually appeared! Al, we're setting up the cameras here tomorrow night. If it happened once, it'll happen again. You kids will be here, of course, and we'll have everything we need to film it. Bring the Dracan egg contraption. It might have been the key to opening the doorway."

I can't stand to listen anymore and turn to walk back to the vehicles. My friends fall in behind me, followed by Wolf and the men. Jewel hurries to catch up with me. "I saw her. I know what she really is."

18
STORM

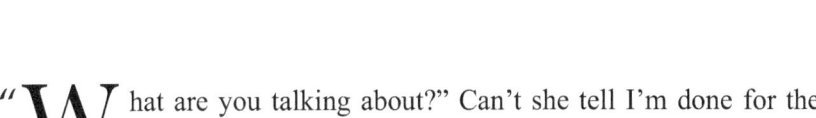

"What are you talking about?" Can't she tell I'm done for the day? I need to regroup, and I certainly don't want any more surprises.

"Jaina Chen. She isn't human. I saw her real form in the blue light."

"Why don't you open the link and share this revelation with all of us?"

"I would, but I suspect she somehow uses the link to read our minds."

Great. Isn't that just great. "Fletcher, Sky. Hurry up. We need to talk."

When Pax and his sister catch up, the others are far enough behind they won't hear us if we talk quietly. Sky taps on her wristband, but closes the link when Jewel vehemently shakes her head and puts her hand over Sky's.

"Why not?" Sky asks.

"Jaina was in her true form in the blue light, and I believe she taps into the link and listens in. I wonder now if what we saw was real or a projection from her mind after she heard about the dreams."

"It was real to me," I say, but I'm not as certain as I was.

"What is her true form?" Pax asks.

"She's insectoid, and her aura indicates she must be Terran."

"What do you mean by insectoid?" Storm asks.

Jewel pauses, as if she's trying to find the words. "Her head is larger than in her human form, wide at the top and angling down to a point, like a triangle. Shiny black eyes wrap around and up the sides of her head. Two slits in the middle of her face could be a nose, and her mouth must be located where the face comes to a point. Her neck and body are long and thin above the waist, and rather thick on the bottom. Spikes run the length of her skinny arms. The fingers of her hands are long and curved, more like claws than fingers."

"I didn't know you can see the auras of insects," Sky says. "I thought you only saw human ones."

"You know I don't. Only their life force is visible to me, but something sets her apart. I wish I knew what it was. I wish I knew more about her kind. I don't understand why she hasn't appeared that way until now. I've always been able to see through disguises."

"She sounds like a praying mantis," I remark. All I know about them is the females bite the heads off the males while they're mating. It makes me glad she called me a child. Not that I'd consider her as a mate. The thought makes me shudder.

"Yes," Jewel answers. "Only much bigger."

"When we get back to the compound, let's ask our folks if they know anything about an insectoid race, if we can drag them away from Jack and his team. Let's ask Murphy and Juliana, too. They might have heard of them," I suggest.

On the way back to the compound, Al drives in silence, and I'm tempted to ask him about Jaina. He appears to be the most level-headed of the crew, but I can't get a clear reading on him. I'll ask Sky and Jewel what they've observed about him. It would be helpful to have one member of the team on our side.

As soon as we arrive, Jack's native helpers scramble to load up the backs of the Hummers with boxes of equipment. He must have been serious about shooting an episode of his series. It's probably a waste of time. If the portal opens at random, why would it open again tomorrow night? Oh, well. It isn't my money.

Thankfully, Jaina and Al stay with the vehicles while the rest of us make our way into the house. I don't know how I'll react to her now that I know about her alter-ego.

My stomach growls as soon as we enter the dining room and the aroma of Peruvian dishes on the sideboard hits me. I take a plate and fill it with some roast chicken, potato balls stuffed with ground beef, and roasted vegetables.

Jack Austin can't hide his excitement all through supper, while the rest of us eat quietly. It finally dawns on him, no one is sharing his enthusiasm.

"What's wrong with all of you?" He throws his hands up and turns around, glaring at each table. "We witnessed a miraculous event tonight, the gods coming through the Aramu Muru. Tomorrow night, we're going to film it."

"They weren't gods," I say. "They were giants. Didn't you meet one at Tierra del Fuego? Wasn't he just as human as you are?"

"All right. Let's say they were. They still came through the gate, didn't they?"

"Maybe," Charles says. "Something was off about them. They flickered as if they were holograms."

"The Dracans use a lot of holograms in their underground and undersea cities," Jewel says. "They give them the illusion they're above-ground."

"Are you saying the Aramu Muru is a gateway to a Dracan city?" There's no dampening Jack's enthusiasm. Gods, Dracans, what difference does it make? It should be great TV.

"The question is whether we somehow triggered the hologram, if that's what it was," Charles says. "What are we going to do about it if it happens again tonight?"

I have an idea, but I'll keep it to myself. Meanwhile, I'll have a talk with Juliana. If my sister hasn't told Jewel what her Dracan friend told her, I'll find out why. If she won't tell her, then I will.

19
SKY

The sound of weeping draws me out of a dreamless sleep. Jewel's anguish snaps me fully awake and I rush to her side.

"Jewel, what is it? Are you hurt? Did something happen?" In her despair and confusion, she isn't receiving the peace I'm pushing at her. She's scaring me.

"What can I do to help?" Juliana asks, throwing off her covers and padding over to Jewel's bed.

"Get back!" Jewel shouts. "It's you, Juliana. Why are you doing this to me?"

I'm hit by Juliana's shock and disbelief. She staggers and backs up to her bed, where she abruptly sits and starts crying, too. It's too much for me, like it was when Triton's emotions nearly killed me.

"Everyone quiet down," I shout, sending out what I hope is a blast of calmness. The sudden silence startles me and I realize I've shocked them both. I guess it wasn't calm that hit them. I can't help it. I start laughing hysterically.

"You should see your faces." I gulp and hold my sides, sinking to the floor.

Jewel's startled laugh joins mine and suddenly we're back in North

Carolina, playing the silly "other than" game again. It gives me an idea.

"Other than Juliana's parents going missing, a sick artifact somewhere around here and giants wanting to kidnap me, everything is fine, right?"

Juliana wipes her eyes. "Are you insane?" she asks.

Her question sends Jewel and me into gales of giggles, and in moments, Juliana is laughing, too. There's nothing like contagious laughter to lighten the atmosphere.

When we're finally reduced to an occasional giggle, Juliana says, "I think I know what's bothering Jewel."

We listen intently as she tells us about the locator beacon her Dracan friend gave her before we came here.

"He said only Jewel can open it. I didn't understand at first, but now I know Jewel wasn't reacting to me, but to the beacon in my backpack. This one is keyed to Shaula. If you're the only one who can use it, Jewel, it's because Shaula has marked you."

The blood drains from my friend's face. I get up from my perch on the floor and sit next to her on the bed, putting my arm around her.

"What the heck do you mean?" I bellow. I swear, if that evil thing has touched her, I'll kill him personally.

"He's claimed her as his mate, using a biochemical marker that can't be erased or negated in any way."

"He raped her?" I want to throw up. Jewel is silent, but her trembling shakes the entire bed. I wrap the quilt around her.

"In a sense," Juliana explains. "When a Dracan male marks a female without her full consent, it would be considered rape. I've never heard of it happening until now, which is why I didn't make the connection sooner. Murphy and I are a marked pair because we love each other, and it's a matter of time before we're together. Dracans don't force themselves on women as a rule."

"How do we get rid of it? Jewel loves Pax and he loves her. Shaula will just have to deal with it."

"It can't be erased, Sky. She'll never be free of Shaula, and when he claims her, she'll have no choice but to go with him."

Jewel finally speaks, her voice shaking like a leaf in a hurricane. "When did Shaula mark me? I was never alone with him. Where is the mark? Can I cut it out of my skin?"

"It would be on the back of your neck, and you can't get rid of it while you're alive. The chemical seeps into your spine and infuses your nervous system. Do you remember the night you spent in the jail cell? The guards piped in a gas to put the prisoners to sleep. I'll bet he did it then."

"The locator beacon will work for me because he wants me to come to him. He's holding your parents hostage, Juliana. He'll trade them for me."

"I don't know what to say, Jewel. Normally, I'd say it's a fair trade." I slam her with a fist of fury, right in her gut. It's as effective as a physical fist, and she doubles over and gags. I'll have to remember I can use my gift as a weapon.

"I said, normally," she squeaks, stifling a moan. "Most Dracan males are wonderful mates. Shaula is pure evil. We can't let Jewel do this."

"How do we stop it?" I ask.

"We kill him," she says.

"We have to tell the boys. When Pax hears about this, he'll figure out a way to end Shaula. Storm is already on board. He's been out for Dracan blood since he was ten years old. Murphy might know how it can be done."

I glance at the clock on my wristband. It's only 4:30 am, but I don't care. I throw the door open, march to the boys' room, and bang loudly on their door. If Dad and the others were down here with us, I would have woken them up, too.

I sense Pax questioning me, so I send him a blast of anger. That should do it. The door opens in seconds and Storm is there, bare chested with his black wavy hair all tousled and gorgeous. Heat shoots through me, and my knees get soft and mushy and try to propel me into his arms. His scowl stops me cold.

"What's up?" he asks.

I am, you idiot. My mind refuses to settle down for a few long seconds. "All of you need to come to our room. We have a crisis, and we need your help."

I turn my back and march back to our room. A flurry of activity assures me they're following.

My brother spots Jewel's tear-reddened face and rushes to wrap his arms around her. Murphy plops next to Juliana on her bed and Storm sinks to the floor next to the door. I send him a blast of annoyance, longing to wipe the smirk off his face.

Jewel breaks down and sobs against Pax's shoulder, clinging to him. His eyes question me, and I say, "We've found out what's been bothering her."

20

PAX

I hold Jewel's shuddering body close and send her the peace I send my sister when she's upset. The trembling slows and she slowly relaxes. My jaw tightens and I grit my teeth, fighting a surge of gut-wrenching fury as I listen to Juliana explain about Shaula and what he did to my Jewel.

Storm growls low in his throat. Or maybe the growl is mine. Now I understand his need to tear that lizard limb from limb.

I tap my wristband. We'll need cooler and smarter heads to help us figure this out.

Dad, are you awake?

I am now. What's up?

Get the others and come down here now. Please.

He must have heard the desperation in my mental voice, because he answers, *Be right there. Hang on.*

The men are fully dressed when they come in ten minutes later. They listen while Juliana explains it all again. I can smell their anger as she answers their questions, even with my guard up.

Charles sums it up when she's finished. "If we use the locator beacon, it will lead us to Shaula and Storm's parents. He wants Jewel.

We assume he'll trade her for them, but we can't allow it to happen. Murphy, would you be able to enlist Thuban's aid?"

Murphy answers, "Perhaps. I will certainly let him know about the mark and the beacon. He and his people are very interested in capturing the traitor Shaula. This crime will motivate them even more."

Charles moves to Jewel's other side and I let her go so he can hug her. "Jewel, if we set a trap for him, you would have to be the bait. If you aren't up to it, we'll find another way."

"I'll do anything to catch that creep," she says. "I'd rather die than be with him."

"It's nearly time for breakfast," Dad says. "We can't let Dr. Austin and his people know anything about this, especially about Juliana's possession of the beacon. I don't trust them, so we'll play along with his plan to revisit the Stargate tonight. After you came downstairs last night, we talked about visiting the floating islands today. I say we act like tourists for the day. We'll use the link to make our plans."

"I wouldn't," Jewel cautions. "Jaina Chen isn't human, and I believe she can read us when we're linked."

Dad and Charles say nothing, waiting for her to explain. Wolf nods his head. I wonder if he knows, or just suspects Jaina is different.

"If she isn't human, then what is she?" my dad asks.

"She's insectoid, like a praying mantis. She has an aura, so I assumed she was human, and I didn't see through her disguise. How is that possible?"

"Tell him what you told me about her aura," Sky says.

"There's an odd metallic grey in it I've never seen before."

As if she's been listening on the other side of the door, it opens and Jaina Chen enters the room without knocking.

"Breakfast is ready," she says, giving each of us an intense glare. "Family meeting?"

"We're just finishing, Jaina," Dad says, his voice carrying a tone of authority. "We'll be up in a moment."

She whirls and marches out of the room, shutting the door behind her.

"Do you think she heard?" Sky asks, her voice trembling. "I can't feel her emotions at all."

"We go along with their plans," Wolf says, getting up from the floor and dusting his pants off. "For now. We can discuss strategy when we return tonight. Murphy, I don't know how you contact your people in Atlantis, but now would be a good time to talk to them about Shaula."

Murphy nods, smiling as usual. I wonder if anything bothers him.

BEFORE WE LEFT HOME, once it became clear we were coming here, I researched Lake Titicaca. It's the world's highest navigable lake, home to the Uros people and their floating islands. They built them hundreds of years earlier to protect themselves from the war-like Incas. Later, the Spanish conquerors left them alone, considering them sub-human.

The fact that totora reed islands have survived for centuries fascinates me. We wait on the dock in Puno for the boats Jack commissioned to take us out to the islands. I watched the special program he filmed about them on "Mysteries of the Ancients." The Uros are a simple people with an entrepreneurial drive. Since Jack's episode aired, the number of tourists visiting the islands grew exponentially. The Uros have taken full advantage of the booming tourist trade.

The girls are uncharacteristically quiet. I hope Jack and his people chalk it up to fatigue. Jaina keeps glancing at them, so I doubt we're fooling her. She knows something is up.

We step off the boats after a short ride, onto a strangely solid surface. Sky and Jewel step gingerly, as if they're afraid their next step could send a foot through the island to the water below. The reed mat is probably around twelve feet thick, constantly replenished with fresh reeds scattered on top as the ones on the bottom rot, so there's no danger of falling through. The decaying bottom is more pungent than the odor of most lakes. All of them have some measure of decay happening close to shore.

Houses, outhouses, boats, and even a watchtower, everything is made with the totora reeds. I understand parts of the plants are even edible. Human resourcefulness amazes me.

The islanders dress in traditional Andean costumes from the Inca period to impress the tourists. They've embraced tourism, along with the modern devices money can buy. Some homes are topped with solar panels, and I spot an antenna or two on some rooftops.

"Meet Henry," Al says, introducing a short, tanned islander dressed in white slacks, a loose, white long-sleeved shirt and a vest woven with a lot of colors. His straight black hair hangs like a helmet on his head, framing high cheek bones and a long nose. Could this be the same one who spoke with the giant?

"Welcome," he says in accented English. "I welcome you to my home," he says, sweeping his arms out wide toward the middle of the lake, "where the gods created the world."

His eyes suddenly widen, and his face goes pale as he stares at the place he pointed to, the sharp bitter stench of fear coming off him in waves. I turn to the lake.

A dark, pitted triangle is rising slowly from the water, blotting out the sun as it lifts into the sky and hovers over us without making a sound.

"Take cover," Storm shouts, and I run to grab Jewel's hand and duck behind one of the houses, while he and Sky run for another. Juliana and Murphy remain where they are. When the ship doesn't fire, I venture back out to the square. It's not one of the bad guys, I reason.

Henry falls to his knees, wailing loudly in a language I've never heard before. The other islanders do the same, arms lifted high and faces reflecting their terror. Is this the first time they've seen a Dracan ship? I've read there's a lot of UFO activity reported here, with strange lights and orbs flying in and out of the lake. I guess seeing an actual alien ship up close isn't a common occurrence.

A priest rushes out of his reed house, frantically adjusting an ornate headdress topped by a sun emblem outlined in multi-colored feathers. He hops and twirls in some ritualistic dance.

Al and Jack are frozen in place with their mouths hanging open.

The only one of the team who doesn't appear surprised is Jaina, whose mouth is turned up at the corner in a sneer as she stares at the ship.

I jump when Murphy's voice sounds right behind me. "I guess they heard me."

"Did you call them?" Sky asks.

"Yes. Charles asked me to."

"Is that Thuban's ship?" I ask.

"No. These are allies. I believe they're going to meet with Thuban." As I watch, the craft pulls away, speeds into the sky and disappears out of sight in a few seconds.

The islanders let out a long wail and drop their arms and faces to the surface of the island. Henry is the first to get to his feet.

"Viracocha," he says, his voice thick with reverence. "We have seen the creator."

21

JEWEL

Pax takes my hand and we walk over the solid mat to a bench made from the same reeds as the island. All around us, excited people chatter in groups, and several children come over and stare curiously. I love the multi-colored tops and skirts of the women. Even the vests both the men and women wear are woven in colorful designs. Pale greens and shades of brown and tan streak along the ground, creating a living design on the reed carpet floating on a pristine jewel of a lake.

A young girl comes to the front of the small crowd of children and asks in English, "Who are you?" A floppy cloth hat, in shades of pink and red, half-hides her face. A blousy periwinkle top and long red skirt with a blue and green design embroidered above the hem, complete her outfit. Her aura shines with green and blue interweaving strands.

A tiny boy tugs at her skirt and she turns to say something to him in their language. Her waist-length hair is neatly arranged in two braids down her back. It reminds me of the ridges that run along the head of my half-Dracan friend Marla.

"Are you gods?" the girl asks.

"Why do you ask?" I ask in return.

"You come, and gods come out of the water. We never see them until you come."

"No," I answer. Pax squeezes my hand and grins at me. I explain, "We're people just like you. Other people are in the aircraft. Not gods."

I'm sorry when her face drops. She takes the little boy by the hand and marches away, toward a group of adults. Unhappy with her account of my answers, they head back to their homes.

"Maybe I should have agreed with her."

He laughs and says, "I hope you didn't cause an international incident."

"I doubt it. They'll think we're just ignorant Americans. I wonder who taught her English."

"I think Jack is ready to go." He helps me up at the sound of Dr. Austin's sharp whistle. I'll be glad to get back on solid ground, once the boat gets to the dock. This odd island would take too much getting used to, and I'm happy to leave it to the natives.

SKY AND JULIANA share the back seat of the Hummer as we head to the Stargate. I've glanced at Jaina several times, again disappointed I can't see her as an insect. She remains silent, her hand clenching the stick shift when she notices my glances. I don't mind the silence, but Sky likes to talk, and the dam finally breaks.

"What does Dr. Austin hope to accomplish tonight?" she asks our driver. Without waiting for an answer, she continues. "Does he really think the blue light will show up again? Has it ever happened two nights in a row? Isn't it a rare phenomenon? Frankly, I hope we don't. I don't want anything to do with those oversized women."

There goes Jaina's clenching hand again. I turn in my seat and shoot Sky a warning glare. She's unstoppable.

"Why do you think they mentioned me? Of all of us, I think I'd be the last one they'd want to contact. And where do they want to take me? Do you think they know where the artifact is? But then, wouldn't they want all of us? I can't fix it by myself."

Juliana grabs her wrist and shakes her. When Sky keeps talking, I realize how nervous she is about tonight. Too nervous to remember Jaina isn't human and is probably not on her side.

She says, "What if the giants aren't holograms? What if they come after me?"

"We'll find out tonight," I try to reassure her. "We're all here, and you know Storm and your brother won't let anyone take you."

"Neither will Murphy," Juliana adds. "Or your father, or Wolf, or Jewel's father. You have us, too. Don't worry."

"You forget we were there when Jewel was abducted. A crowd is no guarantee they won't get what they came for."

I've been thinking the same thing. We don't know what powers or weapons those scraggly women have. My gut turns to ice. Her fear is infectious.

Jaina's hand relaxes on the stick shift, and my stomach drops at her expression. She's smiling.

The parking area is clear of tourist vehicles. Jack must have alerted the authorities we'd be filming tonight. When we pull in and get out of the car, two more Hummers join our little caravan. The film crew starts unloading, and Storm and Juliana help them move some of the heavier equipment. I recognize Henry among the native crew members.

No one appears startled when their gear floats out of the cargo hatches. We make our way along the path to the Stargate, with an assortment of oddly shaped packs floating alongside. The men behind us chatter in their language and the rest of us walk in silence.

Dr. Austin's team assembles the equipment like a well-oiled machine. By nightfall, they're ready. He calls the four of us to stand with him in a circle of light in front of the cameras. The wall and surrounding desert are dark in contrast. Storm pulls up short, out of the cameras' range, and we gather with him.

"You know you can't go public with our story, don't you? No one can know about the aliens, either."

"I don't plan on telling the world about your gifts. At least not until you've done what you're supposed to. I understand about not wanting undue interference." Jack's tone is meant to placate us, but I hear it as condescending. He irritates me. His aura is a sickly puce in the bright lights, and I trust him less than before.

"Then why do you want us in front of the cameras?" Pax asks.

I nod. Good question.

"I'm going to introduce you as the ones who helped open the Stargate, nothing more. I hope our program will gain a new, younger audience. Our funding comes from quite a few wealthy benefactors. There's a good chance some of their money will flow towards you once the ratings rise, which would help your cause, wouldn't it?"

While Jack is explaining the logic of his scheme, I watch the life-forces of my father, Dylan, and Wolf fan out closer to the wall. I spot Murphy, too, even though he isn't lit up like the rest. They're up to something. Otherwise, they'd be the ones arguing with Jack.

"We'll pass," Pax says in a firm voice. "Broadcast without mentioning us, Jack, and there may be a time when our alien friends use your program to announce their existence. It would certainly boost your ratings."

Jack's shoulders slump, but then he straightens again and turns to the camera Jaina is manning. He begins the introduction I've heard many times before.

"I'm Jack Austin, and we're coming to you from Peru. Tonight, we bring you something magical. Something impossible. Something that will defy everything you know about our universe. Tonight, you will witness the unfolding of one of the great mysteries of the Ancients."

He gestures dramatically toward the wall, suddenly illuminated by filtered spotlights casting a bluish shadow in the small doorway. The effect is stunning.

"Cut," Al calls from behind his camera.

"What now?" Sky asks.

"Now we wait for the thing to open," Al answers.

I hope we won't have to wait long.

22
SKY

The word "butterflies" comes nowhere near describing the quivering of my innards right now. It's like tiny rodents are running around, taking nips of my sensitive stomach from the inside. I think I might throw up.

"Calm down, Sky," my brother says, sending me some much-needed peace. "What are the chances it will open again tonight?"

"Normally, none, I suppose," I answer. "But if we're the ones triggering it, then it will open." I'm afraid to tell him what I'm planning, but it turns out I don't have to. He knows.

"You aren't going in alone."

"We'll all go," Storm says, coming up behind me. "Wolf and the men are in position. While Jack is hamming it up in front of the cameras, we'll go around the sides and wait with them."

"Won't they spot you in the bright light?" I ask.

"Al explained to us how they'll film it when the blue light appears. They'll shut off the spots. We'll make a run for it, then."

"What about us?" Jewel asks.

Juliana answers, "I'll be here with you and Sky. When the giants appear, we'll walk toward them. It'll make for some good footage for Jack. He won't notice the men are gone."

"It's too risky," I say, my anxiety rising. Pax squeezes my shoulder.

"Don't worry, little sister. It'll all work out." I hate when he calls me that. He's only ten minutes older.

I gratefully sink into one of the canvas folding chairs the crew provided for us. Storm pulls his closer to me. Shouldn't he and Pax be getting ready to make their escape? At this point, I don't care. All I can think about is whether my legs will carry me into the blue light toward those nasty hags.

~

"WAKE UP, SKY. IT'S HAPPENING." Storm nudges me and I smile at his sexy voice.

Then I wake up. Oh, God. Help me do this.

Pax grabs my hands and pulls me to my feet. He sends a blast of comfort and I regain a bit of confidence. Still, my knees are shaking.

"Gotta go," he whispers, and he and Storm head out in opposite directions. Juliana takes my right hand, and Jewel my left.

"We've got you," Jewel whispers in my ear.

The blue glow is shaped like an enormous blurred bubble hovering in front of the wall. I wonder if the cameras are capturing the shimmery rainbows flowing within it. I wish I had Jewel's vision right now.

We walk between two of the cameras and wait next to Jack. Once again, the one in the lead walks out, the vague forms of others behind her where they remain in shadow.

"Fire Hair. You come." Her deep voice booms, the surrounding rock formations amplifying it. Vibrations pulse through my friends' hands, still holding mine.

"Where?" I shout back.

The woman's eyes roam the desert in front of her, as if she can't tell where my voice is coming from. If this scene is, as I suspect, a hologram, then she probably can't see any of us from where they're projecting it.

"You are one of us. You come alone."

"Sure," I shout back. "Right away." I hope my voice isn't shaking with fright. Jack's eyes widen in shocked approval.

"Let's give them something to boost their ratings," I say to the girls. Together we walk toward the blue light. A spotlight remains on us while the cameras roll. The closer we get, the more I want to cut and run.

The edge of the glow begins to recede, and I wonder if we'll reach it before it fades completely. When the hairs on my arms stand up and my skin tingles, it dawns on me this isn't a hologram.

The giant sees me now. When she spots my friends, she screeches, "Alone. You come alone," and points her staff at Juliana.

Before she can fire, or do anything else with the staff, Dad dives into the bubble of light, followed by Charles, while it shrinks around them, leaving us on the outside.

"Run!" I yell, and the three of us sprint and leap into the bubble. A blur of wings flies in from the right of the dwindling light.

I quickly get up and run to stand close to the leader, trying not to stare at the knees directly in front of my face. "Don't hurt any of them. I will come willingly, but only if they come with me."

She bends down to my level, and I nearly gag at her stench. I hope Pax has his guard up. I turn away from her to search for him and freeze in shock. He isn't here, and neither are Storm, Murphy or Wolf. But there's Jaina, staring at me, as she usually does. How the heck did she get in here? Then I remember the flying blur. She has wings?

The four giants we couldn't see well in the blue light are now crystal clear: gaunt sallow faces, stringy hair, uncured skins for clothing, and long, curved, lethal, blood-red fingernails, like in my dream. The one in the lead grins at me, grisly remains of her dinner stuck to her pointed teeth. At least it isn't bloody. I try not to breathe too deeply. I wish I had Pax's ability to stop smelling right now.

I recognize the massive cavern we're in as the one in my dream. Since there are no stalactites or stalagmites, I assume it was either a cave formed underwater, or man-made. Pale daylight streams in from a wide opening in the ceiling, so high up I can't judge how big it is.

"Where are we?" Juliana asks. Jewel remains silent. I wonder if she's reliving her own captivity.

"It's daylight here," I answer. "I'm pretty sure we're not in Peru anymore, but if we are, we've traveled in time."

One of the women grunts and the rest follow her to an opening in the rock.

"Come," says the one now taking up the rear. "All come."

23
STORM

Screeeeee. The sound those things make when I smash them against the rock sets my teeth on edge, like I'm running a cheese grater across them. I shudder and set the rage free, letting the force of it give me strength as another claw sinks into my shoulder. How many are there?

I whirl and jab with my elbow, feeling it thud on thick armored skin when I connect. I toss it over my head and let the telekinesis throw it at the rock, just like the others. I crouch and spin, ready for the next attack, but the ones around me are gone.

"Fletcher!"

I spot Pax, holding one in a chokehold, its enormous head writhing on a skinny neck, claws ripping at his arms until he lets it go.

At that moment, the spotlights come on, momentarily blinding us. When my eyes recover, Wolf and Murphy are surrounded by bodies of giant insects resembling praying mantises. Where are the others? What happened to the girls?

I slap my wristband to open my link to Sky.

Where did they take you? Are you alright? Jewel warned us Jaina might be able to read our thoughts, but what difference does it make now?

Storm? Her mental voice sounds distant, like there's static inter-ference.

A loud twang reverberates in my brain like a snapping cable and sends a lightning bolt of pain through my head. The link breaks, but at least I know she's alive.

Pax doubles over, holding his head.

"You tried it too, didn't you?"

He nods. "Jewel answered, but something broke it. I hope it didn't hurt her the way it did me."

"Oh, man. Oh, man." Jack hurries toward us sounding excited, and I want to kill him. The cameras are tracking him. Were they filming the whole time?

"Don't," Pax warns. He knows me well, or maybe he spots the cameras coming off the ground and assumes I'm about to smash them. He's right. I ease them back down instead. They could show us exactly what happened to Sky and the others.

"What the heck are those things?" Jack asks, sounding out of breath.

Wolf answers. "They are the same as your camera-woman, Jaina. They're Mantoids, a race that has lived on this planet far longer than humans."

"Jaina?" Jack chokes out. "Impossible. She's one of us, not one of these creatures. Jaina?" he shouts, this time directing it toward his team.

Al answers, "She's gone, Jack. No sign of her."

"What do you know of the Mantoids?" I ask my uncle. "You never told me about them." I thought he'd shared all the Cherokee legends with me. Why not this one?

"Let's go back to the crew. I'll tell you all together."

"What about the bodies?" Pax asks. "Don't we want to bury them, or burn them?"

"What bodies? They've disappeared," Murphy notes, scanning the area. I march back to the wall, where I know I tossed a bunch of them. Sure enough, there's no sign of them. Not a single cracked carapace, not one body part and not a drop of blood. Do they even have blood? Did they melt into the ground? I growl in sheer frustration.

Al comes into the light to meet us on our way back to the cameras. Pax is the first to get to him.

"What did you see, Al? What happened to my sister, my dad and the others?"

"The girls disappeared," he says, sounding more grave than excited. "The blue light swallowed them up. The giant was mad and shouted something, then the light just retreated, the way it did last night. I guess the stories are true. They've gone to the land of the gods, or wherever those giant women came from."

"Did anyone other than the girls go with the giants?" Wolf asks. If Dylan and Charles didn't go with them, where are they?

"It happened too fast, Wolf," Al says, "but it's all on film. We can replay it in slow motion."

Wolf turns his attention to the hybrid. "Murphy, is there any way we can track them and find out where the giants have taken them?"

"Yes," Murphy answers. "I will always be able to find Juliana, no matter where she's gone."

"Using the mark?" Wolf asks.

"Yes, however, the mark presents one more problem. If I can find Juliana, then Shaula can track Jewel. We have to find them first."

I have the strongest desire to smash everything around me and force myself to calm down before things start flying. I promised Sky I would protect her. I failed, just like I failed my parents. If anything happens to her, I'll never forgive myself.

"How does it work, Murphy?" Wolf asks.

"Unless you want everyone here to know your story," Jack suggests, "let's get the gear packed up and head back to the compound. Our native friends would spread the word faster than a fire in dry brush."

The men watch, wide-eyed, as I help lift the heavier equipment into the cars. Henry drives Jaina's Hummer back to the garage, where he and Al take two of the cameras inside.

Every time I think of Sky or the others, my blood boils, and I stuff the rage back into its cage. It's the only way I know to control it.

Jack leads us to a media room set up like a small theater, with four rows of plush seats facing a wall-sized screen. Wolf and Jack each take an aisle seat in the second row. Murphy and Pax find seats in the row behind them, and I sit in the back.

I hear activity behind a wall at the back of the room and guess it's the projection room. Al joins us and sits in a front-row seat with a series of controls built into the arm rests.

"Henry went home," he says. "We can talk now."

"Now, Murphy, please tell us how this tracking thing works between you and Juliana," Jack says, turning halfway around in his seat, resting his feet in the aisle. "What mark are you talking about?"

Wolf stops Murphy with a gesture and turns to Jack. "Do I have your word you will not share this information with anyone? Your public cannot learn of this. Our entire world is at stake."

Al says, "Nobody's gonna hear it from me. What about you, Jack?"

Jack drums his fingers on the table and frowns. He gets up and paces in front of the screen, finally stopping in the middle to address his audience. Maybe he needs to be the center of attention. He disgusts me.

"If I keep quiet about it now, will you give me the exclusive when it can be revealed to the public?"

"If we survive," Wolf says, his voice somber, "and all parties agree, then yes. Keep in mind, there are several races involved here, and they must all agree to the exposure."

"Then you have my promise," Jack says and turns to Murphy. "Spill it. What is the mark and why would it lead you to your Juliana?"

24
SKY

We emerge into bright sunshine, to a field where bare-chested men are harvesting some crop. I can't tell what it is and don't have the breath to ask in our hurry to keep up with the enormous strides of the women ahead of us. The men appear to be normal sized, but there's no way of telling how far away they are. They could be giants, too.

My head still rings after our connection snapped as soon as we entered the tunnel. When we were kids, Pax and I made rubber band slingshots using our fingers. They worked great for spitballs but hurt like the dickens when they snapped back the wrong way. That's how my brain felt when the link broke. When Jewel's hands flew to her head, I knew the same thing had happened to her.

If we've moved in time, I'm surprised the wristbands worked at all. I wonder if we might be in a different dimension. Something is wrong with the sky, but I can't put my finger on what. I need answers. I glance at Jewel, but she's concentrating on the ground, her face pale.

I'm lost in my thoughts until Juliana stumbles after we've been walking for what feels like hours. I reach for her emotions, but nothing comes back. How strange. I reach out to Jewel, which is easier because

I'm tuned in to her, but again feel nothing. What's happened to my gift?

"Hey," I shout. "We have to rest." I need to talk to Jewel.

The giantess ahead of me stops and turns back to us. She pulls a flask from a belt at her side and offers it to me. "Drink. Good water."

I cup my hands and hold them up to her. She laughs, opens the flask and pours some of the contents into her tipped-back mouth. "You. Same."

I shake my head and say, "It's too big for us. We'll use our hands," and I demonstrate by sipping air from my palms. The thought of putting my mouth on something she drank from revolts me.

She nods and carefully pours, while I lap it up until I've had enough. I gesture to the others, and she calls the other giants over. They readily share with us all.

"Where are we?" Dad asks.

"You no speak," the giant says, glaring at my father. "Only Fire Hair speak."

I've had enough. "I am Sky, not Fire Hair, and this is my father, Dylan. He has every right to speak for us."

I point to Jewel and her father and say, "Jewel, Charles. They also speak."

I grab Juliana's hand and pull her forward. "This is Juliana, who also speaks." Then I point to Jaina, skulking by herself after bringing up the rear during our trek. "She does not speak."

The giant throws back her head and roars with laughter. The others join her. I fail to get the joke.

"I am Agateno. We go to truth-sayer. You tell who speaks. She say yes or no."

At least we have a destination. I don't know what a truth-sayer is, but we're going to meet her. I am not excited about it. The giants settle on the ground a short distance from us. Dad pulls me next to him and strokes my hair, soothing me. Charles draws Jewel close, with his arm around her shoulders. Juliana leans against a tree with her knees drawn up and shoulders slumped.

I turn to my friend, who's tossing bits of grass and pebbles at a rock. "Jewel, I can't feel anyone. What's wrong with me?"

She doesn't answer, but Juliana says, "We're under a Dracan dome. Our gifts don't work here, and neither will your wristbands."

That explains the odd sky. Jewel doesn't glance up, only continues rhythmically tearing things up from the ground and tossing them. I can't imagine how frightening this is for her. At least she isn't alone this time. We're in the same boat.

After a short rest, the giants get up and start walking. We have no choice but to follow. We could run, but how far would we get, and even if we made it back to the cavern, how would we get back home from there?

The light turns a rich reddish gold as the sun begins to set, only there is no sun in the cloudless sky. Could we be underground? Under-sea? Are we even on earth?

PAX

M urphy addresses Jack and Al, "Before we begin, you need to know I am half-Dracan. My mother is human. Dracans are shapeshifters, with the ability to transform their bodies to appear completely human when they choose to. Most prefer to remain in their true reptilian form. I am comfortable in either persona."

Al fidgets in his seat, decidedly uncomfortable. Jack leans against a narrow stage in front of the screen, with his arms crossed and his narrowed eyes fixed on Murphy.

"Dracan males mark their mates with a bite on the back of the neck, injecting a biochemical which quickly fuses with the female's nervous system."

"When you bite them, are you in your reptilian form?" Al asks, his face turning a little green.

"Yes," Murphy answers. "We have a set of recessive fangs for that purpose."

This is the first I'm hearing about the process. Shaula bit Jewel like a snake. I will rip him apart.

"It's quite painless for the female," he says. "In fact…" he starts to say then snaps his mouth shut as if he's thought better of it.

"Jewel would not have felt it had she been unconscious, as we suspect. She was in a jail cell overnight, and after sleeping gas was administered, he would have had access to her."

"What if he raped her? With Jewel unconscious, she couldn't have fought him off." I can barely get the words out of my constricted throat.

"He did rape her, but not in the way you mean," Murphy says with certainty. "We consider what he did as criminal as physical rape, which is impossible for Dracans. We cannot mate without our female's full consent."

"What would happen if one of you tried?" Storm asks.

"In Dracan physiology, a gland located within the brain stem receives signals from the marked female. If she's unwilling, the enzymes from the gland prevent the male from mating."

"If Jewel rejects Shaula, which she will," I say, "then he can't touch her. Is that what you're saying?"

"He can't physically mate with her. What he did is an unspeakable crime punishable by death in our culture. However, if she does become willing, the charge will no longer stand."

"She won't change her mind. She hates him and she loves me." My hands curl into fists and I'm aching to break something. Storm shoots me a sympathetic look. Our combined rage pheromones make my heart pound with adrenaline surging through my body. I jump up and start pacing in front of the screen. Jack quickly moves out of my way and takes a seat in the third row, watching me pace.

"Murphy, how would you track Juliana?" Wolf asks.

"You could compare the mark to a GPS signal that works anywhere in the universe. Our gland is like a satellite constantly pointing at the signal."

Jack asks, "Can anything interrupt the signal?"

"Yes," Murphy replies. He frowns, glancing at me. "The same thing that can break the mark. Death."

Storm asks what we all want to know. "Where are they, Murphy? If you know, then tell us."

"They're south of us. If you have a map, I can pinpoint their location."

Al quickly leaves the room to find one.

"While we're waiting for the map," Wolf says in the controlled voice he uses when Storm is about to lose it, "I'll tell you what I know about the Mantoids."

"Yeah," he answers. "I thought you'd told me all the Cherokee legends."

"We have no stories of these people because they are not a part of our history. The Hopi Indians have legends of the Ant People who helped them survive cataclysmic events in the distant past. Ancient rock drawings depict Mantoids alongside Ant People."

Wolf stands and stretches, remaining on his feet as he continues. "It is believed the Mantoids worked with the Ant People to save the Hopi by bringing them into vast caverns where they taught them life skills and fed them until the surface of the planet was again survivable."

Jack interjects, "Nowadays when you hear of giant praying mantises, they're usually kidnapping people and doing horrifying experiments on them. Until I met you and witnessed the UFO flying out of the lake, I thought those stories were nonsense, but people have long been saying they've been abducted by those creatures. None of them consider them benign."

I don't like his stony expression when he again turns to Wolf.

"You accused Jaina of being one of them. Why?"

I answer him before Wolf can, "The first night at the Stargate, Storm had Jaina Chen suspended in a floating bubble because she'd been rummaging in his backpack. Do you remember?"

Jack glances at him with a hint of fear in his eyes. Storm stares back, and I continue. "Right after he let her down, the Stargate caught our attention, but Jewel was watching Jaina and saw her as a mantis. Even before that, I knew something was strange about her. She emits a pheromone in some sort of odd frequency. I don't recognize either."

"Sky senses everybody's emotions," Storm says. "Any human's emotions, I should add. It doesn't work with aliens, and it didn't work with Jaina."

"And now the Mantoid, Jaina Chen, is in there." Murphy gestures in the general direction of the Stargate. "With Juliana and the rest. I hope, for her sake, she doesn't mean them harm."

"What do you mean, for her sake?" Al asks, returning with a map he lays out on the mini stage. I detect a hint of eau-de-rage coming from him, too.

"I assume Dylan and Charles are in there with them. Sky's father is a Karate Master, and the three girls have all been trained in combat. Jewel's father is strong and motivated to keep his daughter safe. Unless Jaina has some alien tricks up her sleeve, she's outnumbered. I hope, for her sake, she proves to be their ally and not their foe," Murphy explains.

Storm stands in the back, stretches, then heads down to the front where we gather around the map. "It's a shame the Mantoid bodies disappeared after we destroyed them. They aren't that hard to kill. After Murphy shows us where Juliana and the rest are, why don't we watch the film, so Al and Jack know what we're capable of."

"Good idea," I agree. "I want to be sure Charles and my dad definitely went with the girls."

"Show us, please," Wolf asks, stepping back to give Murphy room next to the map. He nods when Murphy points to a spot among the islands just south of Ushuaia, the southernmost city in the world. The girls and our fathers are in Tierra del Fuego.

"Sequoia was right," Storm says. "She knew something important was going to happen there."

"Yes," Wolf acknowledges. "She has told me she and the women are coming to Ushuaia."

"Isn't she close to her time?" I ask, concerned for her and her baby. I suspect Wolf and Sequoia are in nearly constant communication with each other.

"Our baby is the one who is making it impossible for her to stay away. As soon as Sky's link was cut off, Sequoia says the baby has been sending out waves of anguish."

Al and Jack are completely baffled. They don't know about the baby's empathetic abilities. She's a stronger empath than Sky, and I always believed Sky was the strongest on the planet.

"I don't pretend to know what you're talking about," Jack says. "Let's go ahead with the film. We're not going anywhere tonight."

Al pushes a few buttons on his arm-rest controls, and images appear on the screen. There's no sound, other than the faint whir of the projector behind the wall.

The blue light grows out of the small door and expands to cover the screen as the cameras focus in for a close-up. We watch the giants move forward in a pool of pale light. Is that daylight? Are they in a different time zone?

The camera zooms in to catch the backs of the girls walking toward the giant in the lead, while the others remain faint in the background. It stays focused on them as they walk.

The girls approach from where I was supposed to jump in with them. Storm had the same plan on the other side but the Mantoid attack stopped us and I didn't see what happened next.

"What's that thing the giant is pointing at them?" Storm asks, standing up and emitting strong pheromones.

What the heck is wrong with my scent guard? I remember when I first learned to use it for self-preservation. It's nothing more than a mental ability, and my mental state is messed up right now.

As the giant points her spear, the light starts rapidly shrinking. Two blurry shadows enter from the left side just before the girls start sprinting to leap into the light. Another blur flies in from the right.

"Can you go back and slow this part down?" Wolf asks.

Al nods and presses more buttons. The film rewinds to the point where the girls appear, moving in slow motion. Al stops it just before they run, then moves it forward frame by frame. There. Two of the shadows resolve into Dad and Charles, taking a flying leap into the blue light. I watch them tuck and roll when they hit the floor. The shadow on the other side resembles a giant bug with wings. Jaina, the Mantoid.

I'm relieved, knowing the men are there with the girls. Al pushes a button, and the film resumes at normal speed. We wait through a couple of minutes of darkness, then the floods come on, and we watch as Wolf, Murphy, Storm and I slaughter the attacking bugs. Only we didn't.

I hear Al exclaim "Wow" several times during the battle. When it ends, and while our attention is drawn away from what we thought were carcasses, the cameras catch them standing up, one by one, and disappearing behind some boulders next to the cliff. They were a diversion to keep us separated from the girls.

Al stops the film and Jack clears his throat and says, "Do you…" He chokes, and I know his throat is constricting. He tries again, "Do you think Jaina is behind this?"

In my opinion, Jaina's role in this is not as important as the two questions running through my mind. What do the giants want with my sister, and how do we rescue them?

2 6

JEWEL

I can't shake this dread weighing on me like a lead blanket. The closer we get to the truth-sayer, the heavier it gets. I drag each foot through the dust on the trail, one after the other, as if every step is my last. I can't lift my head, and after losing my gift of enhanced vision again, I don't want to. I suck in air and have trouble blowing it out, wheezing like an out-of-shape old woman.

"Hang in there," Dad says, holding my elbow for support. "I've got you." The concern in his voice makes me want to weep. Understanding why my emotions have been so raw lately isn't helping me control them.

It's becoming increasingly dark and harder to see the trail directly in front of us. The holographic day is being swallowed up in holographic night. Don't these scraggly people ever sleep?

"What are those lights?" Sky asks, fatigue dulling her voice. We've rounded a hill, and spots of light flicker in a deeply shadowed valley below. Campfires dot the forest, some visible and some reflecting off trees. I breathe deeply and get a whiff of pine. After walking along a nearly shadeless path, a forest would be more than welcome.

"We wait," Agateno booms. "Sit."

I gladly drop to the ground, not caring where I land. Dad slides down next to me and wraps me in a hug. I bury my face in his shoulder, overcome with sobs. "What's wrong with me?" I wail.

"It isn't you," Juliana says quietly. "It's the mark, Jewel. Shaula is reeling you in."

"Maybe we need to get to him first," Dad says. His voice sounds distorted, full of rage. I've never heard him sound like this in my entire life. I wonder if it developed while I was in Atlantis, lost to him and Mom. "Do you still have the locator beacon, Juliana?"

"It's in my backpack. I suggest we wait until we're out of here and can use our abilities again. What can we do against Shaula and his guards, unarmed and powerless?"

"I assure you, we are not powerless," Dylan says. "You've been in training and Sky holds her black belt. With my skills and Charles's determination to protect his daughter, we have a chance against the Dracan."

"I doubt it, Dylan," Juliana says. "I've lived among them all my life. A Dracan male determined to have his female is stronger than you can imagine. It would take all of us, with our abilities in operation, to take him down. Even then, we might not succeed."

"Jewel." Juliana's voice softens. "You must resist his call with everything you have. It won't be easy. You must continually force yourself to think of Pax. Remember your love for him when Shaula tries to cloud your mind and force your will."

Pax. I picture his beautiful eyes lined with thick, dark lashes, intense shades of green shot through with gold lighting up when he looks at me and darkening as he moves in to kiss me. I picture the way his hair falls over his left eye and gleams gold and yellow in the sun, outlined by waves of his blue aura, shot through with magenta when he's with me. I remember his finely sculpted mouth against mine, and I wrap myself in the strength of his muscular arms. Energy returns to my limbs and body. She's right. I can fight Shaula if I hold Pax in my mind and heart. I'm glad to note my sobbing has stopped.

Dad's grip on me loosens and he says, "Jewel, they've sent a wagon for us."

I must have been too absorbed in visualizing Pax to hear them approach. Four enormous horses paw the ground and snort, hitched to an equally huge wagon. They resemble Clydesdales in a variety of colors, but the ones at home and on commercials have nothing on these.

The giants' heads aren't as high as the horses' backs. If you took a picture of them without any of us around, you wouldn't know they're twelve to fifteen feet tall.

A male giant who must have come with the wagon stands next to a jet-black horse and pulls down on its harness. I admire its long yellow mane, matching tail and matching hair falling from its knees to the ground, more like soft feathers than horsehair. It whinnies and nuzzles him, and the others bob their heads, as if impatient to pull the wagon home. I'd love to see them with my full sight.

The man is bare-chested except for an open leather vest. His pants are also leather, tucked into knee-length fringed moccasins. Feathers and leather thongs decorate his braided black hair, and even in the darkening light of dusk, his skin is darker than the females. These must be the Indians Al told us about.

"Get in wagon," Agateno commands, pulling the back panel off and leaning it against the wagon bed to make a ramp for us. I pull up with my hands and push with my feet, crawling up the steep incline. Sky and Juliana are also struggling, but we make it with our dads' help. Jaina simply walks up and sits down. She's an enigma.

As soon as we're seated along the sides, the leader replaces the panel, and the man makes clicking sounds and maneuvers the horses around to a trail I hadn't noticed, heading down into the valley.

I sit close to Dad, and he drapes his arm across my shoulders, holding tightly to keep us from bouncing too much. The rutted, rock-strewn path doesn't make for a smooth ride.

Jaina is sitting across from me, her face turned toward Sky. She hasn't spoken a word since we came through the light. I wonder again what she's doing here. The red-haired women walk behind us, talking to each other in a language I'm unfamiliar with. They're more relaxed than before.

My eyes droop despite the wagon's bouncing and jerking and the uncomfortably hard floorboards. I'm physically and emotionally exhausted, and I'm tired of fighting sleep. I snuggle closer to Dad and let myself drift off.

I couldn't have been asleep for more than a few minutes when the wagon creaks to a halt, and I wake to a camp filled with noise and activity. My stomach growls at the aroma of roasting meat. A whiff of pine sap, barely discernible over the cooking fires, relaxes me and I breathe deeply.

Several children as tall as we are come crawling over the sides of the wagon and squat in front of us, reaching out to touch our heads and our clothes. It's disconcerting when a three- to five-year-old's face is on a level with my own.

A child grabs my hand and abruptly pulls me to my feet. She laughs when she realizes I only reach the bottom of her chin. A boy about a foot taller grabs me around the waist and lifts me up.

"Hey!" I shout as loudly as I can. "Put me down."

I've startled the kids, and the boy drops me on my rear. Dad helps me up and dusts me off, trying not to laugh. The giants don't even try to hold it in. I stomp my feet as the adults near the wagon burst out in roaring laughter. At least they have a sense of humor.

When Sky speaks, the laughter instantly stops, and the camp fills with an eerie silence. I have the oddest feeling they revere her for some reason.

"We're hungry and tired," she says. No one responds.

"Food," she says, pointing to her mouth, and several of the men turn toward the nearest campfire, where some small animals are roasting on a spit.

"I guess we're eating before we can sleep," she says to us.

A female, not one of our escorts, removes the back panel and helps us down the ramp. Dylan steps out first, followed by Dad then the rest of us. Jaina, as usual, brings up the rear.

The giantess, dressed in a cream-colored knee-length fringed dress, leads us to a clearing ringed with small boulders. When it becomes obvious to her we won't be able to sit comfortably on them, she points to a pile of pine needles under some trees. I gratefully sink to the spongy ground and lean against a tree trunk, using my backpack as a cushion behind me.

"I'm afraid I'll fall asleep with my face in my supper," Juliana says, stretching her arms as she yawns loudly. Yawns are highly contagious, and we're soon following her lead.

"They have interesting homes," Dylan notes. "I'd expect log homes in woods like these, but theirs are made of clay, or perhaps stone. The campfire flames reflect off glass windows. The roofs are metal, and they have brick chimneys. These aren't primitive people, as I'd first thought."

"You are correct, little man," a deep voice says, coming from the shadows under trees about ten feet away. An old woman, leaning on a branch, hobbles into the light of the campfire and takes a seat on one of the boulders across from us, close to the fire. Her hair, although faded with age, is still red, and in much better condition than the giants we followed here. As large as she is, she appears frail, wrapped in a fringed gray shawl covering a floor-length white doeskin dress.

"I am Gienika. My people know me as Truth-Sayer. You," she points at Sky, "are very small to be our Fire Hair."

27

STORM

I jump out of bed at first light, glad we're no longer sleeping in the subbasement. After last night's screening, Jack moved us up here, to a suite next to Wolf's. I toss my gear into my backpack and wake the others.

"Murphy, did you call your lizard friends?" I ask, pulling his covers off.

"Grrrrrr," he answers, and takes a swipe at me. I've come to like the good-natured hybrid, and today he's going to lead us to Sky.

Fletcher needs no prodding. He went to sleep fully clothed, with his pack loaded.

We find Wolf, Jack and Al in the dining room.

"Eat up," Al says, pointing to the feast on the sideboard. We fill our plates and join them.

"We've launched several expeditions from Ushuaia," Jack is saying. "Our compound there is like this one. Did you watch our episode featuring the pyramids in Antarctica? We did a short segment in the piece about Tierra del Fuego."

"I did," Pax answers. "I'd love to know more about the pyramids, but right now we have to concentrate on getting to Ushuaia."

"It's about two thousand seven hundred miles from here," Jack says. "It will take our cargo plane around five hours to get there."

"Is your compound in the city itself?" Wolf asks. I think I know what he's getting at.

"No," Jack answers. "It's a little over a mile from the airport, up one of the surrounding hills. It's in a birch forest, hidden from the main road."

"How do you and Al feel about riding in an Allaran ship?" I knew Wolf was thinking it would be the quickest and surest way there.

"Why?" Al asks.

I tell him, "They could get us there in minutes." He shakes his head and laughs.

Jack's eyes light up. "Can we take our equipment along? Would they let us film the inside?" I swear, if he were a cartoon character, dollar signs would be rolling around in his eyes.

"Perhaps they'd allow you to take your cameras," Wolf responds, "but I seriously doubt they'd let you expose them in any way. Secrecy is important to them."

"We have vehicles in Ushuaia. Our film equipment travels with us."

"What about weapons?" It makes sense for Al to ask that. I knew when we met him he's more than a driver and cameraman.

"I'll ask Sequoia what they say about it," Wolf says. "If they agree, Storm and I are trained in the use of pistols, rifles, and bows. If you have any available, we'll be happy to carry them as backup."

"What about Pax and Murphy, here? Don't they get weapons?" Al asks.

Pax says, "Don't need them. We have skills."

Al laughs. "Yeah. I've heard that before." Murphy grins at him. Does anything bother the hybrid?

Wolf excuses himself and walks toward the front room and the door, tapping his wristband. I hope Sequoia and my baby cousin are alright.

Jack and Al leave, too, talking about the gear they hope to bring along. The rest of us finish our breakfast in silence.

I find Wolf sitting on the edge of a fountain in the courtyard. "How is Sequoia?"

"The baby is restless, and your aunt is getting little sleep. The bond between Sky and the baby is stronger than we imagined. If we don't find her quickly, your aunt may go into premature labor."

My gut clenches. Where are the Allarans? Are they sending one ship or two?

"Has she communicated with our ride, yet?" I ask.

"They should be here any minute. Analiese and Coral are coming with Sequoia. I'll check if Al and Jack are ready, and we'll meet the aliens here. Maybe you can come along and help them float their equipment out."

Wolf and I get up and stride into the house, passing Pax and Murphy on the way out.

I can't believe how much gear Jack plans to bring. Lights, camera bags, generators and a host of cables and boxes form a pile in the middle of the garage.

"All of it?" I ask, incredulous. "Unless they send more than one ship, they won't be able to carry the equipment. I think I should warn you…"

I'm about to tell them about our reaction to the males when I'm interrupted by a shout in the courtyard.

"They're here!"

Jack takes off running through the barn doors while Al takes his time. I shrug and float the enormous pile out after them.

The disk covers the entire courtyard, hovering just above the rooftops of the surrounding buildings. The portal opens and a beam of light shoots out, obscuring the inside of the ship from view.

I run when Sequoia floats down the light beam. Wolf gets to her first, catching her up in a strong hug, and I'm right behind him. Coral floats down next, and Pax grabs his mother around the waist and swings her around. When Analiese follows, Murphy reaches out and hugs her, as well. My heart goes out to them. Both their daughters and their husbands are missing this time.

Vega lands then, and the reaction I've come to expect takes me over. Al whips out his pistol and aims it at the Allaran, while Jack's eyes narrow and his lip curls up in disgust. It's too bad I didn't have time to warn them.

A female drops down behind Vega, evoking a completely opposite reaction. I swear Al is panting as he holsters his weapon. You'd think being near both a male and female Allaran together would cancel out our visceral responses, but no such luck. I imagine I'm one of those costumes with male on one side and female on the other, divided lengthwise right down the middle. Weird and awful at the same time.

"You remember Chara," Vega says in his cheese-grater voice. "Baran and Belena are in the second ship. We understand you have equipment to transport."

Chara speaks directly to Al and Jack. "You may ride with us and our friends, or with your equipment. Which do you prefer?" The two men stand slack-jawed, unable to reply. I know how her voice flows over us males, like a hot shower in a tub full of bubbles.

"They will ride with us," Sequoia answers, laughing. Of all of us, she's the one who best controls her revulsion to the female Allarans. I'm proud to be her nephew.

The Allarans enter their ship first. We wait until Al and Jack beam up after them. I can't wait to see their reaction to the bubble seats.

2 8
SKY

The giantess has few wrinkles on her face, but I get the impression she's ancient. Lights float in the depths of her faded blue eyes, as if they're reflecting the universe.

"My name is Sky, Mrs. Gienika, not Fire Hair. The scouts we traveled with called me that, and I explained to them it's not my name."

"Yes. Yes, you did. You may simply call me Gienika." Her eyes crinkle at the corners when she smiles, and I notice she has all her teeth, a bit yellow in the firelight, but without gaps.

"If you're the truth-sayer our escort spoke about, then we need to talk about my companions."

"Speak," she says. Her voice is warm and kind. Maybe we can trust her. Something about her reaches out to me.

"This is my father," I say, pulling him by the hand to stand beside me. "Dylan Fletcher." He bows respectfully, the way he taught us in Karate, and she acknowledges him by bowing back.

"That's Jewel and her father Charles Adams." I point to them cuddled under the tree and dozing.

Juliana comes to stand next to me. "This is Juliana Ryder, whose parents we're searching for. We are a team, Gienika, and each of us speaks for each other. I'm asking you to please, tell your people we are equals in this team. We all speak."

"I apologize for your escorts, Sky. They are not of our tribe. They knew we were seeking you and were kind enough to deliver you to us. Now, who is the other woman with you?"

"Jaina Chen is not part of our team. She does not speak for any of us. In fact, she hasn't spoken since we entered the blue light at the Stargate. Jaina is not what she seems."

"I know what she is," she says, glancing thoughtfully at Jaina, who is curled up asleep a short distance from Jewel and her father. "She speaks, but you do not hear her."

"What do you mean?" I ask.

She closes her eyes and her mouth turns up in a small smile. Instead of answering, she says, "It is important for you to know your assessment of someone may not be accurate, Sky. Do not be too quick to judge. And now, my dear, I will send my daughter Autumn Mahuea to you. She will care for you."

She begins to rock back and forth to get off her seat on the boulder, grunting and pushing up on her stick. I rush to help, but she's far too tall for me to do any good. On the third try, I hear her knees pop and creak as they straighten out.

"Good night, Sky Fire Hair," she says, and lumbers off into the darkness between the trees.

A much shorter giantess hurries over to us. She's a mere ten feet or so tall, with full cheeks, tinted dark rose in her tawny complexion, and startling blue eyes. She smiles and dimples appear in her cheeks. Her hair hangs loose down her back, the fire reflecting off it in auburn waves. As far as I can tell, my hair color is the only thing I have in common with these people. Every one of the women has beautiful red hair.

"I am Autumn," she says, her voice softer than the larger giants. "I will take you and your family to your home."

I don't correct her. We won't be making a home among them.

The doorway is massive, sized for someone twenty feet tall. The house is proportionately a small ranch style cabin, but to us it's large and spacious. Each of the two bedrooms has a modern bathroom, with showers and working toilets. I'm thankful the commode and other fixtures are sized for people like us.

Jewel claims the room with three double beds for us and falls asleep as soon as she tumbles into one of them. Dad and Charles stagger into the other room, where two double beds are made up. If it had been a regular sized place, single beds would have barely fit.

A common room with a couch and two chairs opens on one side to a kitchenette, with a sink, a small refrigerator, and something resembling a camp stove sitting on a cabinet. A picnic table separates it from the common room. Jaina crashes on the couch.

I need a shower, and head straight for the bedroom. The hot water relaxes me, and I'm asleep as soon as my body falls into the bed.

I WAKE up thinking I'm back at home in North Carolina, expecting to smell Mom's coffee. Green-tinged light filters through the window and shadows move as tree branches bob in the breeze outside, just like at home. I come fully awake and remember we're not in "Kansas" anymore, and I understand how Dorothy must have felt after finding herself in the Land of Oz. As soon as I realize where we are, I jump out of bed and get dressed.

"Jewel, Juliana, get up." I give each of them a shake and head to the bathroom to wash my face. When we've each had time to refresh and get to the living room, Dad and Charles are at the table, deep in conversation. Jaina is gone.

"We need some answers," Charles is saying. "Why are we here? What do these people want with us?"

"I want to know where we are," Dylan says. "Juliana says it's a Dracan dome, so we can assume day and night are regulated by some sort of timer and simulated sunshine. We could be anywhere on earth."

"Or under it," Jewel chimes in. "The Dracans build their cities underground or under water. The portal we came through is most likely a wormhole, which could put us anywhere."

"Murphy will find us," Juliana says, sounding very sure of herself.

"How can you be sure?" I ask. "I doubt the giants left them a roadmap or instructions on how to open the wormhole."

"I have his mark," she reminds us. "He will track me and find us."

Jewel pales and abruptly sits on a chair next to Charles. "And I have Shaula's mark. How long will it be before he finds me?"

I long to comfort her. I long for Pax, who is somehow both willing and able to send me comfort when I need it. I want to be back with the boys, where we can use our gifts to help each other. How did Jewel stand it without her special sight for so long? It makes me sick to my stomach when I remember the call of the artifact. What if we don't get back in time to fix it? Will we all die?

29

PAX

Dr. Austin is in high spirits as he takes us to the docks where he keeps his trawler, the Vagabundo.

"She's sixty-five feet in length with a twenty-foot, seven-inch beam. Four staterooms give us plenty of space for crew and camera equipment, and she's a marvel in rough seas. Best purchase I've ever made."

We climb aboard and stow our packs below deck before joining him at the bridge. I'm glad for the jacket as we pull away from the dock into a sharp breeze. It's good to be back on the water, but I hope we won't have to dive. I'm surprised the water temperature this close to Antarctica is nearly as warm as in northern California, ranging from the high forties to mid-fifties Fahrenheit. Still, it's nothing like diving in the Bahamas, where the water was in the high seventies in January and February.

Al navigates in and out among the channels between the islands of Tierra del Fuego, following the coastline of a much larger island. We enter a channel lined with cliffs and can barely hear the engines over the noise of millions of squawking birds nesting in the cliffs.

"Rock shag," Al shouts. "In the Cormorant family. Can't get rid of them." I'm getting used to his weird sense of humor and grin back at him.

It gets much quieter when we exit the channel in a huge bay surrounded with more craggy islands. I'd love to come back here and explore some of the fjord-like channels I spot leading into the interior of a few of them.

Jack points toward the middle of the bay and says, "One day Isla Verde was there, and the next, poof. Gone."

"Did it sink?" Wolf asks.

"If it did, there's no trace of it. The Argentine navy was out here for a couple of weeks afterward, taking soundings and sending down divers. The depth of the ocean floor is consistent with the surrounding ocean. You'd think if it sank, there would still be visible traces of trees and landmarks down below. There's nothing."

"The same thing happened with Sandy Island, between Australia and New Caledonia," Al chimes in. "Now so-called geologists are saying it never existed. I'll bet they'll do the same for Isla Verde. In a few years nobody will remember it. Scientists don't like anything they can't explain, and the media are already occupied with other news."

Jack steers the boat to the spot where the island had been.

"Here," Murphy says, surprising me. "Juliana is here."

"How is that possible?" Jack asks.

"I just know. She's below us. There must be a Dracan city under the sea. Now we simply have to find out how to get to her."

"Murphy, can you contact your friends in Atlantis? Perhaps they can help us," Wolf suggests, walking over to drape an arm over the despondent half-Dracan's shoulders.

"What's this about Atlantis?" Jack asks, intrigued. I'm surprised none of the men have told him about Jewel's abduction and captivity there, especially after the Dracan ship rose out of Lake Titicaca right in front of him.

"I'll get us some lunch," Al says, heading to the galley while Wolf brings Jack Austin up to speed. Murphy, Storm, and I follow him down and he gives us a quick tour of the boat. The staterooms are small but well-appointed. Two of them have double beds and share a head, or bathroom, with full-sized fixtures, including a bathtub. The other two have bunks. A second head with a shower stall is located off the galley, which has a full-sized refrigerator and stove and plenty of cabinets. This boat is built for long voyages.

I help him assemble some sandwiches while Storm and Murphy relax on a bench behind a long table hanging from the ceiling, attached by chains. Drop-down legs secure it to the floor until it's raised up again. I snag a pickle and chew while I work, enjoying the sharp tangy flavor.

"Murphy," Al says, his voice sounding like rocks rolling around in a tumbler. "What are you like in your Dracan form?"

"I'll show you," he answers, standing and sliding out from behind the table.

"No," Storm says. "Not now. You can show him when I leave." He gets up and moves toward the stairs. I admire him for accepting Murphy's company, but he has a serious problem with Dracans in general.

When Storm is gone, I watch Murphy morph into Murphrid, the form Jewel said he always wore in Atlantis. His snout elongates and scales appear on his face and arms. His fingers lengthen into claws, and his teeth grow long and sharp. His eyes are what strike me the most. They've gone from dark brown to yellow with vertical pupils. The eyes, more than anything else, mark him as reptilian. He's grown about six inches taller and I can tell the jeans and turtleneck he wore today are tight and uncomfortable. I wonder how Juliana fell in love with this giant lizard.

Al stares with wide eyes and his face has lost a little of its tan, but his expression reveals no emotion, shock or otherwise.

"Thank you," he says, and nods politely. He walks around the Dracan, looking him up and down, and says, "Did you work out much back home?"

Murphy throws his head back, bares his impressive teeth and laughs loudly.

"I'm a scientist," he says, drawing the sound of the "s" out more than usual. "If I worked my muscles as much as I work my brain, I'd be massive, and you'd have a problem."

"How so?" Al asks, raising his eyebrows and crossing his arms in a challenging stance.

"I'd be dumb enough to challenge you to a fight, just to see who's stronger. As it stands, I'm much too intelligent to want to fight you."

He reaches his arm out to give Al a friendly smack on the shoulder, and Al grins and smacks him back.

"You're okay," he says. "Now change back and help me bring these sandwiches topside." They each carry a tray up the stairs.

Storm looks relieved that Murphy's in his human form.

Jack grabs a sandwich and says, "I have topographical maps back at the compound. They don't show what's underground, but they mark some significant cave openings in the nearby Andes. One of them could lead us to the others.

"How would we know which one?" Wolf asks the obvious. "If there are no maps of underground tunnels, we could spend a lifetime exploring caves with no clue where they might lead."

"I would know," Murphy says with complete confidence.

"Yes, but how many would we have to go to before you know which one is the right one?" Storm asks.

"We fly over them. We fly over the islands, too. We'll find it." I admire his resolve. Nothing we say will shake his conviction. He will find a way to Juliana.

JEWEL

S ky must see how despondent I am, because she grabs me by the hand, pushes the huge door open and leads me outside.

"Deep breaths, Jewel. In through your nose and out through your mouth."

Juliana follows us out and takes a deep, exaggerated breath, stretching her arms up to emphasize just how deeply I should be inhaling. Dad and Dylan come outside and do the same, and I laugh. I love our patchwork family. We breathe in and out together, and I imagine our hearts beating in rhythm. I picture the boys and our moms with Wolf, Sequoia, and Murphy in a circle going through this exercise, and my spirit lifts and grows still.

We've drawn a crowd of the huge children, and before long, every one of them is breathing with us. The bustling camp has grown quiet.

Then Sky claps her hands and breaks the spell, and the children break out in laughter, scattering into groups of three or four to resume whatever activity they interrupted for our exercise.

Autumn hurries toward us, her grin revealing perfect teeth. "Come," she says, sounding excited. "Mother wishes to speak."

She leads us to the clearing ringed by stone seats where we'd met last night. This time, we climb up on the stones, the two men sharing one and we three girls on another. There's room for all of us to sit cross-legged, which is the only comfortable position on the backless stone.

Two men in leather leggings and fringed vests carry an ornate wooden chair to a spot near the fire pit in the center, facing us. I admire the smooth carvings on the back and arms, carvings of trees and vines with faces of animals peeking out here and there.

Women of the tribe file in, chattering in their language, and take seats on the rest of the stones, some arranging themselves behind the back of the chair. A drumbeat silences everyone, continuing a steady rhythm as Gienika hobbles into the circle, leaning heavily on her staff and supported on each side by the tallest females I've seen yet. They help her sit, bow from the waist as if she's royalty and move to stand behind us, near the tree line.

I turn to them, surprised to see Jaina Chen sitting between them on a carpet of pine needles. She appears as unperturbed as always and doesn't acknowledge me.

The drum stops and silence fills the forest. Even the birds stop chirping. Then Gienika says something in nearly a whisper, and everyone bows their heads, as if in prayer. I send up a prayer, too, asking for help to get home and a way to break the lock Shaula has on me.

When I raise my head, a man dressed in a red cape and wearing a matching red and black feather headdress is standing beside Gienika.

"I will speak to our guests in English," she says, and the man immediately translates her words into their language. He must be a shaman of some sort, or maybe just a translator.

"Sky Fire Hair has come to us, just as the prophecy said she would." Gienika pauses to let the man speak. After a few more sentences like this, I no longer notice the pauses or his interruptions.

"She is not what we expected, but the word is very clear. She will save our nation, and not only ours." Gienika gestures toward Jaina, who gets up and moves to stand beside her.

"Jaina Chen is emissary to Jaide Laurelei, queen of the Mantoid race, the oldest race of intelligent beings on planet Terra, or Earth as you know it."

Prickles raise the hairs on my arms and the back of my neck. Jaina is again staring at Sky, who's squirming as if she feels them, too. When I reach for my friend's hand, a spark of static arcs between us, startling her. What's going on?

"Those sensations, Sky Fire Hair, are coming from Jaina, who uses pheromones and supersonic sound frequencies to communicate with her kind." Gienika's eyes crinkle, and she smiles widely. "I have told you she speaks, but you don't hear her."

A ripple of laughter runs through the audience when the man translates. It dies down when Sky stands to her feet on the stone seat.

"I'm sorry, Gienika, but I don't know what you're talking about. I'm smaller than many of your youngest children. I have red hair, but so do many other people where I come from. All of you have it, and I wonder why you don't think one of your people might be the Fire Hair you speak of. I have no talents or special abilities, especially here in your land. Why are you convinced I can do anything to save your nation?"

The man in the cape translates, and all eyes turn to Sky in shock. One person shouts something, another answers, and suddenly there's an uproar in the circle. The stone under us begins to vibrate and I wonder if the giants are stomping hard enough to shake the ground. Gienika struggles to her feet, and the drums beat a rapid, staccato beat. The crowd grows silent again, but the ground is shaking harder. I hear it then, a tone so deep my gut quivers before it reaches my ears.

"Hold your ears, everyone," I shout. I wish Juliana had her gift now. We're about to experience the full force of an artifact's cry.

31

SKY

Crud. I can't believe how messed up this is. I throw my hands over my ears, knowing it's useless to even try.

"Lie down on the rock," I yell at Jewel and Juliana, scrambling down myself and curling into the fetal position. I glance at Dad and Charles, who are both flat on their boulder. The intensity will soon knock us unconscious, especially since Juliana can't put us in an insulating bubble this time.

I wait, but the sound seems distant and isn't growing. It sounds muted like it did in Juliana's bubble. I sit up to find Gienika again sitting placidly in her chair, and Jaina lying on the ground next to her, with her mouth open in a silent scream. Is Jaina dulling it, somehow?

My hair rises in a cloud, prickling my scalp. It reminds me of a science experiment in fifth grade. Each of us touched a globe on the teacher's desk, and our hair stood on end from static electricity. This time everyone in the circle has a halo of hair floating around their heads.

Gienika nods at me and points to Jaina. She is the one making a sound bubble around us all.

As soon as the ground stops trembling and the sound of the artifact fades, Jaina stops and her face goes slack. She could be unconscious. I jump down off our boulder, run to her and plop on the ground next to her so I can pull her head into my lap. She's panting, and her eyes are slits, glittering as she stares at me intently.

"Please, bring her some water," I say, and several of the giants scramble to find some. Autumn hands me a cup that holds at least a gallon. I dip my hand in it and carefully pour a few drops into Jaina's mouth. Her eyes close then, and her lips curve in a small smile.

The man in the red cape bends down and gently lifts her. "I am Jayman," he says, keeping his booming voice low. "I will care for her, Sky Fire Hair."

When I've stood up and dusted myself off, I marvel at the solemn expressions on all the now-silent faces. I've blown it now. They aren't happy.

Gienika clears her throat and says, her voice strong with authority, "Before Terra's cry, you abdicated your responsibility as the Fire Hair of prophecy. You implied you have no special abilities, at least while you are here, and your diminutive size makes you of less worth than our children."

I start to say something, but she shakes her head and holds up her hand. *Do not speak*, I hear in my head. Is it my imagination, or did she just mind-speak to me?

With her next words, her voice grows stronger, and there's a great deal of power in it. I wonder if there's Allaran DNA in her.

"You are the Fire Hair of the prophecy, Sky. You proved it when you rushed to Jaina Chen's aid, even knowing who and what she is. You, my dear, will bridge the races, uniting them. If you do not accept your responsibility, our nation and others will die. We must know...Do you accept the charge given to you, the charge you were born for?"

I have no idea what their prophecy says, or how I can save her people, but something in me responds, and I believe her. We're already supposed to save the world, so why not add saving a few nations to our impossible mission? No. We have too much on our plate. I can't do this.

I fight the words even as they push through my lips. My mouth betrays me and says it out loud. "I accept."

I drop to my knees, the weight of responsibility shoving me to my face. Tears well up from a place I didn't know existed deep in my core. As I weep, each woman touches me as she passes by, each one loaning me her strength and giving me her blessing. Each one wordlessly expressing her hope.

Finally, Dad pulls me into his arms and cradles me. Charles, Jewel, and Juliana form a circle around us, and when I glance up, we're the only ones left.

3 2

STORM

As much as I like being on the water, I'm glad to be back on solid, dry land. Jack's compound is a cluster of cabins on a wooded hillside. Birch trees surround us and the sound of the wind moving through the leaves soothes the raging beast and gives me some much-needed rest.

Sequoia is soaking in the sun, reclining on a lounge chair on the deck behind their cabin when I join her.

"How's my cousin?" I ask, placing a hand on her distended belly. Baby rewards me with a kick and somersault. Her tiny body presses against my hand as she turns. My heart skips a beat and fills with a surge of pure joy. Why would I ever consider leaving my family, especially this little one?

Wolf comes out holding two glasses of iced tea. "Storm, I didn't know you were here. Want something to drink?"

"No, thanks. I just dropped by to say hello to my cousin and found Sequoia here, too."

She laughs. "I believe we're inseparable."

Wolf settles in a deck chair on her other side and reaches out to hold her hand. Contentment floods me, and I sit with my legs propped up on the railing and close my eyes. The rocking motion lulls me into a half-sleep when I remember I'm not on the boat any longer. My eyes shoot open. All around us, trees are swaying unnaturally. Sequoia cries out while her baby broadcasts her alarm before the sound begins to vibrate in my gut. We're about to be hit with an artifact's blast again. How did Juliana protect the girls the last time?

I concentrate on wrapping a ball of air around the three of us then imagine the air becoming solid and sound-proof. My mind pulses in a frequency I can't hear, reinforcing the wall of the bubble. Wolf has his arms wrapped around Sequoia and the baby while her hands cover her ears. He stares at me oddly. We hear the artifact's sound as if from a distance. Judging by the trembling of the deck and the whipping trees around us, it's close enough that it should be temporarily deafening us, if not knocking us unconscious. I have a lot to learn from my sister, as soon as we get her and the others back.

"It appears we have two artifacts to find," Wolf says. "I don't know how you did that but thank you for protecting us. There's no telling what the full force of the sound might have done to the baby."

"Juliana protected the girls in the other compound," I explain. "I figured if she could do it, then I should be able to. I'm not sure how I did it, though."

"Your gift is growing stronger," Sequoia says. "It's changing. Is anything else different?"

"I don't know. I'm more confused, maybe."

"Don't worry about it. Change is hard for all of us, but it can result in much good." My aunt's wisdom always manages to make everything better.

I tap my wristband to check on the others. They had no protection.

Murphy and I are okay, Pax responds. *So are my folks and Analiese. Still deaf, but it'll pass. How about your aunt and uncle? The baby?*

I reassure him and close the link.

Wolf and I help Sequoia down the stairs to a walled-in garden. We walk down a short path flanked by beds of lettuce, zucchini, corn and other vegetables to a gate in the stone wall. Jack's cabin is at the top of our hill, two houses away up a dusty road.

By the time we get there, everyone else is gathered in the main room having a conversation. Their hearing is returning, but judging by the volume of their voices, it isn't yet normal.

"I have contacted Atlantis," Murphy is saying. "A nearby wormhole is causing strong interference. They are unable to come until it passes."

"I guess we call on the Allarans, then," Analiese suggests. "They've been good for transportation, if nothing else." She obviously still resents them for refusing to help rescue Jewel.

"Maybe this time they'll help us find a way to our husbands and the girls." Her face isn't hopeful.

"God, I wish their wristbands were working," Coral says, her voice dropping to a normal level. Her ears must be recovering.

Pax sits beside his mother and puts an arm around her. "It'll be alright, Mom. The girls are strong, and Dad and Charles are with them. Murphy knows where they are. We just have to find a way to get to them."

A deep boom suddenly shakes the house. "What is that?" Al shouts, while the rest of us freeze in shock. A second boom rocks us, and I hear glass breaking upstairs. He and I run to the window on the back wall, and what I see propels me through the door to the backyard, hands out and already pulling up trees and throwing them like spears at the pitted triangular craft shooting lasers at us.

I can't tell if their branches and leaves are interacting with the wind, or my anger-driven aim is bad, but the trees fall short of their mark. I send everything that isn't bolted down at the craft, but like the last time this happened in North Carolina, I can't put a dent in the thing.

Gunfire erupts from the yard behind me. Pax, Murphy, and the men are pointing rifles at it, while Al prepares to fire the rocket-launcher on his shoulder. He checks to make sure no one's behind him and fires. The missile explodes on the viewport, but when the smoke clears, it hasn't so much as cracked it. Nothing we throw at the Dracan ship has any effect on it.

Then I spot the grinning face in the viewport, and the monster inside me explodes out of its restraints. My fury digs into the ground around the hovering craft.

The bedrock smashes and breaks apart as tons of rock and trees fold around the ship like a giant, leafy taco. I aim every loose projectile into the nozzles and watch as the laser beams double back to the holes they're being shot from.

I enjoy the sight of the eyes in the hated face widening in shock and its mouth opening in a scream. I watch it melt inside the ship, along with everything else enclosed with it, and for the first time since my parents were abducted, the monster inside me is satisfied as the ship crashes to the ground.

"Hide it, Storm," Wolf shouts.

I understand and lift the ship to move it into the pit. Why can I move it now and not when I needed to push it away from us? Once it's settled, I bury it under the dirt I'd raised up around it. We don't need a bunch of curious government officials discovering it and sealing this area off.

When I'm finished, my knees buckle and I fall, but Al catches me from behind and eases me to the ground.

"What you did was amazing, Mr. Ryder," he says, He smacks me on the shoulder, and I know he's kidding.

"A rocket launcher?" I kid back. "What would you ever need one of those for?"

"Obviously so he can pretend to take down a Dracan ship," Murphy chimes in. I look at him sharply. We just killed at least one of his people. Shouldn't he be planning revenge on us instead of cracking jokes?

"Chill, Ryder," Pax says, glancing at Murphy. "It must have been one of Shaula's allies."

"Yes," Murphy affirms. "And I was messing with Al. I'm glad you buried the ship. There could be more coming."

"How did I manage to move it?"

"The lasers took out their shield when they burned up their instruments. You moved it the same way you moved me in Triton's cavern," Murphy answers, "with your mind."

33
JEWEL

A soft knock on our bedroom door jars me out of a restless sleep. I glance at the mound under the covers on Sky's bed and get up to answer before whoever it is wakes her up. Juliana throws off her covers, stretches and walks barefoot to the bathroom.

Jaina's fist is raised to knock again when I open the door.

"Would you come to the common room, please?" she asks, more politely than usual.

I step out and close the door behind me. "What's up?"

"I need to explain a few things before you leave here."

"We're leaving? When?" I'm happy to hear the news.

"Today," she says, with a hint of her usual impatience.

"Shouldn't the others hear your explanations?"

"I suppose I can wait until everyone is together, but we may need to leave in a hurry."

The smell of coffee surprises me. Dad and Dylan are already at the table, sipping from steaming mugs. Dad nods toward the counter, where a glass carafe half-full of the dark brew sits in a coffee maker like ours at home. I find a mug in a cabinet and pour some for myself. By the time I'm ready to sit, Juliana and Sky are both following their noses toward the counter.

When we're settled, we wait expectantly for Jaina, who's sitting with her hands in her lap, not drinking coffee.

"When did you know about Sky?" Dylan asks.

"I suspected as soon as I became aware of her gift," Jaina answers. "We had been waiting many years for Fire Hair. At first, I refused to believe Sky could be the one."

I'm offended for my friend and ask snidely, "Why wouldn't she be? What was wrong with her?"

Jaina tilted her head as she turned to me. "For one thing, we expected a giant, like our friends here. In the unlikely event Fire Hair might be a human, then it would have been someone of stature. Sky is small even for a human."

She's serious. Does the prophecy mention stature?

"What is the prophecy, exactly?" Dad asks. I wonder why no one has told us yet. Gienika gave us a general overview, but prophecies tend to be more specific.

Jaina turned her attention to my dad. "It was given in an ancient language, difficult to translate. Essentially, it says a mighty woman of flame red hair will unite the races during the time of Terra's dying. Only then will Terra be saved, and the nations thrive once again. You can understand, perhaps, why I had a problem with Sky's small stature."

"Is this the time of 'Terra's dying'? Is that why the giants thought Sky might be the one?" Dylan asks.

"You know it is. When the tetrahedra fail, Terra will die. I understand Sky, Jewel, and the other two are trying to save the planet by fixing the tetrahedra. It appears to be an impossible task, considering how many are scattered throughout the globe." Jaina paused, gazing at each of us in turn. "And yet, here you are. I have come to admire your determination, even if you cannot succeed."

"How can you say that?" Sky says. She gets up and stands inches from Jaina's face. "We've fixed two of them already. All we have to do is find them, and we can repair the rest."

"Your optimism is admirable," Jaina says. "I will lead you to the ones my people are guarding, but our range is limited. The Dracans have systematically destroyed our tunnel systems and homes in their greed to build cities."

"The Dracans were forced to build underground cities after the great war," Juliana says, coming to the defense of her friends. "I'm sorry your people were displaced, but can't you find a way to coexist with them?"

"They decimated our population, and we are few now. We have homes here in Patagonia and in the North American western desert and mountains. Our Queen Jaide has charged me with the task of finding you and asking for your help to restore our nation and allow us to grow our population back to a sustainable level. You could say we're an endangered species."

"Jaina," Sky says. I hear the sadness in her tone. "If I knew how, I would do anything to help your people. I'd like nothing better than for all the races to get along and share the planet. But I'm just one person, and a person of small stature, as you say. I'm anything but a "mighty woman." Gienika could very well be mistaken. I am probably not the Fire Hair you're all waiting and hoping for."

"Only some of the Dracans might go along with a peace treaty," I tell her. I'd love to be more optimistic about Sky's ability to fulfill such an impossible prophecy, but I've had first-hand experience with the complexities of Dracan politics.

"Thuban, the King of the Atlantic Ocean, is one of them, and he has allies. I suspect the King of North America is one of the few behind Storm's parents' abduction. If he's on Shaula's side, he wants nothing more than to have all of Terra under Dracan control. It seems unlikely they would reach a consensus about uniting the races."

A heavy knock at the door interrupts our conversation. Charles opens it to the giant Jayman.

"Come in and join us," he invites him, gesturing toward the couch. The giant smiles, steps in and when he realizes the couch is made for our size, sinks to the floor cross-legged.

He keeps his voice deliberately soft when he says, "I am ready to escort you to the transfer chamber."

"Transfer to where?" I have no idea what he's talking about.

"It is where you entered, at what you call the Stargate. You will be returned to the same place."

"Jayman," Dylan says, "where did you learn your English? Where did Gienika learn it?"

"Jaina tells me you have heard the story of the injured giant who received aid from Jack and his team. I am he. When I realized only one of the small people understood my language, I asked Jaina to teach me yours. Her queen assigned some of her people to teach those of us who were eager to learn. Not many were. Most learned some basic words, but Gienika, Autumn, and I picked it up easily."

He stands up and opens the door. "Gather your things. I will accompany you and help you through the Stargate."

I'm glad the wagon is ready for us. The horses snort and stamp impatiently while we climb the tailgate ramp. Autumn is there to see us off, wiping her eyes and sniffling.

"Goodbye," she says. "Come back."

"If it's possible," Sky assures her. "We'll see you again."

Jayman takes the reins and urges the horses on. They easily pull the wagon up the steep trail to the rocky path leading to the cave. All of us humans together probably weigh less than one of their largest people.

I wish I were happier about getting back to the others, but the tug tearing me up inside is getting stronger. I try to follow Juliana's advice and concentrate on Pax, but instead of romantic thoughts, I can only picture Shaula hurting him.

34
SKY

T he horses stop at the cliff face where we exited the tunnel on the way in. Its shadow is visible behind a boulder that appears to have broken off the cliff and come to rest standing up. Jayman jumps down and makes a ramp of the tailgate for us. I enjoy a good stretch after sleeping through most of the long ride.

Dad follows the giant into the tunnel, and Charles takes up the rear as we head in single file. Jewel is in front of me, and I hear her gasp as she enters the large cavern.

"I can see again," she says, her relief evident as soon as I follow her in. I tap my wristband gingerly, afraid of the snapping pain from before. It doesn't happen, thank God.

Pax? Can you hear me?

Sky, where are you? Are you okay? Is Jewel with you? Where have you been? The communal link opens, and I know Storm is also listening, even though he isn't saying anything.

Slow down, please. We're fine, and we're all here. No one was hurt, and we've learned a lot. We're coming out of the Stargate. I know it'll take a little time for you to get there, but please come pick us up.

It won't be possible. Now he speaks, and Storm doesn't have anything good to say.

I'm annoyed, not paying attention, and nearly run into Jewel's back. She's come to an abrupt stop, and I'm slammed with waves of her fear. A Dracan ship is parked in the middle of the cavern, about forty feet in front of us. How did it get in here?

Pax? Storm? Are you still there? My frantic mental shout is met with silence. We're too close to the ship, and our wristbands have stopped working.

A tall man dressed in a dark robe stands by the ship, arms crossed over his chest. Jayman gestures for us to stay where we are and strides toward him. Our fathers stand in front of us protectively.

"He's Dracan," Juliana says softly, standing between Jewel and me. "He's in human form. I don't recognize him, but then I've only seen most of them as Dracans."

"I recognize him," Jewel says in a strangled voice. "Shaula. He's tugging at me."

I quickly move to her other side, putting her between Juliana and me, and pull her close to my side. Juliana closes in, too, trying to loan her strength. I've never seen Jewel so pale.

I peek around my dad to get a better look at the evil Dracan. He's beautiful, with dark wavy hair falling to strong, broad shoulders. He has a Roman face, with a straight nose, full lips and large brown eyes under heavy eyebrows drawn together in a frown. High cheekbones and a strong chin complete the image of a man who will let nothing stand in his way. His posture and the upward tilt of his chin speak volumes about his self-assurance.

He turns to stare at Jewel, his gaze cruel, and I decide he's not beautiful at all. He's terrifying, and my gut clenches at the thought of him putting his hands on my friend. No. My sister.

"Back up slowly," Charles says. "Get back to the wagon. We'll hold him off."

I start to obey when I bump into a solid wall behind me. I whirl and nearly smash my nose into the chest of the large Dracan grinning down at me. I stomp on its foot and watch the grin disappear, but it's too little, too late. It swipes at me and knocks me to the ground. So much for my Karate training.

I can't do anything but watch my Dad take a flying leap at the thing when its attention is on me. He knocks it flat, but another comes out of the shadows and quickly overpowers him. Charles, who's had no training, is struggling in the tight grip of another lizard, fists flailing harmlessly off its scales. The Dracan knocks him out cold. Jayman is on the ground, clutching at a bloody hole in his shoulder, while Shaula holsters the weapon that put it there. It's over quickly.

I'm mesmerized by the sight of Jewel walking toward the man/lizard. She fights against each step, but it's as if she's in a tractor beam. He's grinning at her, and I want nothing more than to kill him right now.

Where's Juliana? She tugs on my shirt and I turn to see her half-hidden by a boulder. I scoot closer, hoping for a chance to escape. If we can get out of here, we can get the giants to help us.

"Stop." Shaula's command rings through the cavern, echoing off the walls. "Juliana, come to me and bring your backpack."

She stands up and defiantly shouts, "No!"

I watch Shaula, afraid he might shoot her like he did the giant. I wonder if she can hear my heart pounding.

Instead, he smiles and says in a voice that sends shudders through me, "You will obey me, Juliana, because I have your parents."

"Where are they? What have you done with them?" she asks, her voice strained. I imagine how her throat must be closing in fear for them.

His answering grin is pure evil. "If you wish for them to remain unharmed, I suggest you move now."

Juliana bends to pick up her pack and walks toward him with defiance in each step. She drops the pack at his boot-clad feet, and one of the other Dracans opens it and removes an egg-shaped object, like the one Jack and his team found at the mandala. He hands it to Shaula who examines it carefully.

"Yes. Exactly what I wanted. I am taking Jewel, but I'll leave the rest of you to get to wherever you were going. Now I have the locator that is keyed to me. You will never find us. Say goodbye to Jewel. She is mine, now. You will never see her again." He laughs and guides her into the ship, his hand on her back. Four other Dracans follow them in, and the ramp closes.

As we watch, the craft silently rises and glides to the opening in the roof, momentarily blocking the light. Then it's gone. Jewel is gone. Again. And this time we might not find her before…what? Before she's the bride of Dracula? Oh, God.

Then I remember the artifacts. Shaula may have doomed us all to certain death.

35
SKY

"Sky, bring my pack," Dad shouts. He's squatting next to Jayman, putting pressure on the wound. Juliana spots it near her, scrambles to grab it and tosses it to me. I run to the giant and set it down next to my father.

Charles stirs and moans, holding tightly to his head. "What happened? Where are they?"

Juliana helps him sit and offers him a sip of water from her canteen. She doesn't say anything, and I don't blame her. No one wants to tell Charles his daughter has been abducted again.

"Come help me clean and wrap this wound, Charles. I'll explain as we work."

Juliana and I crawl back into the depression where she'd hidden. I can't imagine trying to force words past the boulder-sized lump in my throat, and she just stares at her hands, clasped around her knees. I think about contacting my brother, but what would I say?

The despair she's emitting is soon eclipsed by a tsunami of anguish from Jewel's father. If my heart weren't already shattered, new shards would certainly have killed me from the inside as the wall of his pain hit. I bury my face in my arms and sob. Juliana pulls me close and sobs with me, both of us trying not to be heard. The men need to concentrate on helping the giant.

Eventually, our sobs become an occasional hiccup, and we listen to Dad and Charles murmuring softly. I can't hear their words, but their voices are soothing.

"Thank you." Jayman's voice booms through the cavern. "I am forever in your debt, gentlemen. Now, if you will, pull the lever you'll find behind that outcropping of stones." He pointed toward a section of the wall.

I wipe my eyes and crawl out to watch what the men are doing, with Juliana right behind me. Charles is sitting cross-legged next to Jayman, holding his head in his hands. Dad has disappeared.

I'm relieved to hear him call out from behind a cluster of rocks, "I found it. Do I pull it down?"

"Yes, when you are ready," Jayman says. "It will open the portal, but it will not keep it open more than a few minutes. You must be ready to run when you pull it."

Juliana and I scramble to get close to Charles. She helps him to his feet, and I grab both his and Dad's backpacks. We walk to where Jayman is pointing.

"The desert will appear there. Go quickly when it comes into view."

"Will we see you again?" Charles asks.

"I am sure of it," the giant responds with a smile. He gently lays his huge hand on Charles's shoulder. "I am sorry, my friend. Do not despair. We will not stop searching for your daughter until she is found. I can assure you the Mantoids will also help."

A glimmer of hope flickers through Charles. I send my own little bit of hope to him, as well. We found her before, and we'll find her again.

"We're ready, Dad," I say, standing at what should be the edge of the blue light when Dad flips the switch.

The light moves outward from the rocks like an expanding bubble. Dad runs to join us, and we soon see the desert spread out in the glow of the setting sun. I grab my friend's hand and run. When we hit the wall of the bubble, a rubbery resistance gives way, and we tumble through.

"No one's here." Dad reports the obvious and taps his wristband.

Charles practically crawls to sit on a rock, and I watch a variety of expressions flit across his face. He's deep in a mental conversation with Analiese, no doubt. I pull Juliana to sit close to me with our backs against a boulder.

"I need to speak with Pax and Storm, to find out why they aren't here and to let them know what's happened. I really wish you had your wristband ready, but since you don't, are you okay with this?"

"Of course," she says. "I'll just rest my eyes while you talk to them." She crawls away a few feet, adjusts her backpack behind her head and closes her eyes.

Pax? Storm?

Pax answers, *what on earth is going on there? Mom and Analiese are wailing like banshees, and the baby's screaming is making everyone crazy.*

Screaming? How can the baby scream? Did Sequoia give birth?

Soundless screaming, Sky, like you used to do as a child, making everyone miserable without making a sound. It's a special gift you empaths have. The baby is still snug inside her mama. Now stop wasting time. What happened?

I dread telling him but can't postpone it any longer. *Shaula took Jewel. I'm so sorry. We tried to stop him, but we were outnumbered.* His shock washes over me in a surge of pain.

What about the rest of you? Storm chimes in. *Were any of you hurt?*

He shot our escort, Jayman, in the shoulder, and Charles was hit over the head hard enough to knock him out. He might have a concussion. Otherwise, we're fine.

We'll track him, Storm says, *with the locator beacon.*

No, we won't, I say, knowing I'm projecting my discouragement through the link. *Shaula took it. He also confirmed he has your parents, Storm.*

Are they alive? he asks, alarmed.

He assured Juliana they are. Now, why aren't you here? What's holding you up?

He replies, *We're in Tierra del Fuego, waiting for the Allarans to pick us up. They haven't responded to Sequoia's call yet. Can you hitch a ride with some of the tourists around there?*

It appears they've all gone home for the night. Pax? Are you alright?

He's in shock. I've got him. Storm breaks the link.

I relay the conversation to Juliana as best as I can and watch the shadows quickly lengthen as the real sun sets and darkness drops like a curtain over the desert. I'm glad for my jacket, and soon begin to shiver as the temperature plummets. We're high in the Andes, over twelve thousand feet above sea level, and it gets very cold at night.

Dad and Charles take out small packets from their backpacks and shake out survival blankets. Each of us has one. We lay our two blankets on the ground underneath us and cuddle close, with Dad and Charles putting us between them for protection. They spread the remaining thin metallic sheets over us, and we use our packs as pillows. I'm amazed at how quickly we warm up.

The thin atmosphere this high in the mountains makes the Milky Way appear so close I could reach out and touch it. How small we are in this magnificent expanse of space, filled with an impossible number of galaxies, each at least as big as ours. Billions of stars and planets fill this tiny slice of universe. How many of them no longer exist, and how many more are there whose light won't reach us for thousands of years? Why is our planet Terra any more important than the trillions of others circling their own suns? If Terra dies, will it even make a tiny ripple in the universe? My thoughts expand outward until I sense a presence of such love that my restless, fearful spirit is comforted, and I sleep.

The sound of tires on gravel penetrates my mind and abruptly ends my dreamless sleep. Dad throws off the cover, letting a blast of cold air in to jar me fully awake. I'm blinded by headlights that abruptly shut off when Charles yells.

When my eyes again adjust to the dark, Dad is speaking with a small Peruvian I recognize as one of Jack's crew. Henry.

They've brought two of the Hummers to take us back to the compound. I cannot wait to fall into a real bed again. I want to sleep until Jewel is found, and Storm and Juliana are reunited with their parents.

3 6

PAX

I can't believe she's been taken again. What is that monster doing to her? How can I fight against his mark and rescue her? The thoughts whirl faster than I can catch them, and my mind shuts down in a daze. A gray fog is swallowing me whole.

"They're here." Storm's hand on my shoulder shakes me awake. I want to crawl back in the fog but now is not the time. I get up and help Wolf pull Sequoia to her feet. Mom and Murphy are gathering our supplies, while Analiese remains curled up in a fetal position facing the back of the couch. Al and Jack have their pile of filming gear ready for pickup.

I sit on the edge of the couch and rub Analiese's back.

"Do you think you can walk?" I ask her, knowing the pain racking her. Her only daughter is in danger again, and she can't help her. She shakes her head.

I carefully roll her over and scoop her up in my arms. If there's any chance at all we'll rescue her daughter and save the world, I'll make sure she becomes my mother-in-law. She wraps her arms around my neck and buries her face in my chest. I'm surprised at how light she is.

"Pax," she murmurs. "Jewel loves you. Find a way to save her, please."

My gut clenches and fills with rage. "If I can't," I say so only she can hear, "I'll die trying."

She nods.

Mom floats into the Allaran ship first, followed by Murphy with an armload of goods. Still holding Analiese, I float up after him, followed by a whirlwind consisting of groceries and blankets. I envy Storm his telekinesis right now. The portal closes, and I assume he's elected to go on the next transport with the others.

As soon as we get into the observation room, I bend to lay Analiese on the floor when a bubble slides over and molds itself to fit under her body like a couch. I wonder when humans will invent smart furniture like these chairs. Maybe Vega or Baran, or, better yet Belena, will share their secrets with us. I wonder if they're forbidden to help us find Jewel this time, too.

Minutes later, we're floating down the portal beam. Dawn bathes the courtyard in a rosy light as we descend. The ship carrying the others has already dropped them off, and the house staff is scurrying like ants carrying boxes and bags of equipment inside. I'm grateful Storm waited around to help us unload our supplies. I carry Analiese to the portal, and he floats her down and over to her waiting husband. Dad grabs Mom around the waist, and they hug for a long moment before going into the house together.

"Are you alright?" Storm asks, throwing his arm around my shoulders as we walk inside together.

"No," I answer truthfully. "And neither are you. We need to find a way to get Jewel and your parents back quickly."

"I know, but I'm fresh out of ideas. We need sleep and clear heads for this."

I agree in principle, but how can any of us expect to get any sleep? I hope Jack gives us our basement room back, or at least some black-out curtains.

Sky and Juliana are still sleeping, and I don't want to bother them. I imagine it's been especially hard on my sister. My already aching heart breaks a little more for her.

~

I WISH I could say things are better when I wake up, but I'd be lying. It's like I've been hit by a train. I'm surprised to discover I've slept through most of the day to supper time. The meal is as substantial as always, but my appetite isn't. I grab a plate and sit next to Storm and Murphy, who are both shoveling food into their mouths.

"How long have you two been awake?" I ask, picking at the roast chicken.

"Many hours," Murphy says, messing with me.

"How many?"

Storm answers for him. "About half of one." So, they've slept nearly as long as I have.

Sky comes bounding into the room and throws her arms around me from behind.

"We have so much to tell you! A lot happened before Jewel was taken, and you need to know we'll have help finding her."

Murphy stands and holds his arms wide to fold Juliana in a long hug. Tear tracks smudge her face, but she's smiling at him with shining eyes.

I'm a tin can slowly being crushed by a giant Dracan claw.

"It's good to see you, too," Storm says, with a hint of sarcasm.

Sky rushes over and throws her arms around his shoulders. I can feel the love she's sending him, and from the way his eyes are shining, so does he. Great.

Dad is sitting at a table in the corner with Wolf, Charles, Al, and Jack, who's pointing to a spot on a map spread out in front of them. I walk over to see what's going on.

"This is where the Gate of the Sun is, in the ruins of Tiahuanaco. Some of my colleagues are excavating a buried pyramid, and they've found evidence of subterranean monoliths. The ruins are fascinating, and I've filmed some of my specials there and plan to do more as they uncover the underground city.

"Since I've learned about the Allarans and Dracans, the ancient machined slabs scattered over much of the area are no longer a mystery to me. It's a shame we can't share that knowledge with the rest of the world."

"Not yet," Wolf says.

I can understand why the slabs baffle modern archeologists. They look like parts of a modular building, cut with precision so they would easily slide together. The indigenous people would not have had the tools to cut them with that degree of engineering.

"Do you think the underground pyramid and monoliths might lead to the artifact?" I ask.

Sky's curiosity has brought her over to see the map.

"The Mantoids will lead us to the artifact. It's one of the things we learned in the land of the giants." She has my attention.

Storm and Murphy pull up chairs for the girls, then some for themselves. We all gather around to hear what happened to them. Juliana and Sky take turns describing the massive children and the village, but when Sky fills us in about Gienika and how she's something called a "truth-sayer," her brows draw together, and she stops talking. Wolf and Charles stare at her as if willing her to continue, but they also remain silent. A sense of Sky's dread comes over me, and I instinctively send her calm.

Juliana speaks up, "If you can't tell them, then I will. The giants think Sky is the fulfillment of a prophecy, that she is Fire Hair, the one who will unite the nations."

"No," Dad says emphatically. "Our priority, after we find Jewel, is to find a way to fix all the artifacts. Sky, you can't focus on two things at once. You know none of us can do what you four do, and you can't afford to spread yourself too thin trying to help everybody."

I agree. I've seen how drained Sky can get around groups of people.

"Dad, what if I can accomplish both by doing what we're already doing? In North Carolina, the watchers guarded the artifact. It was Triton, the dragon, and the Sea Dwellers who guarded it in Andros. Here, the Mantoids have that duty. By working with the different species and races, aren't we uniting them in a common mission? What if all I have to do is prove each has a vital role in caring for our planet?"

"It sounds good in theory," Storm says. "But not everyone will agree. Take Shaula and his kind, for example. No offense, Murphy. They'd try to silence you."

"Not to mention the divisions among the humans on this planet. No offense, Storm," Murphy counters.

Jack opens his mouth to chime in when we're interrupted by the door opening so forcefully, it hits the wall. Henry rushes in, as white as a sheet, pointing toward the door and shouting in a shaky voice, "Viracocha! Viracocha!"

I have a bad feeling about this.

37
STORM

"Viracocha" is what he called the Dracan ship by the floating island. I run out after him, hands ready to do everything I can to repel the vessel or stop it like the one in Tierra del Fuego.

I hear the others running after me. The triangle completely covers the courtyard, blocking out the sun. I search around for anything I can use against it, but short of ripping out the fountain or destroying the buildings, there's nothing to throw at it. I think about the barn and the four Hummers in there. If I open the doors, I can float them out one at a time and toss them, but it would only ruin the cars and rain gasoline and oil down on the natives kneeling and bowing everywhere.

The portal in the center opens, and light bathes the area on the other side of the fountain. I stop short and wait. Whoever is in there is about to pay us a visit.

"Marla!" Sky shouts, running toward the girl floating out of the craft. Marla Snow? She grabs her in a hug then turns and hugs Max, who touches down right behind her. The two of them are dressed in matching green tops and tan pants, but where her top is a tunic, his is an open vest exposing his bare chest. He's more muscled than I remember.

Marla turns to Juliana and draws her in for a long hug. I know from

Jewel's account of what happened in Atlantis that she and my sister grew up together.

"Where's Jewel?" Marla asks as if she'd just stepped out of a car instead of an alien spaceship.

"Yes, where is she?" a woman, dressed in a gold floaty gown and wearing a golden headdress, calls out. Her voice turns my insides to jelly. I've never seen her before, but she obviously knows Jewel.

The Peruvians are prostrating and trembling with awe. I want to join them.

"Forgive me, Meissa," Marla says. She straightens and announces in the snooty voice I remember from school, "This is Meissa, Dracan Queen and Supreme Ruler of North America."

I give in to my impulse and bow in a Karate salute, and she rewards me with a smile. Since when do Dracan females have the same effect on humans as the Allaran women? Or is it just me?

Sky sends me a shaft of pain. She's getting better at weaponizing her ability.

Charles steps forward and addresses the queen. "Our daughter has been kidnapped by a Dracan named Shaula. Are you familiar with him?"

The queen bares her teeth, and I suddenly hope I won't have to see her in her Dracan form.

"Oh, yes," she says in a purr. "And when I find him, I will tear him into little pieces. Where is Jewel's mother? I have something to say to both of you. To all of you."

Jack rushes forward, bowing and nearly tripping over his own feet. He guides the queen into the common room. Al stays in the courtyard and yanks a couple of the men to their feet. The rest get up and scurry to get some refreshments for the guests.

The Dracan craft lifts and streaks off at an impossible speed. It's out of sight in seconds. I go to greet Max and his girlfriend.

"You're older," Pax observes. "Has the wormhole near Atlantis affected the way time is passing?"

"It's been four years," Marla says, glancing fondly at Max, who takes her hand and kisses it. No wonder he's more muscled. He's fully grown.

"We've been married six months," he announces. I nearly choke.

"A little young, aren't you?" I ask. When we last saw Max just about a month ago, he was eighteen, or very close to it. They've had four years together in our one month. This time anomaly thing is insane.

All through middle and high school, Max was a bully, the leader of a gang Sky called the "lost boys." The kids were either afraid of him or fought to be a part of his gang. He and I were always at odds. I understand rage, but I keep mine subdued and don't use it to hurt or intimidate other people. At least, I hope I don't. He had no filters, and because he's the sheriff's son, he got away with more than other kids would have.

After Marla enrolled a little over a year ago, he swaggered more, bragged more and became insufferable. Marla attracted nearly every male in the school, but she chose him, and her hard, arrogant attitude turned everyone else off. They were suited to each other, except for one thing. Marla was a lot more intelligent than that goof. He had trouble stringing three words together.

This Max is different, more mature. Where he used to swagger, now he carries himself with confidence. I wonder if Sky notices a difference in him. Marla also seems softer. Jewel admires her. Maybe it's time I give the two of them a chance.

Sky takes Marla's hand and leads the couple into the house. Murphy follows with the rest of us.

Meissa's regal dignity turns Jack's oversized armchair into a throne. He's even put a pillow on the floor under her feet. One of his house staff hurries in with a tray of refreshments, and Meissa graciously accepts her offer of some fruity concoction.

When Wolf and Sequoia enter, the queen kicks aside the pillow and stands to her feet, staring at Sequoia's belly. My aunt stands still, tall and proud, and my chest swells with pride for her. She's every inch a Cherokee warrior. The part of her that is also a compassionate, loving medicine woman shines from her eyes as she regards the Dracan.

"Your child," the queen says, reaching out for Sequoia. My aunt makes waddling graceful as she glides to Meissa, grabs her hand and places it on her belly.

Meissa closes her eyes and smiles as my cousin moves against her hand. When she opens them, she puts her arms around Sequoia and draws her into a hug. She lets her go, throws her head back and when she again looks at Sequoia, her pupils have contracted to pinpoints.

Her voice sounds hollow as she says, "Your child will cross the bridge of hope, built by another to save the nations."

I hear Sky gasp next to me and I wrap an arm around her. She immediately grows still. Maybe I have some of Pax's brother magic.

Meissa continues. "The light she brings will never be extinguished, so long as Terra survives. The time may be short, or it may stretch for eons. The future of the planet is not yet determined."

Dead silence fills the room. I hold my breath along with everyone else until the queen shakes her head and says in her normal voice, "Now, where are Jewel's parents?"

Charles and Analiese move into the room from the doorway where they'd witnessed the queen's strange proclamation over Wolf and Sequoia's baby. I'm glad she's regained some of her strength. Jack and Al get up from the couch, making room for them. Meissa greets them with a bow and sits back in her chair.

Max and Marla take a seat on the second sofa, and the rest of the adults bring in chairs from the dining room. Pax, Sky, Murphy, Juliana, and I sit on the floor against the wall, where we can observe everyone.

"You must be proud of your daughter," she says, once everyone in the room has settled. "I have never met a human with such courage. It is our hope Jewel will one day become an ambassador between our peoples."

"She won't have the chance unless she breaks away from that snake," Charles says.

"Yes," Meissa agrees.

Juliana stands up and says, "If you please, Queen Meissa, allow me to tell you what we know."

The queen acknowledges her and nods.

"Shaula has marked Jewel without her knowledge or consent."

Meissa jumps to her feet, bares her teeth and transforms. I wonder at her change from a tall, beautiful woman to a taller, fearsome beast. Her face elongates into a snout and a huge mouth filled with menacing teeth. Her eyes become larger and turn red-streaked yellow, slit with black, vertical pupils. Her brown hair solidifies into ridges starting from over her eyes and running over her head and down her back, lost in the folds of the dress that's grown with her. Her scales gleam golden in the low light of the room, and her fingernails have become six-inch claws, which she clenches into massive fists. Her headdress nearly scrapes the beam holding up the fifteen-foot-high ceiling directly above her.

A tray clatters, and I hear shattering glass as one of the staff drops to her face and wails something in her language. I can understand why they think this creature might be a god.

Meissa roars and my gut clenches. I can't believe Jewel stood up to this thing.

"Shaula will pay for his crime," she shouts. At this moment, I'm almost sorry for Shaula.

3 8
JEWEL

"Where are we?" I ask as we step away from the ramp. It's obvious we're in a Dracan docking bay, but where? Neither of the two guards answers me, and I wonder if they speak English, like everyone in Atlantis does. Maybe they're under orders to ignore me.

I follow the brown-scaled one out of the bay and into a hall lined with dull gray metal. It's disorienting. The seamless walls, ceiling and floor are the same uniform color, with no contrast and nowhere to focus the eyes. I concentrate on the guard to avoid getting dizzy. The scrape of boots behind me reminds me the other won't let me escape even if I knew where I was going.

I try to picture Pax, but the images won't stick. Please, God, get us out of this endless corridor soon.

We follow the hallway around a bend, and the Dracan leading me reaches out and presses something hidden on the wall. A door slides open and we enter an equally bland room lined with uncomfortable metal chairs. My spirits drop lower every minute.

"Sit," Brownscale says. He does speak English.

I obey and plop into one of the metal chairs, praying I won't be here long. My back already aches from the angle of the seat back, and the edge of the seat puts too much pressure on the back of my legs.

Hemmed in with bolted-on arm rests, it's too narrow for me to sit cross-legged. Both guards stand at attention at the far wall, staring at me. There must be another invisible door there. I stick my tongue out at them. Grayscale bares his teeth and I turn my face away from them.

After what seems like hours, the wall opens, and Shaula strides in, no longer in his human form. I stand up in a vain attempt to show some courage. He terrifies me.

He's as vicious as ever, with his cold eyes and cruel teeth. All the Dracans have large alligator teeth, but Shaula's are more like a crocodile's, sharper and longer than the others. His scales are dark gray with little sheen to them. Everything about him reminds me of creepy shadows in horror movies.

He says nothing but stares at me intently, and I have the sudden urge to kneel. When I don't, the urge increases, along with a sharp pain at the back of my knees.

I resist again and a heavy weight comes down on my shoulders. He's using the mark to manipulate me, and I fight it with everything I have. I grunt with the effort, and he laughs, releasing me.

"You will be mine, Jewel Adams, and no amount of resistance will help you."

I don't answer. If Pax can't find me in time, Shaula might be right. I'll fight him as much as I can, but what if I'm not strong enough?

"Come. I'll show you to your quarters. I hope they're to your liking." He whirls and the guards nudge me after him. I hope there's something decent to eat and a comfortable bed to sleep in.

After a short walk through more of the disorienting corridors, Shaula leads us into an ornate room paneled in a rich dark wood. A breeze comes in through two open picture windows on the wall opposite the door, assisted by a ceiling fan with blades shaped like giant leaves. The air smells fresh, although I'm sure it's recycled like all the air in Dracan cities. I walk to the window and take a deep breath, admiring a garden filled with green plants, some flowering, that ends at a distant wall. The garden and plants are real, but the perspective to the wall may be a hologram.

Couches and overstuffed chairs sit in three groupings around the room. Floor-to-ceiling bookcases cover two walls. A library.

Shaula walks to a door between bookcases and gestures for me to follow him inside. A marble dining room table, flanked by high-backed chairs with royal blue upholstery, is set for two. Textured sky-blue wallpaper covers the walls in this room, and a garden breeze blows in through another set of picture windows.

"Eat. I will show you the rest when you're finished."

I'm grateful he doesn't join me at the table but leaves through another door instead. I have little appetite, but my stomach growls and I take a little of the stew bubbling in a silver tureen. It's good, and I eat more of it, glancing around at some landscapes hanging on the walls.

When I'm full, Shaula returns and leads me to the next room. Where I expected windows, a screen covers the wall. It's very much like Marla's media room in Atlantis, with plush theater chairs and controls in the armrests.

"I'll show you how to use the equipment as soon as we're mated. Until then, I am all I want you to think about. You will have no distractions. You will be confined to your bedroom. Your meals will be served there, if I decide you need to be fed." I want so badly to wipe the grin off his face. He's horrible, and I will die before I give in to him.

The bedroom is a stark contrast to the other well-appointed rooms in the suite. Bare white walls, uninterrupted by windows or artwork, frame a floor of black and white tiles, reminding me of an old fifties diner. Like the jail cell in Atlantis where I spent one night, a sink and toilet sit in one corner, half-hidden by a plain white screen. A card table and two metal chairs like the ones in the waiting room stand alone in the opposite corner. A large bed is pushed against the wall to the right with a small nightstand next to it. It's topped with a thin mattress, two flat pillows at the head and a rough blanket folded at the foot. There are no sheets. This is more like what I expected from this monster.

I walk over to the bed and sit down, bouncing a little on the mattress. Shaula has no idea how this prison has cemented my determination to resist him or die trying. He wants to break me. Maybe he will, but the result won't be what he expects. I smile at him and say with sincerity, "Thank you."

39
SKY

I t takes several minutes for Meissa, still in her Dracan form, to cool down enough to take her seat. Her face gradually relaxes as Juliana tells her about Gienika and the giants and how kind they were. Jewel had told me the color of their scales changes in hue and intensity depending on their moods. Her coloring is softer, and so is Murphy's, who is no longer human. His clothing, unlike hers, did not expand when he changed, and he looks uncomfortable.

"Go change clothes," I whisper to him. "She won't miss you for a few minutes." He nods and leaves, and Meissa's eyes follow him.

I wonder why Juliana hasn't told her about Gienika's prophecy, especially since she uttered one over Sequoia's baby that appears to tie in with mine. If I'm Fire Hair, then I'm the bridge. Baby O'Connell is the one who will cross over the bridge. Come to think of it, it's best not to bring it up. What if I'm not the Fire Hair they were hoping for?

"When Murphrid returns," Meissa says, after nodding her thanks to Juliana, "I have a message for you from his mother. Considering Shaula illegally put his mark on Jewel, I believe the news will be welcome and could offer a way to find both. I understand he is also holding others of you as prisoners?"

Storm gets to his feet, as do Wolf and Sequoia. He puts his arm around his aunt, and the three of them face the queen.

"Queen Meissa," Sequoia says. "Shaula abducted my sister and Storm's mother, Salali Ryder, along with his father, Tom, when our nephew was a ten-year-old boy. He took them to Atlantis, where King Thuban cared for them as he does all refugees, believing, as they did, their son had died in the accident from which they were rescued. I learned this from Juliana. Perhaps she can tell you the rest of the story."

"Please sit, Sequoia. You must be fatigued."

Wolf helps Sequoia back to the couch, where he sits with her, but Storm remains standing.

His sister joins him. "King Thuban treated my parents well," she says. "They are scientists and were assigned to work with Murphrid's mother, Ashley Jenkins. I was born nearly two years after they arrived in Atlantis, and they raised me with love. They grieved their son and made sure I knew him through their stories. When Jewel reunited with her friends and the four of them repaired the artifact in Triton's cave, I discovered my brother is alive and well, and, because of the time anomaly caused by a long-lasting wormhole, he is only a year older than I am."

I'm surprised Dracan faces show as much astonishment as human faces do. Meissa's impressive jaw is hanging open, and her eyes are wide under arched eye ridges.

"And this is your brother," Meissa notes, pointing a claw at Storm. "Sky's mate."

"I'm sorry, your majesty," Storm stammers, losing the cool confidence he wears like armor. I don't think I've ever seen him blush before.

He clears his throat, but his voice sounds tight as he explains, "Neither of us has decided on a mate yet. In our society, we're too young, and we don't use a mark like the Dracans do."

I'm delighted at his squirming and let him know it. He turns and flashes a glare at me, and I send him another jab of joy. Whether he likes it or not, I believe Meissa may have hit on another prophecy.

Murphy comes in then and slides down the wall to sit next to me, dressed in loose pants and a colorful Peruvian vest he must have borrowed from Al. He's shirtless, and I admire the soft blue and yellow scales on his chest. He's grinning, I think, and I know he heard the exchange between Storm and Meissa.

"What has happened to your parents?"

Juliana replies, "Shaula took them when he escaped King Thuban. The last anyone saw of him, until now, was when his ship and one of Thuban's disappeared into a rogue wormhole."

"If he's reappeared, then Thuban's men may also be nearby. We will find him, and I will destroy him. I sincerely hope he does no harm to his prisoners before we rescue them. And now, Murphrid, I have a message for you which may have a bearing on this."

Murphrid gets up and goes to stand in front of the queen. "I'm at your service, Queen Meissa."

"Your mother sends her love and says she's missed you these four years."

Murphy's head droops, and he answers, "It's only been a few weeks for me. I hope the anomaly is soon over. I miss her, as well, if not as long."

Meissa nods. "Marla Snow is the first Dracan female to choose a human mate. It would not have been possible except for two discoveries. The human blood in her became dominant as her love for Max grew, nearly overriding the genetic programming of her Dracan blood. And yet, she would not have been able to accept Max as her mate without the mark, which he, as a human, was unable to produce.

"Ashley used Marla's blood to manufacture a serum mimicking the mark of the Dracan male. When it was injected into both Max and Marla, they became true marked mates."

The newlyweds smile at each other. How romantic. They went through so much just to be together. I glare at Storm's back and send him a spear of annoyance. He jumps and squares his shoulders, refusing to look at me. Why does he make it so hard for us? We don't need a serum to be together. I wonder if Dr. Jenkins can make a human love potion.

Pax jumps to his feet and tries to control the anger in his tone. "What does it have to do with Jewel and getting her away from Shaula? He's already marked her. Only death can break it, and what if we don't find him and he doesn't die? What if…"

His knees give out, and he collapses back to the ground. The peace I send him meets a wall of grief so thick it can't penetrate.

"Paxton, you and Jewel are meant to be a marked pair and Shaula stole her from you. What Ashley discovered is hope for you. The mark Jewel carries can be transferred through her blood to you, and through it, you will always be able to find her."

"How can I get her blood if she's missing?" Pax cries out, fighting tears.

"I have some." Analiese's quiet voice brings the room to dead silence again. "You know I'm a geneticist, and when Jewel came home, the first thing I did was draw several vials of blood to test for any negative effects from her captivity."

"What did you find?" Meissa asks.

"I could not identify a certain element in her blood. It matches nothing in my experience. Now I know it's the biochemical marker Shaula injected her with. Would it be possible for me to work with Dr. Jenkins to produce the necessary serum?"

Marla stands up and goes to hug Jewel's mother. "I'm sure she'll be honored, Analiese. Do you have a laboratory here?"

"Not here," she says. "All of my equipment is at home. Perhaps it's time for Sequoia, Coral, and me to return. We can work better there than here, and Sequoia doesn't need any more adventures right now. Marla, would you and Max please come with us? I want to study your blood and how the mark works in Max."

Marla glances at Meissa. "If it's alright with Meissa, we'll be happy to come along. Max can spend some time with his father, and I'd love to help you as best I can."

Meissa stands to her feet, and this time everyone in the room stands with her. "We will take our leave. Analiese, prepare what you and the women need for the journey, and we will take you home. Marla, you and Max go with the women. I hope you resolve this quickly for Jewel's and Pax's sake.

"I thank you, Dr. Austin, and your staff for your generous hospitality. I suppose the word of our visit is out by now. I am sorry to leave you with the task of quieting any rumors. It is not yet time to reveal our existence to the human world."

"I understand," he responds. "I can't promise the natives won't talk, but I'll do what I can among the archaeological community."

Meissa transforms back to her human form before leaving the room, and everyone follows her to the courtyard, where the ship is once again hovering. Everyone but Murphy, whose pants nearly fall off when he changes back to the familiar movie-star persona we all know and love. He needs some clothes that automatically resize with him.

"Wait a minute," Pax shouts, stopping her as she approaches the ship. "You said Murphy's mother made two discoveries. What was the second one?"

The queen's eyes soften as she turns to him. "The chemical marker in the human male is more potent than in a Dracan male. Max immediately reacted to the injection, bonding him to Marla. He was the first. We do not know if the effects will be as positive in you, but we have hope. If the marker doesn't kill you outright, it may give you what you need to fight Shaula."

The queen enters, followed by Max and Marla. The vessel waits for the men to bring their wives out with packed suitcases. We hug and say goodbye and the women disappear into the ship, which takes off as suddenly as it did before.

"They'll be home in fifteen minutes," Storm says, coming up behind me. "I hope it doesn't take long for Dr. Jenkins and Analiese to get the serum ready. I don't think your brother has any patience left."

"Marla told me a ship is already launching from Atlantis with my mother on board," Murphy says, back in his regular clothes. "Knowing my mother, she won't take time to sleep until the serum is ready."

"That makes two of us," Pax murmurs as he walks toward the house. The shards of his breaking heart penetrate my own, and my energy bleeds through the punctures. We can't crawl into a hole and just wait. If we don't do something, we'll drain away completely.

"Dad, let's spar," I call out, surprising myself.

Dad's expression makes me laugh, which makes him even more astounded. Am I losing it?

"What a great idea, Sky," he says and turns to Jack. "Is there a gym nearby, or at least a sandy beach? We don't have mats or protective equipment handy."

Jack looks thoughtful. "Maybe it's time to visit the Bolivian side of Lake Titicaca and take a trip to the Isla del Sol, which has a couple of decent sandy beaches on the east side. Some of the Inca ruins there have indentations that resemble our Stargate. The ruins of Tiahuanaco, where the Gate of the Sun stands, lie east of the lake. Henry believes there are tunnels under the Sungate, possibly leading to another artifact."

"Why waste time at Isla del Sol, then?" Pax asks. "Maybe those tunnels are a portal like the one in the Stargate. If there's even a slight chance they might lead to Jewel, we have to explore it."

"He's right," Charles says. "Finding my daughter is more important than anything else right now."

"Besides," Jack says, "don't you need her to fix those artifacts?"

We need her alright, but not just for the artifacts. My heart aches for my friend. Sparring is out for now, but I badly want to punch something or someone.

40

PAX

I f I didn't know about the aliens and their role in building ancient civilizations, I'd be as stumped as modern-day archeologists by the Gate of the Sun. The ten-ton single block stands alone, nearly ten feet high and thirteen feet wide, as if it were once a doorway in a wall. On the front, carvings frame an open door leading nowhere. A figure some believe is Viracocha sits in the center, over the doorway, with rays surrounding his head and tears carved on his face. Other figures with wings and curled tails fan out on either side of him, some with human-like faces and others with the faces of condors.

We know from Vega, the Allarans and Dracans had built this temple complex and a spaceport at nearby Puma Punku for their mutual benefit. Both locations were destroyed around twelve thousand years ago, in the great war between the alien races. Many of the inter-locking wall slabs at Puma Punku still litter the ground and baffle modern experts.

Jack's voice pulls me out of my thoughts, "Henry has arranged for us to have this place to ourselves tonight. He believes the priests who practice the ancient religion will be able to open it by ritual chanting. We'll be the first foreigners to see them in action."

"It would make a great episode for your program," Murphy comments.

"Unfortunately, we're forbidden to film it. Still, it'll be exciting to experience it first-hand, cameras or no cameras."

"Meanwhile, I'd love to examine the excavation of the underground pyramid you told us about," Dad says.

"The excavation stopped after the first of the mysterious sounds nearly deafened the archeologists working the site. They've been surveying the area with ground penetrating radar, trying to find its source, but the clay makes it difficult. They don't know about the artifacts, of course. I'll show you what little they've unearthed. Follow me." Jack whirls and leads us away from the gate which stands near the northwest corner of a temple terrace, down ancient steps, and east toward a roped-off area of the digs.

He's right. There's very little to see, so I wander away to explore the rest of the site. The ruins are amazingly well-preserved, although parts of them, like the wall in the sunken temple, were reassembled by archeologists in the 1960s. I'm fascinated by the stone faces in the wall. The heads are original, but their placement may not be. They appear to be an interstellar version of the United Nations, and I spot a Dracan, an Allaran, and a Watcher. One of the more worn faces could even be a Mantoid. I lose myself in imagining what the world was like when all the races interacted. Did they have problems with racial divisions?

Jewel has had more experience than any of us with the Dracans. Icy bands close around my heart when I think of her with Shaula. What if we can't get to her soon enough?

"Didn't they find a tunnel under one of the pyramids they've been unearthing?" Sky must have followed me. I'm sorry she can't help but feel my pain.

"Yeah. Under the Akapana pyramid," I answer, grateful for the internet and my research. "It's narrow and steep and they have no idea what it was used for."

"Remind me to ask Vega, or whoever is on the next ship we ride in," she says. "Why haven't the Allarans done anything to find Jewel? Didn't Vega say the Creator hasn't forbidden them to help this time?"

"You're asking me?" I sink down in the shade of the wall. Sky joins me and rummages in her backpack for a bottle of water. She offers it to me, and I take a long swallow before giving it back.

"Do you think the priests will be able to open the Sungate tonight?" She sounds more defeated than hopeful. I send her peace. She relaxes with a sigh and leans back against the wall.

"We'll find out. Jaina said there's a system of tunnels under the Stargate, but when it opened, it led to someplace different. This could be another wormhole, or it could be the entrance to a tunnel system. I don't care which it opens to, if we get some answers," I reply.

ANGRY VOICES WAKE me from a restless nap. Jack and Henry are deep in a heated argument. Juliana, sitting next to Sky, is busy stacking loose rocks in a pile and scattering them, using her telekinesis. Al watches her with focused interest, while Dad and Charles examine the sculpted faces.

"What's going on?" Sky asks, and I shrug. I don't know, and I don't really care unless it concerns Jewel. Dad comes over to sit next to me.

"The priests aren't coming tonight," he says. "It has something to do with the phase of the moon. Jack says Henry should have known about it and never consulted with them, and Henry is adamant he did. I wonder if something spooked them."

"Are we going back without trying?" Juliana asks.

"No," Sky replies, sending a surge of anger and determination. "We'll use the wristbands to amplify my thoughts, and I'll call to Gien-ika, much like we did with Triton. If it doesn't work, we'll come back and try again until it does."

"If there's no other way to get to the tunnels," Juliana comments, "Storm and I can use our gift to dig an opening pretty quickly. We'd probably ruin the digs, but we'd get the job done."

"No," Dad says. "We'll find another way. Besides, if the tunnels were made by Dracans, you might not be able to get into them even if you dig down to them."

The sun is setting by the time the argument dies down. Jack calls out, "Let's get over to the Sungate. If nothing happens tonight, Henry says he'll talk to the priests tomorrow."

Sky opens her link to the rest of us. *I've included Dad, and he's relaying the message to Charles. We'll form a circle around the gate, with me facing the carving over the lintel. I don't know if this will work, but it's worth a try.*

Why should you be in the center? Storm sounds annoyed. I drop my guard and get a whiff of fear. He's worried about Sky. So am I.

Remember the prophecy? If I'm the bridge, then whatever comes through that gate won't be able to hurt me. At least, I hope so.

Jack, who has no idea we're communicating mentally, directs us to form a loose circle around the gate. Sky positions herself in the middle against his protest he should be there.

"I've been through the Stargate, Jack. If this links to the same place and we succeed in opening it, then the giants will recognize me."

Al nods, agreeing with Sky. "Jack, you should be on the other side in case this goes south."

Jack agrees and moves, shooting a glare of resentment at Sky and at Henry, who's already on the other side of the gate.

Dad, Charles, and those of us with linked minds close our eyes, while Henry chants in his language. Is he one of the priests?

Sky sends her thoughts into the gate the same way she reached out to Triton, but Triton had strong empathic powers, and the gate is inanimate. I don't see how this can possibly work. Then her mind stretches beyond the gate. I pour my strength into her and sense the others doing the same. A blue glow begins to form in the doorway. She's reaching something or someone on the other side.

The glow expands beyond the confines of the doorway, and the figure of a giant appears. I hear Henry gasp, "Jayman."

The giant takes a leap into the air and tumbles in the dirt outside of the light. The glow snaps into itself and disappears while he staggers to his feet and dusts himself off.

"I told you we would see each other again," he says, grinning at the astonished faces around the circle.

41

JEWEL

I wish the red lights on the video cameras at each corner of the ceiling would at least blink in unison. I imagine the random pattern was meant to help drive me insane or at least bother me enough to make me want to surrender. Shaula is nothing if not supremely confident. I roll over to face the wall and close my eyes. I still see them through my eyelids.

After a few sleepless minutes, my fingers begin to tap out the sequence of blinks on the wall. Tap, pause, tap-tap-tap, pause, tap-tap, pause. Tears fill my eyes as I remember how I used to connect with my mom and dad on the wristband before I met my best friends. Dash-dot-dot, or "D," was my code for Dad. I tap it out over and over until it overrides the haphazard blinking. Next, I tap dash-dash for "M," Mom's code. After Dad made the wristbands for the rest of us, he changed the way we connect to each other, from using Morse code to touching specific buttons around the screen, which normally doubles as a watch and fitness monitor, and tapping a certain number of times. I try one now, knowing it won't work. Not even the watch works here. I'm thankful the band won't come off without a special code only the parents know. I'm also thankful Shaula doesn't know anything about our ability to link mentally. Not that it matters now.

Still unable to sleep, I run through the alphabet, tapping quickly. Finally, I spell out Pax's full name, Paxton Hunter Fletcher. The ache in my heart spills out of my eyes, and I sob until exhaustion takes me into blessed oblivion.

~

THE CLICK of the door wakes me, and I sit up to see Brownscale with a tray. He sets it down on the table and leaves without saying a word. I lift one of the two fancy covers off a dish and find a plain chunk of dry bread. The second cover reveals a bowl of nasty, watery oatmeal, or maybe rice cereal. Since there are no utensils, I assume I'm supposed to dip the bread in the cereal or drink it out of the bowl. I stare up at one of the cameras and laugh out loud. I take the bread and with exaggerated slowness, dip it, throw my head back, and let the gruel drip into my open mouth. Then I smack my lips and do it again. After each dip, I stare at the camera, defying my captors. I imagine the next meal, if there is one, won't be as palatable. Shaula's cruelty will have no restraints here, unlike in Atlantis. I refuse to give him any satisfaction.

When I've eaten it all, I get up and carefully set the tray by the door and begin practicing my karate moves. I run through my katas twice, then do fifty sit-ups and twenty push-ups. I have no way of knowing how much time has passed. Last night, the light went out, and I went to bed. I hope it'll go out when it's time to sleep again. Meanwhile, I have nothing to read, no one to talk to, nothing to watch, and nowhere to go. I might just die of boredom.

The water in the small sink tastes slightly metallic, but there's nothing else to drink. Breakfast didn't include a beverage. My stomach growls, letting me know it's time to eat again. I bang on the door and shout until I realize I'm doing what Shaula wants me to do. I refuse to panic, sit down cross-legged on the bed and start singing some of the old songs my dad used to sing to me.

"I'll be working on the railroad, all the live-long day…" I sing, the words unfolding in my brain as fresh as the many times I'd heard them as a child. "Someone's in the kitchen with Dinah, someone's in the kitchen I know-o-o-o…" I sing it over and over, each time louder until I'm shouting the tune and words.

Finally, the door opens, and Grayscale glares at me as he picks up the tray. He doesn't leave anything to eat.

"Shut up," he growls, baring his teeth.

I bare mine back at him and say, "Not until you feed me. Tell your leader."

When I start the song again, as loud as my weakening voice will go, he stalks over to me and raises his clawed hand. I close my eyes but don't stop. I don't open them again until I hear the door slam shut and he's gone. Apparently, Shaula won't let them hurt me.

My voice is hoarse by the time the door opens, and another tray slides in. I pick it up, and open the lid on the one plate, expecting another dry crust. I'm surprised it's a bowl of the savory stew I ate yesterday and a spoon. I wink at the camera before relishing the first bite.

After the meal, I lie back down, face the wall and pull the blanket up over my shoulders. I hum a meaningless tune in time to the beats as I tap the Morse code alphabet on the wall. There's no point in letting Shaula know the taps are in a deliberate pattern. I know he can hear them, but I hope he doesn't understand what I'm doing.

I tap Sky's name followed by Pax and Storm.

Thump. Thump. I hear the sound before I can tap out Juliana's name. Someone is on the other side of the wall.

Dot-dot-dot, dash-dash-dash, dot-dot-dot, I tap the sequence for SOS. Whoever is there taps it back. Do they know the code, or are they mimicking me? I tap out, *who are you?* I don't know if there are dots or dashes for punctuation marks.

You first, is what came back. They do know it. Are they friends or foes? Is it one person, or are there more? If it's Shaula or one of his lackeys, then he's playing with my mind, but what if he has other prisoners? I decide to take the chance.

Jewel, I tap out. *Now your name.*

Are you prisoner, came back. That's something only a prisoner would ask, isn't it? My instincts tell me to trust the tapper.

Yes. Now you.

Tom. Isn't that Storm's father's name?

You alone, I tap.

No. Wife here. Salali.

My heart leaps. Storm's parents are here, in the room on the other side of this wall. I keep my expression neutral in case I'm being watched.

Juliana. I tap. I'm slowly getting comfortable again with the alphabet, but it's slow going.

Ours, he responds. *Is she ok.*

Yes, I tap. *Storm too.*

Who is Storm.

Your son. They must have called him by his first name, Darrock, before they disappeared.

The door opens before they can respond and I grow still, pretending to be asleep.

"I know you're awake, woman," Shaula's voice grates on my nerves. "Your tapping on the wall is annoying me. Stop it."

I sit up and face him. "I'm playing tunes in my head and keeping time on the wall. If you give me nothing else to do, I'll continue tapping, unless you want me to go insane. What good would I be to you, then?"

"Do not push me," he says and my blood chills, but I refuse to be quiet.

"I know you're watching me, Shaula. Since I have no one to talk to here, why not just turn down the volume on your end? Of course, you might enjoy the few songs I know. Shall I sing you one?"

I bellow out the words, "She'll be coming 'round the mountain when she comes. She'll be coming 'round the mountain when she comes…"

"Stop. No singing. No tapping. I don't care if you go insane. You will be mine, and the sooner you break, the faster it will happen. I am warning you. There are worse places I can keep you, Jewel Adams, and I won't hesitate to move you there." I turn away from the snarl on his face.

When he leaves, the air clears and I can breathe again. Does Shaula know Storm's parents were tapping a message to me? Did they know their son is alive before I told them? I'm afraid to ask them, not because the Dracan threatened me, but because he might do them harm.

When the lights go out, I let the tears come, thankful for the darkness. I'm terrified of Shaula, but I refuse to show him any weakness if I can help it.

Tom or Salali taps out a message. *Thank you.*

I don't answer, but the message soothes me. I'm glad I told them about their son. I let myself drift off.

THE ROOM IS STILL DARK when I wake up to a vibration in my head, sparking and buzzing like an electric current. Watchers? No. When they spoke, it was more of a steady buzzing.

Who are you?

I get no answer.

Are you watchers? Please speak to me.

The current increases, making me want to reach in through my ears and scratch the inside of my eyeballs. Again, there's no answer.

Stop! Please, stop, I beg in my mind. I'd never beg out loud where the Dracans might hear. Somehow, I know this isn't another one of Shaula's torments. Someone or something is trying to communicate with me.

It stops. I breathe deeply and lie there, unable to get back to sleep. Do I have allies in here? Who or what are they?

When the door crashes open, I don't get up. The light snaps on and I hear the guard setting the tray down on the little table. After he leaves, I eat the dry toast and gruel. I guess I'll have to get used to it.

I move through all the katas I know three times and increase my other exercises. If nothing else, I should be more fit when I'm rescued. I refuse to dwell on any other outcome.

My teeth again begin to vibrate, and I grind them together in a vain attempt to stop the current now coursing through me, as if I've shoved a fork into an electric outlet. I fight the urge to scream.

If you can hear and understand me, please talk to me, I send to the source of the current.

The current snaps and crackles then slows and coalesces into words. *You are Jewel?*

Thank God. It knows who I am.

Who are you? How do you know me?

Jaina searches.

Jaina? We left Jaina back with the giants. How does she know Shaula abducted me?

Are you a Mantoid, like Jaina? I ask. I was right about her picking up our telepathic communications. She must communicate with her own kind this way.

A black and white picture forms in my mind. An insect-like creature resembling Jaina wears a flowing robe with a collar that fans out behind its head. I'm aware the buzzing has quieted.

Your queen? I ask.

I am Queen Jaide. The answer comes with a shock of electricity.

I send back an image of Jaina, and she shows me Jaina leading a group of her people. The pictures form more easily than words, without the teeth-rattling vibrations. I've experienced this kind of mental communication before, with Cruiser in Atlantis. This can work.

Thank you, I answer. *How? When?*

The buzzing stops and I receive no more images. The conversation is over with my questions remaining unanswered. There's nothing I can do about it, so I start singing to annoy the Dracans.

42
STORM

S ky and Juliana run toward the giant and throw themselves into his massive arms. He laughs as he hugs them. Henry reaches out his hand, which the giant carefully grasps. The two jabber at each other in Henry's language.

"We're happy to see you again, Jayman," Charles says. "We hope you can help us find Jewel and Storm's parents."

"What makes you think they are here?" the giant asks. "This is another portal to our land. If they were here, I would know."

"Doesn't this gate also lead to a tunnel system directly below us?" Wolf asks. "Are you familiar with the tunnels and do you know how to access them?"

Jayman walks around the gate, scratching his chin, deep in thought. Henry asks him something in his language and the giant says something in return.

Jack watches the exchange between them and shakes his head. "Jayman. Henry. Speak English, please. Do you know about the tunnels and how to get into them?"

"Yes," Jayman says, rocking on the balls of his feet. "However, we cannot access them without Jaina. Her people guard the secrets of the tunnels."

"Where is she?" Al asks. "We haven't heard from her since she disappeared into the Stargate."

"Her queen has called her to action, my friends," Jayman says. "She is gathering an army against Shaula and the Dracans allied with him."

I press my wristband and open the connection with Sky and Pax. *I want to be a part of that. They're fragile fighters and won't stand a chance against a Dracan.*

I agree, Pax answers. *They didn't put up much of a fight against us. How do we volunteer?*

"Jayman," Sky asks, "how would we contact Jaina?"

He sits and pats the ground next to him. Sky sinks to the dirt to his right. Murphy and Juliana follow, sitting next to her. Jayman nods to Charles and Dylan, and they wordlessly do the same. I sit next to Pax and across from Sky. Al and Henry find a spot, and we each sit cross-legged on the ground, forming a loose circle. Jack is the last to drop down on the left side of the giant.

I stare at the ground to avoid Sky's eyes. My gut twists with the effort, everything in me wanting to turn to her. I can't afford to love her when there's a chance I'll lose her. She jabs and I grit my teeth. I'm glad she's learned to use her annoyance as a weapon, but I hate being her target. I want to grab her and run as far away from all this as possible. It'll never happen.

Jayman starts humming low in his chest and pats the ground in a drumbeat rhythm. He nods to Sky, and she does the same. The rest of us take up the cadence.

This may be his way of calling Jaina and her kind. Pax, didn't you say they communicate through vibrations?

Vibrations and pheromones. Can't send the latter, so I'm guessing you're right. The vibrations might draw them out.

I get the drumbeats, I tell them, *but the droning is putting me to sleep. I hope he gets a response before we're all snoring.*

I cut off the link and fight a losing battle with my heavy eyelids. Sky's sharp jab jerks me awake and makes me want to lash out. I can't block what I can't see coming, but I restrain my impulse. I'd never use my gift against her. I glare at her, and she points to a portal forming in the middle of the circle, wavy and silvery like a vertical puddle. A huge Mantoid dressed in armor materializes out of it. Is the armor real gold?

The creature's triangular head bears a crested helmet stretching down to cover the middle of its face, open on the sides to allow for the eyes that run half its length, and ending above its pointed mouth. A living goatee of small mandibles moves and clicks beneath the mouth. A breast plate, more tubular than shield-like, covers its upper body, leaving its serrated arms and hook-like hands exposed. It carries a wicked barbed spear. This isn't one of the creatures Fletcher and I so easily disposed of in front of the Stargate. The eyes are different, and it's much bigger.

The link opens, and he says, *He's sending out an alarming pheromone I've never encountered before. Open your mind, Sky, and communicate like you did with Triton.*

She closes her eyes and forms a mental picture of Jaina in her human form. The creature turns to focus on her, and the air vibrates. It steps aside, leaving the portal clear.

Al jumps to his feet and shouts, "Jaina!" A grin splits his face, and I'm relieved she's in her human form. The creature bows and she nods at it. Al watches the exchange and growls, his eyebrows drawn together in a fierce frown. Pax sniffs.

She's emitting a similar pheromone as the Mantoid, and it's relaxing him, he says.

It isn't relaxing our friend Al, I retort. The man clenches and releases his fists as if he can't make up his mind to attack or wait for a better time. I have no doubt he's eager to fight the creature.

Pax, I think she can hear us in the link, Sky cautions.

If she does hear us, there's no indication of it.

She turns to me and says, "Don't go using your power on us, Storm. We mean no harm and have come to help you."

"What the heck do you need a body-guard for?" Al's gruff voice interrupts her. "Send it back where it came from."

"Relax, Al," she says in a soft voice I hardly recognize as hers.

"We need him and the rest of the Mantoids. Don't forget, I'm one of them."

Al turns and walks away, but stays close enough to hear her say, "The artifact you've heard is in the tunnels below us. We can take you there, but I understand no one can repair it until you have Jewel back. That's a problem. We don't know where Shaula has imprisoned her but suspect they're below the Perito Moreno Glacier in Argentina."

Wolf stands and brushes the dust off his pants. The rest of us take our cue from him and get to our feet. He takes a step toward Jaina, and her guard stiffens and swings the spear to point at him. The spear jerks out of the guard's hands and spins to point directly at his left eye.

Juliana. Her eyes narrow in fury and, for its sake, I hope the Mantoid doesn't try anything stupid. Her reflexes are faster than mine.

She jumps, and the spear clatters to the ground when the Mantoid opens four wings hidden along its abdomen, and shoots straight up in the air, extending its arms over its head, each one nearly the length of its entire body. I'm impressed with its attack form.

Murphy jumps in front of her, growing to his full Dracan size in seconds. He bares his teeth, growls at the thing and extends his claws, ready to rip it to shreds. Is this what they call the transforming power of love? What happened to our mild-mannered friend?

"You know I mean you no harm, Jaina," Wolf says, raising his hands in the air. "Please call off your soldier."

Pax sniffs again and tells us, *There's a change in their pheromones. I wonder if I can learn this scent-based language.*

Jaina nods and the guard lowers to the ground, folds its wings into the armor, and picks up the spear, standing it on end with the tip pointed upward.

Its face remains impassive as Murphy takes a step toward it and warns, "Death to anyone who threatens my people. Do you understand, Jaina?"

"Stand down, Murphy," Jaina answers. "He takes his job of protecting me as seriously as you do yours. Now the misunderstanding is over, let's all relax."

Wolf asks, "Do your people have tunnels under the glacier? Can they help us get to her?"

"If she's there, the Dracan picked one of the few spots under which we have no tunnels," Jaina answers, turning to Charles. "If we were to dig deep enough to prevent the weight of the glacier from crushing the tunnels, the magma flowing underneath would destroy them, or cook anyone using them.

"Magma?" Pax asks. "I know the Andes are in the Ring of Fire and volcanos have been erupting more frequently lately, but how can a glacier grow over a magma field? The Perito Moreno glacier is one of the very few in the world still growing."

"The magma is deep, but our tunnels would also need to be deep. No viable pathway exists between the two. Jewel has been communicating with our queen. Her mind has been finely tuned by using your invention, Charles. We are working on a way to help you save her, but our lack of access is proving to be troublesome."

"Invention?" Jack interjects. "What is she talking about?"

"It's nothing important," Dylan breaks in. "Charles found a way for Jewel to exercise her brainwaves."

It isn't exactly a lie, but I hope Jack doesn't pursue it. If the wrong people knew telepathy is possible through technology, we'd all be in trouble. Jaina gets the message and changes the subject.

"We're devising a plan along with Gienika's people, and we'll need Sky to work with us. Her gifts don't work where the giants live, but they will work in our tunnels. Storm, we need you and your sister as well. Pax, you must go to Jewel's mother. She must test the serum on you."

Pax goes pale. What's up with him?

"Juliana isn't going anywhere without me," Murphy says, transforming back to human.

"I'm going with you, Jaina. I can protect you better than this bozo," Al says, glaring at her bodyguard.

Jack's face turns beet red. His voice sounds lower when he speaks through clenched teeth, "Al, let me remind you, I'm your employer. You'll stay here with me, or risk losing your job."

"You'll miss me, won't you?" Al says, grinning at his boss. "I'm not worried, Jack, but it's nice to know you care."

Dylan interjects, "Jack, why don't you come with us? You could use a break, and I'd love to show you the alien tech in our homes. I'm going with Pax, and I suggest Wolf and Charles come along. How do you know all this, Jaina?"

"My people communicate with the deep earth dwellers, including the Dracans and the Formicians of North America. Very little happens on Terra without our knowledge. The Dracans have sent ships to transport you to your various locations. We'll gather Gienika and her people."

"Formicians?" Jack asks. "How many different species are there?" His face has returned to its normal tan. The prospect of going to North Carolina apparently appeases him.

"The North American plains Indians know them as Ant People," Jaina explains and her face breaks into a grin. I don't remember seeing her smile.

"Are you surprised, Jack? There are secrets you haven't yet discovered."

He glares at her and puffs his chest out. "If I keep hanging out with this crew, there won't be any secrets left to discover. Ant People. I know about the rock drawings and the Hopi legend. Just didn't know they were still around."

I grab Pax's arm and tug him away from the rest. We walk down the temple steps and back to the sunken temple area.

"What's wrong, Fletcher? You look a little sick."

He spins away from me and strides along the wall, stopping in front of a worn face that could be Dracan. His bunched muscles and clenched fists show the strain he's under to keep from smashing the face off the wall.

"If the monster has Jewel under a glacier, and there are no tunnels underneath it, then how do we get to her? The Mantoids already know where she is, so why do I need the serum? What good would it do if the injection fails and I die? What if it works, and we're too late?

Shaula's hold on her will break as soon as I kill him. I need to go after him, not go home to the women."

"Wherever she is under the glacier," I reason, "you'll need the mark to locate her, like Murphy did with Juliana. The Allarans said they aren't restricted from helping us find her. We can use them. Do you love her?"

I can't see his face, but his shoulders hunch and he bends over like I hit him in the gut. He's silent for a few minutes then chokes out, "You know I do. I'd do anything for her."

"Then get the injection. You're too strong to die. If Max survived it, so will you."

43
PAX

The Dracan ship lands us in the field in front of Jewel's home. You'd think we'd been away from the women for months rather than days, judging by the happy reunions with their husbands. If we don't rescue Jewel, I'll never have what they do. There will never be another woman like her. Rage is filling the deep hollow her absence leaves in me. If I'm not careful, I'll be as full of it as Storm.

Marla gives me a quick hug and grabs me by the arm. "Come on, Pax. Analiese has isolated the biochemical marker and needs some of your blood to finish the serum."

"What? No hello, let's eat, enjoy a little down-time?"

Her answering grin lifts my mood a little. She doesn't have Sky's gift, but the fact she cares about Jewel is comforting. That, plus the fact she's now older than we are, makes me think we can be friends.

"Where's Max?" I reserve judgment about him.

"On patrol with his dad. Shaula has people in the area stirring up the locals. The sheriff thinks they're plotting a distraction. Shaula knows something is up. If he knows about the serum, he'll do anything to prevent you from finding Jewel."

"Why would his causing trouble here distract us?"

"I don't know, but my father-in-law thinks they're cooking up something big. I wish Storm or Juliana had come back with you."

Marla backs away when Mom approaches, squeezing me in a strong hug. I drape my arm around my mother's shoulders, and we walk toward the house. At the door, I turn and take a deep breath, inhaling the fragrance of growing and decaying forest. The warm animal trace of deer mingles with a whiff of something recently dead, the cycle of life and death in one breath.

Jack drops his pack inside the door, and Charles leads him to the pantry. He examines the secret door covered by narrow shelves where Analiese keeps her spices.

"What are you protecting by making the door a part of the pantry wall?" he asks.

"Our downstairs lab," Charles answers. "We keep it hidden for security reasons since most of our work is top secret. Even so, it's an open secret on the reservation. Analiese has been working on the serum there."

They disappear down the stairs to the office and the lab. I'm uneasy about revealing too much to Jack. I don't trust him to keep anything quiet for long. There's a glint of greed in his eyes, and I suspect he's gathering intel for one of his future shows. Dogs can detect dishonesty in a human. I wonder if I have the same ability. Something about his scent bothers me, and it isn't body odor.

Sequoia breaks away from Wolf to give me a hug, and the baby kicks. Her joy reminds me baby O'Connell is at least as strong an empath as my sister. My misgivings about Jack fade and I send love back to the little one and turn to Jewel's mother.

"Analiese, how soon can you inject me? I don't want to waste a minute. As soon as I have the marker, we need to find Jewel." I don't finish my thought out loud. Who knows how much time she has before Shaula breaks her? It would be the only way she would ever give in to him.

"I need to draw your blood. It shouldn't take long to complete the serum, but we don't know how this is going to affect you," Analiese says. The concern in her eyes and the worry line between her brows make me more determined than ever. I already love her and Charles like family.

"It could make you very sick, and you might not survive it. I've talked to your parents about the risks, and they agree the decision is yours to make. Are you sure you want to go through with this?"

"The sooner, the better," I answer her. She has me sit in one of the recliners. The alcohol swab cools my arm, and it doesn't even pinch when she skillfully finds the vein. The deep red liquid fills the container on the syringe, reminding me of my sister's hair. I pray Sky and the others who've gone with Jaina are successful.

"When the serum is ready, I'll call Doc Townsend. He's agreed to administer it and monitor you. My guess is, we'll wait until tomorrow morning before you eat anything. We've made everything ready for you in Jewel's room. Surrounding yourself with her fragrance may enhance the effects of the serum. Meanwhile, you'll sleep in the guest room."

I'M eager to go as soon as the sun comes up, but it's close to nine before Doc and the others are ready.

I watch as Mom and Analiese lay a rubber sheet on Jewel's bed and cover it with clean sheets. I'm shirtless, in sweatpants, and glad to get into bed and pull the sheet up.

"Doc," I ask, "are you okay with this? Won't you get in trouble for helping us with something the FDA hasn't approved of?"

"Don't you worry about it, son," he answers. "After what you and these good people did for my people during the flood, I'm indebted to you. Sequoia will administer the serum, and I'll be here in case you need me. As far as I'm concerned, every one of you is Cherokee. We'll do anything to help you complete your quest."

Dad sits in the desk chair while Analiese gets me hooked up to an EKG. Sequoia has already started an IV drip. The rubber under the sheet nearly overpowers Jewel's unique fragrance in the room, but I ignore it and focus on her scent, spicy citrus and honeysuckle. Doc checks my eyes and ears and listens to my chest through his stethoscope. Sequoia injects something into the IV line, and my eyes grow heavy.

"This will make you sleepy," she says, patting my arm. "The more relaxed you are, the easier this should be."

I give in to the heaviness and let myself drift off.

I'M BEING CRUSHED. I shove and punch the weight covering me. An image of a grinning Shaula fills my brain. I push and roll trying to get out from under him. My teeth chatter hard enough to shatter my skull, and I'm burning hot under the heat of my enemy. The urge to kill overwhelms me. Voices buzz and scream and my eyes won't open. Ice pours into my veins and darkness rolls in. Shaula is gone.

I wake up shivering under a heavy blanket, my body covered in sweat. The beep-beep of a monitor tells me I'm still alive, but I almost wish I weren't. Everything hurts. Doc gets up from the chair my dad had been sitting in. Then gray fog closes in, dimming my vision. Vibrations in the air and an odd smell tease the periphery of awareness. A thrumming grows inside, setting my teeth on edge, and my body thrashes.

"He's seizing," I hear as if from a great distance. The voice becomes garbled. Someone takes my hand and hums into my head. Mom? I don't know the tune at first, but it steadies me, and my rigid muscles relax. I remember it then, a lullaby from childhood. The warmth of it covers me like a blanket, and I drift off.

Jewel. Her aqua eyes widen in surprise as I reach out to hold her close. My arms meet air and I open my eyes to see the ceiling of her room and my mother's face hovering over me.

"Pax? Here. Take a sip of water." She holds a straw to my mouth, and I drink. It goes down like razor blades when I swallow.

"Is it over?" I croak. My sweats are drenched, permeated with my own stink.

"I think so," she answers and turns to call Doc Townsend. Dad follows him in.

"You've had a rough go of it." Doc speaks in the tone doctors use when they're telling you it's only a head cold when they really mean you might not make it. He can't hide his worried frown. Judging from his uncombed hair and scruffy face, he hasn't slept in days. In fact, Dad looks just as bad. How long have I been sick?

"We almost lost you a couple times," he murmurs. "The worst appears to be over, but you'll need to rest a few days before we can be sure."

I struggle to sit up, but the most I can do is prop up on one elbow. I drop back down to the pillow. "No. We have to move fast. She might not have a few days."

"We'll go as soon as you're ready," Dad says. "You've been out of it for two days, son. We all need to sleep and recoup some of our energy if we're going to help Jewel."

I'm okay. Please rest and get better. I need you. My breath catches in my throat. Her voice is clear in my mind. How is this possible? How did she get her wristband to work? Has she already escaped?

44
JEWEL

I toss the sweat-drenched blanket to the floor and sit up, holding my spinning head between both hands. It feels like a mule kicked me in the head, and my chest burns. I cough deeply until I gag and nearly wretch. There's nothing in my stomach to throw up. Did the snake Shaula try to poison me? The swirling fog in my brain begins to clear, and I remember Shaula in the room, accusing Grayscale of doing just that. He was furious. I wonder if I'll see his goon again.

Another memory surfaces and warms my heart. Pax, his face as clear as if he were here, standing inches from me. His shocked expression probably matched my own. How was it possible? He must have been an illusion caused by this illness.

Sensations and scenes zip through my mind, cold and heat, body aches and extreme thirst. I was shivering one moment and throwing off the cover in the next. I recall Shaula standing next to me then leaving, and how relieved I was when he was gone.

My shaky hand reaches for a pitcher of water and a plastic cup someone left on the nightstand. Trembling, I manage to pour a small amount of water and take a sip, warm and soothing as it slides down my throat.

As soon as I drop back to the thin pillow, I hear Dylan's voice, as if he's speaking in a tunnel. "…if we're going to help Jewel."

How odd. Then I sense Pax, his worry for me, his frustration. I don't understand how it's possible, but I respond as if our link were open, *I'm okay. Please rest and get better. I need you.*

His surprise washes over me. *Can you hear me?* I ask.

Jewel, he responds, *are you using your wristband? Did you get away?*

The hope in his voice breaks my heart. I tap my wristband to open the channel to all my friends, but I get nothing. This isn't real. It can't be.

The wristband doesn't work here. I'm still a prisoner.

Echoing voices fill my mind. I must be going insane. Was Shaula right? Will this bring me to the point of surrendering to him?

Then I clearly hear Sequoia say, "Rest now. I'm giving you something to help you sleep so you can regain your strength."

Is Sequoia there with you? I ask, hoping I'm truly communicating with him and this isn't my imagination.

"Wait, Sequoia, please don't." It's his voice. I hear his actual voice as if from a distance, and not as a projected thought.

His voice fades and I drift away into sleep.

"GET UP." The rough Dracan voice jars me awake. Brownscale has a tunic and pants draped over his massive arm. He's already placed a covered dish on the small table.

"Dress and eat."

"I won't change clothes until I've had a shower first," I reply, getting to my feet.

"No shower."

He drops the clothes on the bed and leaves, closing the door behind him. I stare at one of the cameras. "Shaula, I don't know how long I've been here, and maybe your mother never taught you that you catch more flies with honey than vinegar, but unless I get a decent shower and some decent food, I'll simply starve myself and you'll have nothing."

"Suit yourself, woman." His voice sounds tinny coming through the speaker. "You'll have everything you need as soon as you surrender to me."

Bile rises in my throat, and I get to the toilet just in time. I retch, but nothing comes up, and by the time I crawl back to bed, my whole body is shaking. What is happening? Relapse?

I ignore the covered dish and turn my face to the wall. Now that I've seen Pax, whether real or imagined, I can die in peace.

Don't you dare even think about dying. We're coming for you. Hold on.

Oh, Pax. Don't leave me.

45
SKY

Τ he Sungate wormhole drops us close to the village this time. Agateno and her scraggly scouts lead the way to the village where we're warmly received. The children wave and grin as their parents pass us with armloads of gear they're piling onto wagons. Are they moving?

We follow Jayman to a large cabin near the meeting circle, where Gienika comes out to greet us. Her arms, the size of tree trunks, pull me into what feels like a giant feather bed, but she's gentle, and the hug is quick enough to avoid squashing me.

"Welcome back, Sky Fire Hair. We began preparations for the journey after I saw your return in a vision. Come, you and your companions. Autumn has prepared a meal for you."

Storm walks next to me as I follow her through the open barn-like door. Is he being protective? The thought adds a little bounce to my step. Juliana leads Murphy by the hand while he takes it all in, paying no attention to where he's stepping. Al bumps into him, distracted by the giant-sized furniture. There's something a bit intimidating about being surrounded by giants, even friendly ones.

"What journey?" Juliana asks as soon as we're seated on high stools surrounding a massive table. Like a small child, with the edge of the table nearly at shoulder-level. I need two hands to lift a glass of water to my lips.

Gienika answers, "Jaina has told us Shaula is holding Jewel and two other humans under the Perito Moreno Glacier. We can get close to it using the tunnels, but we cannot reach the base we suspect is underneath. The ice grows in a lake above a thin layer of crust, under which runs a river of molten magma. The space between is not thick nor sturdy enough to support even reinforced Dracan tunnels. Boring through the ice would destabilize the glacier and possibly cause any number of natural disasters, including earthquakes, massive glacial ruptures, and volcanic eruptions."

"How did a Dracan base get in there, then?" I hear Al's frustration in his gruff voice.

"Before the Great War, the Dracans and Allarans were allies. We believe they built the base together during the glacial period of the Pleistocene Ice Age, when much thicker ice covered the Andes," Jayman explains. "The Allarans' ice melting techniques posed little danger of disrupting the area because the ice itself was as stable as an earthen land mass at that stage. Since around eleven thousand years ago, we have been in an interglacial period, where most of the ice has melted, leaving unstable glaciers behind.

"The magma beneath the Ring of Fire has risen closer to the surface in recent decades, and volcanic activity has increased more each year. Although this glacier keeps expanding, the crust underneath grows thinner. Now we know the artifacts affect the planet's balance, we have hope stability can be achieved once again when you and your companions have completed your task."

"In the meantime," Gienika adds, "we must find a way to rescue Jewel despite the natural obstacles."

Storm pipes in, "If the Allarans helped build the base, then they may know a way to get inside without causing damage to the glacier. The Dracans get in and out of there, don't they?"

"I've asked my friends in Atlantis about it," Murphy says, "but they don't know of its existence. Whoever built it did it in secret, or the knowledge has simply been lost over the ages. I wonder how Shaula found out about it."

"When did you ask them?" I ask.

"After Jaina mentioned it as a likely location for Shaula to keep his prisoners. I'd hoped to learn they knew how to get into it. Instead, they don't know anything about it."

"Maybe the Allarans know more," I suggest. "Do your people have a way to contact them, Gienika?"

Gienika doesn't answer but glances at Jaina, who nods. She's been so quiet, I nearly forgot she came here with us. She hops to the ground and transforms. Jaina as a Mantoid is taller than her guard, who has been standing by the door watching the rest of us eat. His eyes bulge out along the side of his face, where hers are more elegant, stretching from the widest part of her head to a couple inches above her pointed mouth. Even with his armor adding width to his body, she's wider, and her spiked forearms are more muscular. I wouldn't want to be her prey.

The two leave silently, and we get back to our meal. Does Jaina enjoy eating human food when she's in human form? I wonder how her digestion and metabolism work as a shapeshifter.

"My friends, you must get some rest now. We leave in the morning. The wagons will take us to the tunnels, and from there we must walk. Follow Autumn to your cabin." Gienika rises to her feet, smiles, and heads through a side door to another part of the house. Jayman gestures toward the open front door, and we file out, following Autumn to the house we'd occupied the last time we were here.

Once again, Juliana and I share a room.

"What's it like to be marked?" I ask her after we've settled into our beds.

She sighs and says, "We can read each other's mind, only without words. I feel what he feels, Sky. His love for me enhances my love for him. It's hard to describe, but I wouldn't want to live if something happened to him."

It sounds romantic, but what if the serum works and binds Pax to

Jewel that way? What if we can't rescue her in time? Would he want to die, too? My mouth goes dry, and I wish my wristband worked here. I want to stop him from doing something we may all regret, but I know in my heart it's already too late.

46

STORM

I hate tunnels. Jaina leads the way since she uses her weird vibrations like echolocation and doesn't need light. Murphy follows, towing Juliana by the hand. At least it's wide enough here to walk side-by-side. He can see in pitch blackness, too. I, on the other hand, need light, and I'm grateful for the heavy lanterns Al and the giants carry behind us. I wish we'd thought to bring our own flashlights.

Thank God these aren't Dracan tunnels. Sky's voice in my head takes me by surprise, and I stumble over a rock and instinctively send it to the side of the tunnel with telekinesis. Man, I've missed it. I can't imagine how Jewel stays sane without her enhanced sight for so long.

Yeah. Why don't you check on your brother while I contact Wolf and Sequoia?

I tap my wristband to open the link to my folks. *Hey, how's our baby doing? Auntie? Is everyone okay?*

Your cousin misses you and lets us know it, and she isn't even born yet, Wolf answers.

Where are you? Sequoia chimes in. *Are the girls with you?*

I explain how Gienika sent Jaina to call the Allarans and how the giants knew we were coming and were ready for this trek into the tunnels.

Jaina contacted them, but she hasn't told us anything. She's only talking to Gienika and Jayman, and all he's said is we're heading to a rendezvous point. He and those female giants from the Star Gate are with us, and so are Jaina and her guard, both in Mantoid form.

We'll see you soon, then, Wolf assures me. *Vega is sending a ship to get us. Since Pax is leading the way, I assume we'll be at the rendezvous as well.*

When? I ask. I can't wait to get back to the surface.

Joy mixed with grief hits me like a tsunami. Oh, yeah. Sky has her gift back.

What's wrong? I open the common line to Pax and Sky. I wish Jewel could link with us.

My brother almost died, she says, anguish in her thought. *But when he recovered, he had his link to Jewel back, and they don't need a wristband.*

Another tsunami, this one of joy. How does she stand the emotional highs and lows? I wait for her to catch up and pull her close. We walk with my arm around her. Warmth fills me, and I wonder why I fight so hard to push this away.

Glad you're okay, Fletcher.

I will be when we have Jewel and the snake is dead. I'm glad you're there for my sister. This won't be easy. I hear steel in his mental voice. Whatever he went through to share the mark with Jewel made him stronger.

Sky and I almost run into Murphy and Juliana when they suddenly stop in front of us.

"Silence," Jaina says loud enough for all of us to hear. We stop shuffling, and I take in shallow breaths like I do in the woods when I'm hunting and close to my quarry.

Vibration starts in the ground under my feet before the low rumble reaches my ears. A sudden breeze in my face smells like sulfur, and I send up a quick prayer, suddenly terrified.

"Drop!" Jaina shouts, and Murphy pulls Juliana to the floor with him. No sooner do I pull Sky down and flatten myself over her than a hot, howling wind roars over us, thick with dust and debris.

What is it? Sky's scream fills my head and blends with my own.

Pull your shirt up over your mouth! Cave-in! I try to follow my own advice, but my arms refuse to let her go long enough. I bury my face in her hair and pray she doesn't smother in the debris. Her tense body goes limp, her terror fading. She sends me one last flicker of love before I lose her.

If she dies, I want to die, too. *Stay with me, Sky.*

Her heartbeat slows, Then I come to my senses. With everything I have, I push the debris and dust off us and send it flying to the ceiling. I flip her over on her back, where she gasps for air and moans. She'll be okay.

From Jaina in the front, all the way back to the last giant in the rear, I push debris to the ceiling, creating a clear space by mental touch alone. The darkness is total. The too-warm air stinks of sulfur. This isn't a simple cave-in.

Juliana understands what I'm doing, and pulls clean air from behind us, away from the wreckage. She lowers boulders and chunks of earth from the ceiling to the floor alongside us while I concentrate on not letting anything crush us in the middle. I don't know where everyone has fallen, but if they're alive, they'll let me know if anything hits them. I hope.

Sky gasps and coughs as she comes to. She squirms, and her fear pierces my heart. *Are you hurt?* I ask.

I'm blind, she says, and turns in my arms. Her fingers find my face, and I hear her sob.

We lost the lanterns. Only Murphy can see in this, and maybe the Mantoids. Can you reach out and tell if anyone is badly hurt?

I'll try, she says. While she's sending out her feelers, I shout for a roll call.

Murphy, Juliana, Al, Jayman, and two of the other giants answer. The Mantoid guard, who brought up the rear, Jaina, and the remaining two giants remain silent.

"Jaina is breathing and doesn't appear to be broken," Murphy calls out. "It's a little hard to tell with her insect body, but at least she's alive. Juliana can sit with her until she wakes up, or until I come back for her. I'll check on the others. There should be a flashlight or lantern around somewhere. I'll bring it to you when I find one."

"Are you okay staying here, Sky? I'll go with him in case they're under some debris."

"No," she answers. "You'll need me to assess how hurt they are. Just hold my hand and don't let go until we have light. Okay?"

When Murphy comes close, I grab hold of the back of his jacket and, hanging on to Sky's hand, follow him to the first fallen giant. I hear Al grunt and expect he's trying to do CPR.

"Not. Breathing," he says between grunts. Jayman is softly chanting something off to our right. Murphy kicks something solid out of the way and bends to retrieve it, all while I'm hanging on to his coat for dear life. I'm not letting go in this pitch blackness.

"Found a lantern," he says. "Glass is broken, but it should still work." I hear a click and blessed light casts long shadows on the walls. He hands it to me and moves away. He lights another lantern and moves down the passage to check on the others.

Rocks and piles of dirt litter the floor, but what concern me are the deep cracks in the walls. That and the growing heat. Another good shake could bring the earth crashing down on us, and I don't think Juliana and I have the strength to hold it. Gienika assured us we were in no danger from the rising magma in these tunnels, but if she was wrong, if we're about to experience a volcanic eruption, we're all toast. Literally.

Just then I hear a gurgling wheeze, followed by a cough and deep groans. It sounds like the CPR worked and our giant is back with the living. Sky drops my hand and bends down to touch her.

Agateno is confused, she says through the link. *I'm sending her peace. She hit her head and has a throbbing pain in her right leg. I hope she'll be able to walk when we're ready to get out of here.*

Hey, what happened? Are you alright? Pax's frantic voice knocks around in my head.

Cave-in at one end, I tell him. *Maybe both. Murphy's gone to explore. We're okay, but two giants, Jaina and her guard aren't responding. We're checking on them now. Where are you?* I try not to think about flowing lava.

Waiting for the Allarans to pick us up. They should be here any minute. We'll find you. Hold on. I'll let you know what the plans are. We'll get you out.

I wish he sounded more confident.

47

JEWEL

S haula's cruel laugh cuts through the cocoon of pain and fog squeezing me, turning my brain to mush. I push off the wall and roll to my other side, keeping my knees curled around the pain in my belly. How long have I been sick?

Hold on. I'm coming. Is that Pax? I don't have the energy to think.

Rough claws grab my arms and yank me to my feet.

"Stand up." Brownscale's voice rasps like sandpaper in my ears.

My legs buckle, and he drops me to the floor. A freezing bucketful of water shocks me. Icy rivulets drip through my matted hair and down my neck. I don't react. Let them think I've lost my mind.

"You wanted a shower," Shaula's voice oozes through the intercom like thick black goo. He laughs again.

"Give it up, woman. Your friends tried to rescue you and failed. We buried them alive in their puny tunnels. No one is coming for you."

"You liar," I croak through my burning throat. It can't be true. I would know, wouldn't I? I'd feel it if they were gone.

"Our explosion set off an eruption. They're burned to a crisp by now."

If you're really coming to get me, Pax, kill him. Please, kill him. I've never wanted to destroy anyone until now. What am I becoming?

With pleasure, he says. I picture my hand touching his face. If I'm hearing imaginary voices, his is the one I want to hear the most. He retreats as if something else caught his attention.

Brownscale laughs and leaves me on the floor in a puddle of water. I don't look up as the door closes behind him.

Since when do teeth get the sensation of pins and needles? Did I somehow cut off the circulation to my gums? When it increases, I realize I'm getting another communication. I bite my tongue in a vain attempt to stop the vibrations and form a mental picture of me violently trembling. The vibration stops, thank God, and a picture of the Mantoid queen forms in my head.

Be still. The words come with a jolt. Static makes her voice sound strange and distant. *Watch.*

I close my eyes and a grainy scene plays out on my eyelids, with shadowy figures trudging through a gray fog. Their faces and the surroundings come into focus. Jaina is leading Murphy and Juliana into a black tunnel. Storm and Sky follow, and Al is behind them, in front of a pack of giants. Pax isn't there.

What happened to Pax? I ask.

Elsewhere, she answers. I wonder why her words come with a current, but the pictures don't. I prefer the pictures until the scene shifts and the tunnel collapses. A gust of choking dust consumes my friends. No. My family. They drop to the ground, motionless, and my heart shatters.

"No!" When Shaula's laugh knifes through the speakers, I realize I've screamed aloud. I fold over and roll on the floor in anguish.

What's wrong? Speak to me. Pax's voice breaks through, and I tell him.

They're gone. They're all dead. It's over.

A sudden calm comes over me, like I'm immersed in a warm bath. It makes no sense. Is this how he helps his sister? My muscles unclench and my body relaxes, all except for the buzzing in my teeth. I don't move from my position on the floor, knowing Shaula is watching. I'm thankful he can't get into my head.

I don't know what makes you think they're dead, Jewel, but they aren't. They're fine. I'm in contact with them.

Watch, the queen says.

Who's that? Pax asks.

The tunnel collapsed. How can they be fine? I'm close to hysteria and wonder if I'm going insane for real.

Not dead. The queen's voice sounds like she's in a tunnel herself.

Who is talking to you? I can hear her.

If you hear the Mantoid queen in my head, then maybe you can see what she shows me.

He's silent as the vision comes into focus and our friends stir in the tunnel. The scene shifts to ants digging through rock and dirt. They must be building an anthill. Why is she showing us this?

Not ants, the voice zaps. *Allies.*

I know about them, Pax says. *I'll tell you later. Let's watch. This is important. We didn't know how we'd be able to rescue them, but the Mantoids and Formicians have it under control.*

Formicians? What have I missed? The scene shifts again, and Jaina is standing with her back to a wall of boulders, serrated arms extended over her head in a battle stance. Storm's hands are up, as if he's ready to throw something at her. The next moment, the wall shakes, and a hole appears. A giant ant pokes its head in, and Jaina steps away. Then it goes black.

What happened next? I ask the Mantoid queen.

Is happening. Rescue. Then you. Each word is a sharp jab. I really do prefer the pictures. Now what? Is she telling me to be patient and wait? As if I had a choice. Are they planning to tunnel me out of here?

Hang tight, Pax says. *The Allarans are picking us up, and we're going to meet the others as soon as they emerge from the tunnel. They'll be working with us, along with the giants, the Mantoids and, apparently, the Formicians. We'll get you out.*

I form a picture of me tapping on the wall. *Morse code,* I say. I don't know if the queen knows what it is, but Pax will.

Storm's parents were on the other side of the wall. We used Morse code to communicate. I told them he's alive and Juliana is well. I haven't heard from them since. I think Shaula moved them.

We'll get them, too, Jewel.

Stay with me. Stay in my head.

I'll never leave you. That sounds creepy, doesn't it? When you're safe, you can set boundaries.

The warm bath covers me again, and I crawl over to the bed and pull myself up. Every muscle aches, but the sickness is gone. I pull the rough blanket over my face. I won't let Shaula see me cry.

4 8

PAX

Baran and Chara float down from one of the two Allaran ships hovering over the meadow. With the two of them together, it's easier to ignore Chara's pull and Baran's repulsion. I wonder if the others notice the difference, or if Jewel's mark is dampening how they affect me. I wonder who's in the other craft.

Baran looks us over and says, "It would be best if Sequoia, Coral, and Analiese remain here."

The argument I expect never comes. Instead, the women gaze at Baran with adoring eyes, eager to do anything he requests. The stiffened backs of their husbands would be amusing if I didn't feel some of the same animosity toward him. Then Chara speaks, and the roles reverse.

"Wolf, your wife is safe here. Coral and Analiese will protect Sequoia and your baby. Max and Marla will also remain. Please introduce your friend."

A drop of drool hangs in the corner of Jack's slack jaw. He snaps it shut and swipes his fist across his mouth as soon as she turns to him. He stands taller, sucks in his gut and grins.

"Jack Austin, at your service, ma'am," he says, his voice deeper than usual. "Maybe you've seen my program 'Mysteries of the Ancients'?"

A tiny frown appears between her brows for a second, then her face lights up with a smile.

"It's a pleasure." She turns to me.

"Paxton, Belena is in a craft over the general area where we believe Shaula is holding Jewel. Vega and the pilot of my craft have gone to the rendezvous point to pick up the others. Belena is joining us there. The tunnel your friends were using collapsed, but our Terran allies have rescued them, and we will join them."

I heard her. I can hear through your ears, if, in fact, you aren't a figment of my imagination. Jewel's voice in my head cancels any attraction I felt for Chara.

I'm not imaginary. Baran and Chara are taking us to the others. Do you hear all my thoughts?

I don't think so, she responds. *I can't know for sure, though, can I? Do you hear mine?*

I believe I only hear what you send to me, unless your mind is blank most of the time. Then I hear her giggle as if she's right next to me.

Baran addresses the men, "There has been an increase of Dracan activity in this area, and we believe Shaula is behind it. Maia's craft will remain here to guard the women."

Wolf and Dad glance at each other. I wonder if they've found out what the Dracans are up to.

Chara says, "It is a short jump to Patagonia. We will be there when your people emerge from the ground."

We follow them into their ship while the other disappears. Jack, walking in front of me, shakes his head and mumbles under his breath. It's too bad he can't share any of this on his program.

We settle in the bubble chairs in the observation room, where a panoramic view of a glacier surrounded by bare mountains fills the screen. Jack is mesmerized by the sight of a wall of ice, where sunlight penetrates in colors ranging from deep royal blue to shades of aqua, like a frozen vertical slice of the Caribbean.

After a few moments, he squirms in his seat. It moves with him, adjusting effortlessly to his body. I can't imagine anyone being uncomfortable in these.

"How long a flight will this be?" he asks.

Baran's voice answers his question through hidden speakers. "We have arrived."

"But we haven't left, have we?"

Charles explains, "The skin of their craft prevents any resistance from air or water, Jack. There's no sensation of movement because the ship remains completely stable as it travels. The Dracan ships are fast, but Allaran technology is more advanced."

"We are masters of the air," Baran says as he enters the room. "Let us meet your friends."

The ship drops us on the rim of a crater overlooking a jagged hole on the bottom, teeming with ants. They're enormous, but not as big as I'd imagined them. That is, until one crawls up toward us carrying the limp body of a giantess in its mandibles, supporting her with its forelegs. I spot Storm and Juliana working with the ants to move boulders away from the opening in the crater. Gray smoke puffs out of the hole, and I get a strong whiff of sulfur. My heart speeds up as it dawns on me what that means. This crater is the mouth of a volcano, coming back to life.

I scramble down the steep incline, dodging rocks and pebbles loosened by the others, who are also hurrying to the bottom. Sky crawls out of the hole, and Dad grabs her in a quick hug and moves past her into the opening.

"What the…" Sky yelps as her feet leave the ground. "Storm put me down!"

By the grim set of his jaw, I know he has no intention of letting her go until she's safely up top, where the Allarans are lifting the injured into their ships.

One of the ants carefully carries a limp Mantoid soldier. I hope Jaina is okay.

"How many more?" I ask, sniffing. As much as I want to put my guard up against the sulfurous stink, I keep it open. I detect fear and pain coming from the opening, but there's no smell of death. Thank God.

"Murphy and Al are helping the Ant People with the rest of the giants," Storm replies. "Jaina's directing them. Everyone's alive, but some are injured. Coming?"

I follow him inside. After pausing a moment to let my eyes adjust to the dim light, I shudder at the stones and small boulders littering the walls and floor, and at the ghostly pallor of everyone who was caught in the collapse. It's hot in here, and I pray they hurry.

Murphy has a giant by the feet, and Al holds her under the shoulders, her head resting against his chest. They nod as they brush past me, heading outside with their unconscious burden. Juliana will probably lift her to the triage area once they clear the opening.

Jaina emits a strange pheromone and odd vibrations as she talks to the ants. Charles hands her a bottle of water, which she sucks dry with her odd mouth. Her scent changes for a moment to something sweeter. Is that "thank you" in Mantoid-speak?

A giant ghost moves toward me, his face a pallid mask, with only red-rimmed eyes showing life.

"It is good to see you again, Pax." Jayman's greeting is out of place in this dark tunnel. "Storm is taking the last of my people out, and it is time to enter the light, is it not?" He gestures toward the opening, where Jaina's pointed abdomen disappears as she exits. I'm eager to get out of the stench and increasing heat. This place is about to blow. Once outside, we climb the loose hillside as quickly as we can.

The Formicians gather around Jaina at the rim of the crater, emitting a cloud of pheromones and making my body thrum with a nearly inaudible vibration. I take deep breaths and detect subtle changes as they communicate.

Can you learn their language? Jewel asks. *Don't be surprised. I know how eager you are to understand them.*

If there's one thing I've learned, I answer, *it's that anything is possible. Yes. I want to learn it. I think Jaina is thanking them and maybe telling them to get out of here. I hope she tells them how grateful we are, too.*

I again get a sweet whiff of what I interpreted as "thank you." It's a beginning.

The Formicians move fast, in a straight line, as they scramble up the side of a flanking mountain. Jaina effortlessly morphs back to her human form, fully dressed as if her clothes are an organic part of her. She follows me into Baran's ship. As soon as we enter the portal room, we watch the ground shake violently, and a plume of black smoke tinged with red pours out of the tunnel.

Instead of rushing away, all four Allaran ships hover over the spectacle below us. The crater explodes in a blast of superheated rock and lava, rocking the ship as we swerve to avoid projectiles. I can feel the motion this time and wonder if the skin has been damaged, or if it only repels friction when moving in a straight line. I'll have to ask Baran or Vega later.

Are you seeing this? I ask Jewel.

Is it real? She answers. *I thought I was dreaming it. Oh, God, we could have lost our friends in that. I could have lost you!*

We're safe, and we're coming to get you. I love you, Jewel. Great. That slipped out. The first time I tell her, and it's through a remote link. This is not how I'd planned it.

I know. I love you, too. Her warmth washes over me, and it doesn't matter anymore. She's my life.

49
SKY

The Allarans have brought us to a grassy meadow in a small valley surrounded by snow-capped peaks. Noxious steam, smelling like sulfur, rises off a bubbling pool surrounded by smooth boulders. Jayman helps Agateno limp to the pool and get in. I lose sight of her in the steam. It'll probably promote healing, with the heat and minerals, but I'm not interested. Something strange is happening with my brother, and it scares me. Has the mark changed him more than anyone thinks? He doesn't feel like himself anymore.

I spot Storm floating another giant out of a ship and open my private link to him.

Have you noticed anything strange about Pax?

Do you mean other than his normal strangeness? He moves the woman over to the pool, where Jayman takes over and helps lower her into the water.

I'm worried, Storm. He isn't himself.

Have you asked him? I hate when he's practical.

I can't. Not until I know what the problem is.

That makes no sense. Seek and you shall find. Ask him.

Right. I cut him off and concentrate on my growling stomach. Something cooking over a campfire lures me to a circle where our alien hosts have flattened the grass. I sit on the ground next to Pax, while a female Allaran hands me a plate topped with some roasted vegetables and a fork. I take a bite and close my eyes in ecstasy as flavor explodes on my tongue. What spice is this? We don't say a word until our plates are empty for the second time.

"The charge that caved in the tunnel was deliberately set," Jaina tells the men who are gathered a little farther from the fire. I move closer and Storm follows.

"How did they know where we were?" Wolf asks, his brows drawn down and a suspicious glint in his eyes.

"I doubt any of us would have told them," Charles says. "We all know the stakes if we don't get my daughter back."

Storm jumps up and runs back to the ship. What's gotten into him?

He returns holding his backpack. Without a word, he reaches in and pulls out the egg-shaped object we found at the mandala.

"They've been tracking us all along with this. I'd forgotten I had it."

"Isn't that what we found in Nazca?" Jack asks. "I'd hoped we could examine it when all this is over."

"We will bury it here," Jaina says. "When it's safe, my people will retrieve it for you, Jack."

He nods, takes it from Storm, and follows Al and Jaina to a spot higher on the slope, where a hole appears in the ground. Did she move the dirt with sound waves? Nothing surprises me.

I turn my attention back to my brother, still sitting near the fire. Sadness rolls off him. I miss Jewel, too, but there's more to it. He's hungry. He ate enough for two. Pain, loneliness, longing, and rage send him jumping to his feet to head away from the fire. I follow, pushing peace at him, but he's erected a wall against me. There's the difference. He's never locked me out before. Pax, what's disturbing you so much? Then I remember that he and Jewel have a telepathic connection none of the rest of us can tap into.

I open our private link, but he shuts it off as soon as he feels it.

"Not now, Sky," he calls over his shoulder as he marches away. Pain stabs me in the gut and I fold to the ground, staring after him.

Storm drops down next to me, throws a blanket over my shoulders and pulls me to his side. We don't speak, but the connection I've been longing for is there. Either he's decided to take the wall down, which is unlikely, or he's as worried about my brother as I am. We're all worried about Jewel.

"We'll get her tomorrow," he says, as if he's been reading my mind. "The Allarans must have a plan."

I snuggle in close and let my eyes fall shut. It's been a grueling day.

IT'S STILL DARK when someone shakes me awake. Juliana. I must have fallen asleep where I sat with Storm, but he's gone. My teeth chatter as she hands me a steaming cup of coffee and sits, covered in her own blanket. I wrap my icy hands around the warm mug.

"What's the plan?" I ask. The Allaran ships are either cloaked or gone.

"They're melting a hole in the ice over the Dracan base. I overheard Baran say something about Meissa finding the location. How odd the two enemy races are working together."

I laugh. "Not to mention the Mantoids and Ant People saving our hides yesterday. Do you realize we know more than the most educated scientists on the planet? A bunch of kids still technically in high school, and we know how the planet works and what's causing the climate craziness, and we can't tell anybody. All we can do is fix it, and only if the interplanetary races will let us do our job. Even then, no one will ever know."

"No!" Pax's shout brings me to my feet in an instant. The anguish he's projecting slams me in the gut. I can barely breathe. Juliana and I take off running toward him, and Storm closes in with us. I hit my wristband, but there's no connection to my brother.

Dad reaches him first and wraps him in a fierce bearhug. "What is it, son? What's wrong?"

"No!" The bellow rings through the camp and echoes off the mountainsides. He turns to Dad, grabs him by the biceps and shouts, "Shaula's taking her away. They've opened another wormhole!"

Four discs appear in the sky and the Allarans scramble for their ships. All but one wink out as soon as they're aboard.

Baran runs over to Dad and my brother, white hair streaming out behind him. I'm mesmerized by the play of powerful muscles in his body-fitting jumpsuit. When Storm smacks me on the back of the head, I'm aware I've come to a stop to stare at the Allaran. I'm salivating. Criminy, these alien men are sexy. Storm's annoyed jab startles me into a grin. He's jealous.

"Come. All of you. Quickly," Baran says. His voice holds less power over me than before, but my insides still melt at the sound of it.

We follow him, floating up the beam by twos to save time. As soon as we hit the floor inside, we run to the observation room and summon our bubble seats. In seconds, we've joined the battle. Our ship dodges and weaves through blazing lights and concussive explosions, and somehow, I can feel it move.

A few years ago, Mom and Dad took us to a theme park, where we rode a simulator. I was convinced we were being chased by dinosaurs and nearly flew into one's mouth. This is the same, only the dinosaurs are Dracan triangles and the lasers we're dodging are real. Even with the odds in our favor, our four ships to their two, they're fighting a ferocious battle.

Glacier ice glints blue as it pops into and out of view. I focus on the sky beyond the mountains, but even that spins and twirls on the screen. Despite the evidence of my eyes, I have little sensation of movement. The disconnect makes me dizzy, and I focus on Storm. He's intent on the action, his hands moving as if he's holding a video game controller. Boys. Still disoriented, I look at my brother.

He's rigid with tension, fists clenched at his sides and eyes focused on the screen, eyebrows drawn tightly together. Tears stream down his cheeks, ripping me open while I try to get beyond the thick wall he's erected. Grief pummels me. My own because he won't let me share his. How deeply linked are he and Jewel now they share the mark? Has their connection broken ours? Is he connected to

Shaula in some way? I'm losing him. My head spins and I shut my eyes.

A silent explosion rocks the ship. The bubble seat compensates, but not before I'm nearly knocked out of it.

Pax shouts, "Watch out!" My eyes snap open. If we're crashing, I want to know it. We're diving, but only to follow one of the Dracan ships falling to the ice, with black smoke pouring from a hole blasted into its side.

"Jewel's in that ship," he says, standing to his feet and heading to the portal room. I jump up to follow him, but Juliana's hand on my arm holds me back. Murphy pushes past her and shoots me a look of sympathy that nearly does me in.

"He has to be first, Sky," she says. "Let him go with the Allarans. His body has fully incorporated the mark and Jewel will always be first in his life. We'll be here when they bring her in."

Storm pushes past us and follows my brother to the portal. "There's no way I'm letting him go alone," he says. Dad and the other men follow.

I start to follow, but Juliana pulls me into a hug and I break down sobbing. Sometimes, I hate being an empath. And a twin. And a girl who can't control her crying.

50
JEWEL

I cough until I gag, over and over as black smoke fills my lungs. I struggle to pull the chain out of the bolt in the wall, but it doesn't budge, and my strength is nearly gone. I can't control the coughing.

"Help me!" my mind screams, but the sound coming through my burning throat and out of my mouth is barely a squeak.

We're coming. Hold on. Don't leave me, Jewel. My heart warms for a moment. Then cold overwhelms me. Spasms of painful coughs interrupt the constant shivers wracking my body. I imagine ice crystals dancing inside my body, tinkling to the rhythm of the tremors. A picture forms in my head, people coming to my rescue. Pax coming to free me. I'm dying.

I half-heartedly pull at the chain binding my wrists to my final prison. Cold. *Pax, I love you.* His terrified face fades from my mind. I'm so tired. I need to sleep.

~

I WAKE UP STRUGGLING, pulling at the chain, frantic to escape the smoke and my captors. Warm hands cup my face, and I hear Pax's voice over me, "It's okay, Jewel. You're safe. You're with us."

My eyelids stick like they've been glued shut, but I manage to get one eye open. His green eyes swim with unshed tears. The other eye opens more easily, and I'm afraid if I look away, he'll fade, and I'll lose him.

"You're safe. You're with me. I'll never let you out of my sight again."

His words warm me deep inside, and I smile through cracked lips. I glance at my wrists, still feeling the chains. The shackles are gone, and only my wristband remains, as much a part of me as my skin, which is covered in an ointment where I rubbed it raw when I tried to get free.

"My darling girl. You're awake," Dad's voice is thick as if he's been crying. He appears next to Pax, who steps aside to make room for him. He touches my face and bends to kiss me on the forehead.

"We've arrived. Storm will float you out of here and into the house. Once the ship is cloaked, the sheriff will let the ambulance through."

"Ambulance?" I ask, in a whisper, my voice completely gone.

"For smoke inhalation and some superficial burns. We have to be sure you're okay."

I'll be with you, Pax says in my mind. *I won't leave you alone.*

Ever? I answer. *You'd better rethink that.* His answering grin cheers me up.

I'm going to help you sleep, Jewel, Sky breaks in. *Riding in an ambulance isn't nearly as smooth as riding in a Sentinel. Trust me. It's no fun.* I remember Sky's own ambulance ride when her car went over a cliff. Was it only a few months back?

Peace washes over me as Sky does her soothing magic. My eyes droop and a warm cocoon wraps around me while everything goes dark.

I WAKE up to the beep of monitors and an IV-line snaking into the back of my hand. My wrists are wrapped in bandages. I wonder if the wristband has been removed. Prisms of light spatter the wall where the sun shines through slatted blinds. I sigh with pleasure at the colors.

Pax's aura glows with blue and yellow. Peaceful in sleep, he's curled on the chair next to the bed. He smiles, and a puff of magenta grows from the vicinity of his heart. He must be dreaming of me. My aura must be flowing with the color. It's one of the few colors I've figured out, since even Storm has magenta moments when he's with Sky, and it overtakes her normal fiery orange when she's near him. Love. Magenta is love. A pang of hunger interrupts my contentment.

A nurse comes in answer to my call button. She glances at Pax and keeps her voice low.

"He's been here all night," she says. "This is the first time he's slept."

I smile and let her know I'm hungry. She nods and leaves.

He wakes up when the food trays are delivered. They've sent one for him, too.

"Let me help you," he says, lifting the lid from my bowl of steaming soup. Soup? I'd been hoping for some real food.

I reach for the spoon, but sharp pain in my wrist stops me, reminding me of my struggle with the shackles and chain.

"You need some time to heal, Jewel. You should be fine in a couple of days."

He lifts a spoonful of clear broth to my lips, and the warmth of the liquid burns my throat, making me glad it's only soup.

"I need some of Sequoia's magic potion," I joke, speaking in a whisper.

"Coming right up," he says, glancing at the door. Sequoia is there, bigger than I remember, and grinning with joy. Her rainbow aura spreads out from her like the rays of the sun. The only other person I've met with a rainbow aura was Lucaya, the Black Seminole healer on Andros, after my time in Atlantis. Perhaps rainbow auras belong to healers. A swirl of purple and violet light covers her baby bump. I wonder what it says about her baby.

She waddles over and I lean toward her for a hug. She's careful to avoid the bandages on my wrists.

"You'll fix me, won't you?" I croak.

"When we get you home, yes, but you won't like it," she answers.

"No kidding," Storm says from the doorway. "Hurts like the dickens but works like a charm."

Pax gives her his seat, kisses my forehead, and leaves with Storm, making room for Mom and Dad. Dad finds two more chairs and brings them in.

"Tell me what happened," I whisper. "Did you get Shaula? Where are Storm's parents?"

The scowl on Dad's face answers my question before he says, "He escaped through the wormhole, and he took the Ryders with him."

Sequoia presses her mouth in a thin line and scrunches her nose as if she's fighting tears. I'm too weak to fight the burn and let the tears come. The aura around her baby deepens to dark shades of purple. Baby O'Connell might be a stronger empath than Sky.

In a moment, she relaxes and smiles again, and my sadness lifts and leaves peace in its wake. "They are alive, and we will find and rescue them," she says, her voice strong with determination.

Dad frowns as he glances from Sequoia to me. "We captured two of his henchmen. A ship is on its way from Atlantis to take them into custody. Thuban has assured us he's sending others to root out any Dracans planning to cause trouble around here."

"Why would they do that?" I ask.

My mom answers, "I can think of at least two reasons. Shaula marked you, and he'll want you back."

I shudder and shake my head. She continues, "Thanks to the vials of blood I took after you came home from Atlantis, Dr. Jenkins and I replicated the biochemical marker and created a serum for Pax. You've marked him, which means if Shaula has any chance of getting you, he'll have to kill Pax and destroy the serum."

"He won't because Pax will kill him first," I croak, with as much passion as I can muster. "Is Ashley still here?"

"She is," Mom says. "She won't leave until she's sure you'll be okay, and I believe she's enjoying her time on the surface."

My eyes grow heavy, and Mom says, "We'll leave you to rest awhile. As soon as they clear you to leave, we'll take you home."

Home. Nothing has ever sounded so inviting.

51
STORM

The reservation has a great medical center, but I've had enough of visiting my friends here. I glance at the line of vehicles ready to pick up Jewel and take her home. It's like a presidential motorcade, made up of SUVs, my truck, and Sky's new red Mini Cooper, which she insisted on driving. Wolf leans against the truck to keep me company while we wait.

"They wouldn't dare attack us on the road, not with you and Juliana among us, and the Sentinels and Thuban's men around," he says for the third time. When Wolf repeats himself, I know he's deeply worried.

"Yeah, you're probably right. Who knows how they think? It's best to be prepared."

He nods, but his eyebrows are tightly drawn together, and he's wound like a knot of wire about to spring loose. He's making me nervous. I scan the sky for any sign of the triangular crafts. I'd have no way of knowing if it were friend or foe from here. It used to be simple. Triangle is the enemy. Disc-shaped is not. Now we have Dracan allies, it isn't so easy.

The plan is to have Juliana and Murphy in the lead vehicle with

Dylan and Coral. Pax and Jewel will be second in line, followed by her parents. Sky and Sequoia will be in her little car, and Wolf and I will drive behind them in my truck. I don't like leaving Sky and my aunt vulnerable in that speck of a car. The Dracans already wrecked her first one. She's an easy target. Sheriff Green with Max and Marla will take up the rear of the convoy. I almost wish Al and Jack were still with us, but they elected to go back to the compound after Jewel's rescue.

The front doors slide open and Pax wheels Jewel outside, grins plastered on their faces. I scan the area like a Secret Service agent, hyper-aware of a possible ambush. The rest of the gang pours out like ants from a disturbed anthill, every one of them chatting and laughing as if this is just another day. I sigh while Wolf goes to open the car for Jewel. From where I'm standing, I lift her out of the wheelchair and gently set her on the seat, pull the seatbelt around her and snap it shut. Pax gives me a thumbs-up and heads to the driver's seat.

The road winds up the mountain, through forest and past plenty of places that would make for easy ambush. As we climb, the edge of the road comes close to a steep drop-off in places. I hope Juliana isn't busy talking up there. The trees offer cover, but also obscure our view of the sky. The higher we go, the more nervous I get.

Dylan's car disappears around a bend up ahead when white light flashes from beyond the curve. A tree uproots and falls across the road in front of Pax's car. He screeches to a stop, and the rest of us swerve to avoid hitting the one in front of us. I jump out, run to Sky's car, and pull the passenger door open.

"Auntie, quick!" I unsnap her seatbelt and lift her out while Sky climbs out the other side. I float Sequoia to a depression in the hillside under an overhanging ledge.

"Stay here, you two. Don't move until it's over." Sky's face is pale, but she nods, and pushes peace to Sequoia. That's my girl.

While I'm settling Sky and my aunt into their hiding place, Pax maneuvers his car through the mess and parks close to the hillside. He helps Jewel out and carries her to a shallow impression in the ground, hidden by bushes. Marla crouches next to her, sandwiching her in between them, while Max and the sheriff take off around the bend.

I catch up and watch a triangular ship hover over the ravine, firing randomly. Shots ping off the metal hull as Wolf fires quick rounds with his hunting rifle. Max, Sheriff Green, Dylan, and Charles shoot at it with automatic weapons, not making a dent in the thing. Murphy, in his Dracan form, is using one of their laser weapons against them with no success.

I help Juliana toss rocks and earth at the ports, hoping to bring it down the way I did in Ushuaia. A silver flash above the triangle is quickly followed by another. The Allarans have joined the fight.

I wonder why it isn't aiming at anyone. I keenly remember the burn of the laser that got me in the leg the first time I came up against one of these. Then it dawns on me.

"It's a diversion," I shout, whirling to race back as a scream pierces the air. Another Dracan ship has Pax and Jewel caught in its tractor beam, drawing them toward its open portal. I grab the biggest boulder I can find and toss it at the portal. As soon as it blocks the light, I lower my friends to the ground and toss another rock in, wedging the portal open. The ship takes off, only to meet a barrage of fire from another Dracan ship. Our allies have arrived.

I float Jewel to Sky and Sequoia under the overhang. Pax sits next to her and pulls her close, while Marla squeezes in, and I run back to join my sister. I get there in time to witness two Sentinels follow the smoking triangle into the ravine. I hope whoever is inside gets what they deserve.

The ground shakes as a ship explodes overhead, and I solidify a layer of air around us while flaming debris rains down. Juliana adds her strength to mine until it's over. Then, with Murphy's help, we search out hot embers and pieces of wreckage and use our telekinesis to bury them.

We've gone a distance from the others when a disc materializes over a clear spot in the road, and I recognize Maia as she touches down and walks toward us.

"One enemy ship has been destroyed, but the other disappeared before we could capture it," she says. Her voice fills me with a strange longing, but this time, my thoughts go straight to Sky.

"Thuban's men are interrogating the ones from the ship that crashed on the glacier. We will discover those who have allied themselves with Shaula and leave it to Thuban to mete out justice. We remain vigilant."

"Thank you, Maia," Juliana replies, gracious despite the animosity of human women toward every female Allaran.

Murphy and I express our gratitude, until Maia holds up her hands, smiling. "We have been charged to protect you as Creator allows, and it is our pleasure to do so." She returns to her ship, and it disappears.

As soon as we're sure there's nothing more to bury, I remove the tree from the road, make sure everyone is ready to go, and we move on to Jewel's house.

"Wolf," I ask my uncle, "where did the Adams and Fletchers get automatic weapons?"

"I believe Sheriff Green has been filling their armory, son. He suspected something like this would happen."

When we arrive, I help get Jewel to her room while the men go downstairs to the Adams' conference room. Sequoia pulls a container of magic paste out of her medicine bag, while Annaliese takes deep breaths, probably to prepare for Jewel's discomfort when my aunt applies her potion. I've been the lucky recipient of Auntie's medicine, and I don't envy my friend. Once the pain fades, though, healing is quick and painless. Murphy's mom, Ashley, greets her warmly and shoos us out of the room while she helps get her settled. The girls are ready to rush in to comfort Jewel as soon as they're allowed.

I join the men in time to hear Jack's voice coming through the phone's speaker. Jaina and her guard are with Jack and Al at Lake Titicaca.

"The last blast just about knocked our compound off its foundation. Watch the news. The Atacama Desert is flooding. It's the driest non-polar desert in the world. I swear the climate has gone crazy. How soon can you get back here with those kids and fix this?"

"In time, Jack," Charles says. "Jewel needs to recuperate before they tackle the artifacts. We know of at least three in your region, and each one takes a lot out of the kids."

"At least this time, they'll have help from the Mantoids," Jack responds. "Jaina is waiting with some of her people."

5 2

PAX

I flinch from the pain in Jewel's wrists when Sequoia applies her paste. Murphy sits in one of the chairs across from the porch swing where I'm holding my head in my hands, both to hide my tears and to avoid his sympathy. Will I cry every time Jewel does? Does he feel everything that goes on with Juliana? How does he stand it?

"It gets easier," he says. Does he read my mind, too?

"In time, you'll be so close, you won't know where she ends, and you begin. Sharing yourself with her will become second nature. At least, that's how it is with Juliana. It may be harder for you. I've never heard of two men sharing a mark with one woman. You're the first."

"Gee, thanks," I mumble. "Like I needed that reminder."

"His days are numbered." Murphy growls softly before going on. "I've heard from Atlantis. They've interrogated the prisoners and now know where Shaula and Storm's parents are."

He doesn't sound hopeful. "Where are they, and how soon can we go get them?"

"Do you remember the island that disappeared off the coast of Tierra del Fuego?" he asks. I nod. He goes on, "They are there. Thuban's men, who followed them into the wormhole off the coast of Andros, are also there, as his prisoners. The problem is, it's no longer on Terra, and while the wormhole remains closed, we will not be able to find him or rescue the Ryders and the others. We must wait until he returns, and pray he brings Juliana's parents with him."

"What are the chances?" I ask. This is getting more and more hopeless.

"He is tied to Jewel. He will return, Pax, and when he does, you must be ready. Your next fight will be to the death."

I heard, Jewel's voice is clear in my mind.

It'll be his death, I assure her. *He's going down.*

Pax, if those ships were meant to capture me, where were they going to take me? They must know how to open the wormhole.

That ship exploded. We'll never know.

Yes, but where did the other ship go?

I ask Murphy, "Do your friends know anything about the ship that went down in the ravine? Did it crash? Were there survivors?"

"Maia said it disappeared. It might have gone into a wormhole, but we can usually detect them when they open. We don't have cloaking technology in Atlantis, but it's possible other Dracan kingdoms have developed it. Whoever is behind this has more resources than Shaula would have access to alone. It could become a Dracan revolt."

Charles calls us inside to get a bite to eat. I smile at Jewel, comfortable in a recliner, and grab a plate for each of us. She moves over to let me slide in next to her. The others settle around us in the living room while Analiese turns on the news.

BREAKING NEWS: **"A massive rescue effort is underway in the Atacama Desert, reaching from southern Peru to southern Chile, where unprecedented flooding and massive mudslides have washed away entire villages. Teams are flying in from the United States by helicopter to help evacuate the injured and rescue as many people as possible. More monsoon-like rains are expected to pelt the region in the next few days.**

"A sharp spike in seismic and volcanic activity throughout

Patagonia has geologists worried about the stability of the region. The Ring of Fire circling the Pacific Ocean has been heating up recently, but this level of activity in South America is unheard of in recorded history. Some native groups are calling it the end of the world, and others are convinced their gods are coming back to Earth. Scientists say it's the result of global climate change. Cayla Knox reporting for News Channel Twelve."

~

"WE HAVE TO GO BACK," Charles says. "Jewel, honey, you let us know as soon as you're up to it."

"I'm already a hundred percent better, thanks to Sequoia. After a good night's sleep, I should be good to go."

"That's my girl," I whisper and nip at her earlobe. She giggles, and I hope her parents didn't see.

53
SKY

The sun is beginning to lighten the sky and we're standing in front of the Stargate again. I'm determined to stay close to Jewel, and not just because my brother is glued to her, but to help her if she freaks out when we go back into that cavern where Shaula abducted her. We're close enough to jump in at the first sign of the blue glow. Jaina has assured us her people know exactly where the artifact is hidden.

Jayman waits beyond the glow, beckoning us to enter quickly, and we don't hesitate. I hope we all make it in before it snaps shut. There are more of us than before. Dad, Charles, and Wolf refused to stay home, knowing Maia and her crew are standing guard over the women. Jack insisted on coming along, promising, as always, to keep this to himself. Al is here, too, because he won't leave Jaina's side.

"The tunnel is too small for someone my size," the giant says, as we gather around him. "You are in good hands with Jaina and her people. I will wait here for you to return. I wish you well."

I tap my wristband, connecting with Jewel. *How are you holding up?*

I'm fine, she answers calmly. *We've done this before. Together, we can do anything, right?*

You're not concerned Shaula might find you here?

Nope. Not with all of you here with me.

"How far is it to the artifact?" Dad asks.

Jaina points to the floor and says, "About a mile straight down. The path is steep, but my people have maintained it and there are no obstacles."

Al groans and comments, "Going down will be easy compared to coming back up."

Jaina shakes her head. "If the young people don't fix this artifact, there won't be a reason to come back up. Time is running out for our planet."

Jaina leads the way along a path hidden behind a pile of boulders, opposite the side leading to the land of the giants. It curves around then begins to drop on an incline nearly steep enough to warrant stairs. We carefully maneuver down the slope by the light of headlamps provided by Jack, following Jaina around tight turns and sudden drops. Al is right about how difficult it will be to come back up. I open myself to each person's emotions. We've lived through one tunnel collapse, but no one is worried. They're all concentrating on putting one foot in front of the other, which is what I need to do.

After what could have been hours, the floor levels and we enter a chamber where a familiar glow greets us. Everyone spreads out around the walls of the chamber while we close in on the wobbling artifact in the middle. Juliana sits on the ground and steadies it with her telekinesis while the four of us gather around it.

Pax sniffs while I search for leaking emotions. Jewel scrutinizes it, and we all come to the same conclusion. There's no crack.

"So, how are we supposed to open it?" Storm asks. "The first one was already cracked, and Triton used fire to break the second. This is intact, and we're missing a dragon."

"My people have guarded the three artifacts in this part of the world for millennia," Jaina says, joining us in the circle. "We can open them for you. Prepare yourselves. It has never been done, and we don't know how much time you'll have."

"You are opening just this one, aren't you?" Jewel asks. "We can only fix one at a time."

Jaina reassures us, "Yes. Only this one for now."

She goes back to the wall, and Pax sniffs as she communicates with the Mantoids. Their vibrations increase as we position ourselves around the spinning tetrahedron.

"Juliana will catch it as soon as it opens," Storm says, "in case we're flat on the ground again. We'll put our hands on the side closest to us when it stops spinning."

Tension builds in my back and neck as I wait for the moment when the artifact's energy barrier bursts open. It doesn't help that only Jewel can see the shell it spun around itself. The first artifact's shell exploded and knocked us down after Storm's telekinesis reached into the crack and forced it open. The second exploded in the intense dragon flames Triton breathed on it. We were safely tucked between the dragon and the wall when it happened, and Storm floated us out to it in a bubble of air. When he lost control and nearly dumped us on the burning sand of Triton's cave, Juliana came to the rescue and saved us. Will this one explode too?

I breathe a prayer and brace myself.

"It's shrinking," Jewel exclaims. "Fast. Get ready to catch it, Juliana."

The artifact slows, holding steady. Storm reaches out with his telekinesis, helping Juliana keep it afloat. The same symbols etched into the triangular sides of the others slowly spin by, until it stops, and I reach out to touch the side facing me. I can't believe it. It's the symbol of four stick figures surrounded by the earth and the sign for love. All the artifacts must have the same symbols, and the ones we've already fixed presented this same side to me.

Jewel has the coyote, star, and butterfly in front of her, and Pax is facing the side with the moon and serpent. Storm has the side with the sun of hope again. This can't be a coincidence, can it?

There's no time to analyze why we get the same symbols each time. We touch our own then reach out to touch the hands of each person to our right, making a human chain around the artifact.

Love builds between us. My heart responds to the vulnerability in Storm's eyes. My connection with Pax has changed but the love is the same. I collect the love and focus on the earth symbol in front of me. It pours through me into the artifact until the symbol glows. Then the artifact responds with a release and a gentle push away.

"Step back," Jewel says. "It's done."

The artifact's gratitude breaks over us, sending its approval. We step back, and it begins to spin, no longer wobbling.

When we turn to face our companions, Murphy and Juliana rush to hug us. Dad and the others are stunned. It's the first time they've seen us do this. I hope fixing the other artifacts will be this easy.

54
STORM

I t doesn't take long before we've slowed to a shuffle going up the steep path. The only sound is labored breathing when Wolf calls a halt. The only one not winded is Jaina. We each slide down the wall and sit where we are. At this rate, it'll take hours to get back, and we still have two more artifacts to get to.

I turn to my sister sitting next to me. "Juliana, do you think we could lift them all the way to the top if we work together?"

"Sure," she says. "I'll start."

A cushion of air lifts me a few inches off the ground. Sky's eyes widen as she rises in the air, and one-by-one, the others are sitting on the same cushion.

"Whoa," Al grunts. "Are you sure this won't exhaust you?"

"When I get tired, my brother will take over. Why, Al? Would you rather walk?"

He grins and shakes his head. "Let the magic carpet ride begin."

Everyone grows quiet as we float up along the path. Juliana sets us down after an hour or so. "Your turn," she says.

By the time we reach the top, everyone is rested except for me. I could sleep for a week. Sky takes my hand, her love and approval energizing me.

We get to our feet and meet Jayman in the big cave. He activates the portal and stays in the cavern while we run into the desert, where Baran's ship materializes. The cars from Jack's compound are gone, driven back by his crew members after they dropped us off here this morning. Henry had used his influence with the Incan priests to keep tourists away from the Stargate, so no one is here to witness the Allaran ship. Our next stop is Ushuaia.

Jaina takes Baran aside and gives him a set of coordinates, speaking loudly enough for me to hear. Jack is on his phone, standing nearby, and I turn to Pax.

"Do you know where she's taking us?"

"Does it matter? We're going to the artifact."

"Probably not, but something is off. It's too easy."

"Relax, Ryder. We're due for something easy, don't you think?"

Once aboard the craft, we arrive in minutes. Baran drops us off in a dry ravine full of rocks and cracked ground. He hands Charles a large pack and takes off. I'll never get tired of watching alien spacecraft disappear.

"Who's hungry?" Charles asks as he pulls sandwiches and water bottles out of the pack. We make short work of the food, shove the wrappings and empty bottles back into the pack and leave it there to pick up on the way back.

"Where's the opening?" I ask, scanning the solid walls of the ravine. A shadow moves overhead, and a blinding flash of light blasts a jagged line in the cliff in front of me, knocking me off my feet. The sun disappears behind a giant triangular silhouette. How did the Dracans find us?

Laser bolts sizzle and flash from several of the nozzles at the apex of the craft. One of the cannons on the edge grows brighter, this one facing my side of the ravine.

I scan the area for our people, spot Jewel crumpled in the middle of the gully with Pax next to her and lift them to the relative safety of a cluster of rocks. Where is Sky? Rage and panic set in when I can't find her. Ice invades my guts and my stomach clenches in fear I've only experienced twice before. The cannon is about to fire.

There. What I thought was a rock squirms and rolls over. I bring her to me, still curled in the fetal position, setting her down under a ledge. No one else is left in the open.

I let the rage take over. Careful to leave sheltering rocks in place, I pick up every grain of loose sand, every unused rock and brush in the ravine and aim the lot at the firing ports, filling the cannon first. This worked once. More debris flies up on the other side of the craft, and I know Juliana's caught on. It wobbles and tilts as if it's trying to get away. The crew tries one last shot at us. It ends them. The explosion contained inside the vessel burns everything.

"Watch out!" Murphy shouts, as the disabled ship drops. I hold it upright while Juliana does the same from the other side. It spears the ground and remains wedged there like a broken ninja star.

"Sky? Are you alright?" I run to the ledge where I left her and wrap my arms around her. She's trembling.

"I'll be fine," she says, but her fear pierces me. "I don't sense Jewel or Pax. What's happened to them?"

"Let's find out." Afraid she might have been hurt in the blast, I float her next to me until we reach the rocks where I hid the two of them. Wolf and the others examine the fallen ship and I know everyone else is fine.

The hiding place is empty.

"Pax!" I shout. "Jewel! Where are you?" The others come running, and her dad is the first to reach us.

"I can't feel them," Sky wails.

"Where did you last see them?" Charles asks, his voice sounding shaky.

"I floated them here," I tell him. "They were both unconscious, but they could have come to and moved somewhere safer."

"Where's Jaina?" Al's rough voice sounds strained. Blood drips from a gash on his head, and he looks like he's about to be sick.

"She stood near this spot just before the attack," Charles says. "Maybe there's a hidden doorway around here. If they entered a Dracan tunnel, it would block their connection to Sky."

His quiet voice brings the level of panic down enough for us to catch a breath and start searching. We need to find them quickly. This might not be the last Dracan ship, and there's not much debris to work with if another attacks us.

55
PAX

W here are we? I sniff and locate Jewel, but I can't reach her mind. She must still be unconscious. I crawl to her and pull her head into my lap. Warm stickiness in her hair smells like copper. Blood. I find a cut on top of her head and press my hand against it to stop the bleeding.

Where is everybody? By the smell, I know we're underground, but even with my guard down, I'm not picking up the normal subtleties I usually get. We must be in a Dracan tunnel.

I hear a scrabbling sound from my left.

"Who's there?" I call out, moving into a crouch. I'm woozy, but trust my training will kick in if I need it.

"Jaina," her voice sounds weak.

"What are we doing here, Jaina?"

"It's the way to the artifact, but the others didn't make it inside."

"Why not? Let them in." Why would she have left them out? What's going on here?

"Do you remember what happened out there? A Dracan ship attacked us. You and Jewel were knocked unconscious, and I dragged you in here."

Another Dracan attack? They'll need my help.

"Jaina, please let me out of here. You stay with Jewel and protect her. I have to help the others."

She sounds regretful when she answers, "I can't. If the Dracans are outside, I can't let them know of the artifact and its location."

"Does this tunnel lead directly to the artifact?"

"No. Farther down, a trapdoor opens to hidden stairs that lead to a shaft. The artifact is in a cave about a mile deep, like the other."

"So, if you open this door, even if the Dracans are outside, they wouldn't know how to reach the artifact. Correct?"

"Perhaps, but they know we are here. We must assume they know about the artifact and will search until they find the trap door. They are persistent."

It's obvious she isn't thinking clearly. Jewel and I can't fix it by ourselves.

"Do you remember what you said to Al? Unless the four of us get to the artifact to fix it, there won't be any reason to keep its location secret because there won't be a planet to protect."

She grunts as she gets to her feet. "You're right. When I open the wall, if your friends are still alive, we have a chance. If not, all hope is lost anyway. Shield your eyes."

I close mine and put a hand over Jewel's while the wall rolls aside. When I open them, backlit shadows fill the doorway, and I hear my sister's cry, "Thank God!"

"Are they gone?" I ask. I'm not willing to take Jewel outside if there's any chance they're still after her.

Storm gently lifts her from the floor but doesn't touch her. "They're gone. She needs attention. We don't have enough light in here."

I follow her outside and watch as her father presses a clean handkerchief to her head. In a few moments, she opens her eyes.

"Pax? What happened?"

Sky tells her while I take Storm aside.

"How did they know where we are? All I can think of is, someone in our group has been feeding them information."

Storm twists his mouth and glares at me. "I told you I was uneasy when I overheard Jaina giving Baran the coordinates. Do you think she's the one?"

"No. She's loyal to the artifacts and knows what's at stake. If you heard her, anyone else might have, too. It has to be Al or Jack, but since we don't know which one, we'll have to watch both."

"Whoever it is, I want to take him down," Storm says.

I turn away from his hard eyes and smell the sharp stink of his fury. I would not want to be at the receiving end when he unleashes it.

We're wasting time. Jewel's voice in my head is like cool rain. The day is more than half-gone. If we get this artifact done, we'll still have to wait until tomorrow to fix the last of the three. I wonder how many more we'll need to find before our task is done. I'm tired of tunnels and darkness.

Jaina again takes the lead, and the rest of us follow with our headlamps turned on.

"If we can get by with just two lights, we should turn off the rest to conserve batteries. The way things have been going, we don't want to risk being caught in the dark," Dad says. We should have thought of this in the first place.

"Jaina and I can see well in the dark," Murphy says. "If necessary, we will lead you to safety."

"Nevertheless," Wolf says, "Dylan's idea is sound. Jewel, you're in the middle, and Al is near the rear. You two keep yours on, and the rest of us will go dark. Two lamps will be enough."

You're the light of my life, I tease her, and she elbows me.

I'm the light of everyone's life right now, she answers. I can't help laughing out loud.

We would have walked past the trap door if Jaina didn't know exactly where it is. There are no discernible seams or handle visible in the dim light, and I seriously doubt the Dracans would have found it. It opens when she hums a series of nearly inaudible notes, revealing a set of metal stairs. We descend to another tunnel, not built by Dracans. I sniff and wish I hadn't. Adrenaline leaves its own stench once it wears off, and I get a good whiff of the aftermath of our run-in with the alien ship before I put my guard up.

We soon arrive at a square shaft topped with a rig of pulleys attached to a free-swinging platform with a narrow handrail.

"I'm not getting on that thing," Jack says. "It isn't safe."

"You forget Juliana and I can hold it up if something happens," Storm assures him.

"Sure," he replies. "As long as you're conscious. Anything can happen."

"The young ones will stand in the middle," Jaina directs. "The rest of us will surround them. My people have maintained this lift, and it will hold us all."

She steps on first, and sets it to swinging, just enough for bumpers along the edges to bounce it off the side an inch or two. Al follows and stands next to her. He tests the handrail and grunts, turning to lean against it. If he's satisfied, we're good to go.

We file in, and Jaina presses a button. We start a smooth descent, faster than a mechanical elevator but not as fast as one in a high rise.

"I didn't see any wires," Charles says. "How do you get electricity in here, and where are the lights?"

"We use Terra's electromagnetism, free and plentiful energy. My people don't need lights."

It makes sense. They couldn't have anticipated our mission, or our need for light, when the artifact was buried here. I pull Jewel close. This mission can't end quickly enough for me.

The artifact chamber isn't far from the shaft, and, again, we're met by a group of Mantoids. Juliana takes her position and steadies the artifact while we approach it. They vibrate the force field away, and it comes to a stop, with the same symbols facing us as before. It's still a mystery why they all do that, but there must be a significant reason. Do the symbols describe us, somehow?

We lay hands on it, send it the love that builds among us, and receive its gratitude. Another one done. How many more are there?

5 6
JEWEL

The Allaran ship is waiting when we emerge from the tunnel exhausted and more than ready for a shower and a good meal. Some of Baran's crew are examining the hull of the downed Dracan ship. He's scowling as he greets us. I'm surprised six more Sentinels are hovering overhead. Why did I assume they only had one for each of us? We could be so far from civilization that no one will ever find the wreck, but satellites will surely spot it eventually. I wonder how they're going to get rid of it before it happens.

"You are far more powerful than we imagined, Storm. We assumed your powers didn't work against Dracan technology. How did you do this?"

Storm's aura shoots out blood red with black lightning streaks. He doesn't like Baran at all. "Juliana helped," he says, without elaborating.

Baran nods and turns away, leading us to the portal beam. As soon as we're settled in our bubble seats, my eyes fall shut. I don't open them again until Pax shakes me awake.

"Let's go, Jewel."

The Sentinel had dropped us off in the courtyard of Jack's compound on Lake Titicaca. Jack's assistant Henry urges us to hurry inside, where the smell of food revives me long enough to eat my fill of the delicious Peruvian meal.

Juliana, Sky, and I are assigned to a room on the main floor. I barely glance at it as I stumble toward one of the three beds and crash. Tomorrow is another day.

∽

I SHIVER in my borrowed down jacket. The seasons are reversed in the southern hemisphere, and Fall comes early at this altitude. It's nearly April, already warm at home and cooling down here. I long for home.

The sun has cleared the mountaintops, and it's promising to be a clear day. We won't be outside long enough to get sunburned, but it's easy to see why the Peruvians wear wide-brimmed hats. We're closer to the sun at this elevation than we are back home.

It's nearly ten in the morning when we reach the Sungate. Again, the Incan priests have reserved the ruins for us, leaving tourists to wait out of sight until they're allowed in.

"Is there some ritual to get it open?" Jack asks Henry, who is staring at the carving of Viracocha over the door.

"Jayman will open it from the other side," he answers. "Any moment now."

The space in the door turns blue, and we run into it, following Henry. Why is he here? Too many people know about the artifacts as it is.

We land in a smaller chamber than the cave at the Stargate, and Jayman greets us with a booming laugh.

"Henry, my friend, it is good to see you again so soon. All of you are welcome here."

Dad takes Jack aside, and I hear him ask, "Is there a reason you've let Henry in on this? Can he be trusted to keep the artifacts secret?"

Jack replies, "I trust him with my life, Charles. He won't talk."

"Before we proceed," Jayman says, "I must have your word you will reveal nothing of what you see here outside the gate. You may not take anything out with you. The time is not yet for the world to know of this place. Do you agree?"

Everyone nods, but his eyes narrow.

"Sky Fire Hair, will you assess each one to be sure they are being truthful?"

Sky steps forward and says, "I'm not like Gienika. I'm not a truth-sayer. I can only sense emotions, and everyone here is nervous. The artifact needs us. We should go."

He nods and leads the way, but the stoop of his shoulders tells me he senses something is wrong.

We go through a series of corridors lined with recessed lights near the ceiling. After all the tunnels, this seems an odd way to get to a hidden artifact, but I'm happy for the light for as long as we have it.

He stops at an open doorway and turns to us.

"You must traverse the city to get to the passageway you seek. Jaina, please take the lead. I must remain here until you return after your successful venture. The temptation to wander and explore will be great, especially for you, Jack. Do not stray from the path. The city is full of traps. Please do not attempt to take anything."

A severe frown makes him appear much older and sadder than the giant we know. I couldn't see his aura under the Dracan dome, but I do now. If the swampy brown color is any indication, he's deeply worried about us.

"We must go now," Jaina says, taking one of his fingers in her hand. "I will take responsibility, Jayman."

He nods and turns away while we follow her past him into a vast cavern. We move along an avenue wide enough for five or six people to walk side-by-side. A squat pyramid at the end of the road gleams golden in light which appears to have no origin. Walls embedded with sparkling gems and topped with gold spikes line the avenue. Evenly spaced alcoves hold priceless statues of Incan deities. I wonder what Jack makes of all this.

I find him staring at one of the statues before he moves on to keep pace with the rest of us. Even his aura is gold. I'm worried about him.

The light itself is different, Pax. Do you see it? I ask.

It's more yellow, I think, a reflection off the gold. Warmer. This reminds me of one of Mad Ludwig's castles in Germany. All the gold leaf gave me a headache. It's ostentatious and a bit nauseating. Did you know he spent all of Bavaria's treasury on the castle and stayed there only a few days in his lifetime?

If it's anything like this, I can understand why. My head hurts. I can't wait to get to the other side of the city.

Keep an eye on Al and Jack. Storm and I think one of them told the Dracans where we were. If they did, then we might have a problem when we're done here.

That would explain why we were attacked twice since Shaula disappeared. Are they after me, or is there something else they want?

When we reach the steps to the pyramid, Jaina veers right, but Henry stops.

"I must go in. I have heard Viracocha's voice."

Jaina walks back and puts her hand on his arm. "Henry, Viracocha's voice is in a chamber along this path. You know our charges must repair it. There will be time to visit the temple when we return. Please be patient."

He nods and reluctantly turns away from the steps, but not before shooting me a glare that sends a shaft of ice through my heart. He hates me. Why?

JEWEL

The soft light in the cool chamber is a relief from the unrelenting yellow glare of the city. Jaina leads us into another tunnel and Storm's groan echoes down the line. If we ever finish saving the world, I will never go inside another cave or tunnel again.

This one is blissfully short, and the artifact bobs in the center of a round cave. Jaina's people are already there, as before. I wonder if they have living quarters nearby like the watchers had back home.

"We are at the third and last artifact in our charge," she says. "When you have repaired this one, I will show you a map of the remaining tetrahedra on Terra. You should know what you are up against."

I'm not sure I want to know, Pax says.

Me neither, I respond, *but once we do, we can come up with a plan to make it easier.*

That's doubtful, considering how deep in the ground they are.

Let's concentrate on fixing this one. We'll worry about the rest of them later.

We take our positions and wait for the artifact to stop spinning. I watch for the familiar symbol of the coyote, star, and butterfly to stop in front of me, and when it does, I reach out to touch Storm's hand while Pax covers mine on the symbol.

Love is an energy flowing through our arms and sparking from our hands to the artifact. We feed it, and it sends back a grateful burp before pushing us away to spin its new force field. How odd. I suddenly feel like a mother with a happy baby. I understand Triton's parental emotions over his "egg."

Jaina, who rarely smiles, is grinning as she gestures us back to her.

"My people thank you, Star Children, for saving our part of the world. Your job is not nearly complete but know we are at your service. And now, please follow me. I'll show you where the rest of the artifacts are."

She takes us to a closed wooden door on the other side of the chamber. The Mantoids hum and it opens to reveal another door, this one divided into four quadrants, each solid gold with familiar symbols etched into the panels and outlined with gemstones.

"Our symbols," Sky says in a soft voice.

"If Creator put the tetrahedra in the earth to act as organs, then he must have put the symbols on them," Dad says, "and they must be extraordinarily significant."

Dylan adds, "The Native Americans had interpretations for them. Do you think the Creator spoke directly to them?"

"He speaks to the Allarans if what they say is true," Wolf says. "We believe he still speaks to us today, but we hear poorly."

The Mantoids open the golden door, and we enter a room with a giant blue globe slowly spinning in the center, floating in white light. A fine silver net with triangular openings covers it. I recognize the power grid the Allarans showed us the first time we rode in their ship. This is Terra, our planet. Continents gradually appear to float by as my eyes adjust to the brightness.

"Watch," Jaina says. The floor pulsates under my feet and the air trembles, but the globe takes all my attention as the net fades into the background while land masses slowly come into sharp relief. I make out the contours of mountain ranges, lakes and rivers. The oceans sepa-rate into stained-glass blues and greens, and it becomes apparent we're looking at the planet's surface beneath the depths. Islands stand out, and we watch them become three-dimensional, right along with the rest of the lands. I'm mesmerized by the brilliant greens of the rainforest and the multiple shades of yellow and brown in the deserts.

Then the colors fade, and we see red dots appear. A dozen, then a hundred, then hundreds of red pinpoints glow around the globe, like a patterned rash.

"This is where we are," she says, pointing to a spot in South America. Three points of light sparkle like diamonds.

When the North American continent comes around again, she points at a diamond in the Bahamas, and another in the southeastern United States. Our artifacts. The ones we've repaired. My stomach drops.

"The red dots?" Wolf asks.

"The rest of the artifacts," she says.

Blood rushes from my head and pools in my feet, and I'm overcome with a sense of loss and hopelessness. There are only four of us, and a gazillion of them. We might as well die right here. Our planet is doomed.

Jewel. I hear the despair in Pax's voice. *Stay with me.*

I reach for his hand and try to pull myself together. *Give me a moment. I'll be okay.* I won't, but the planet isn't dead, yet.

We'll be alright, I tell him, but he doesn't believe me. I don't believe it, either, but we can't stop living. Then it hits me. Sky is projecting.

Pax, your sister. Can you help her? If she rallies, we all will. Get Storm to help.

I tap my wristband and tie in with the others just as Pax is saying ... *not lost. If we couldn't do it, there wouldn't have been a prophecy. Snap out of it, Sky, and help us.*

The load lightens a little and I pour positive thoughts out to the others. I think of Sequoia's baby and Sky's prophecy. They have a future. We have a future. I picture the red lights turning to diamonds, sparkling like stars within the planet. I picture Sky's enthusiasm and show her the colors of her aura when she's happy.

Henry begins to chant and the Mantoids hum tonelessly. Al yawns as if he's merely been asleep, and Jack groans. Juliana and Murphy are wrapped in a hug, his face buried in her hair.

Thank you, Sky says, sounding stronger. I get to my feet. That's more like it.

"I'm sorry," Jaina says with a sad note in her voice. "I didn't know it would affect you this way. Until now, your thinking was limited by your experience. Now you know the magnitude of the task. Perhaps your thinking will expand to find the solution we all need."

"Jaina," Dad says, "can you show us the power grid overlaying the dots?" The tone of the hum changes slightly, and the net moves into the foreground, translucent enough to reveal the light of the dots beneath it.

I spot it as soon as he does. The dots are concentrated at the junctions of the ley lines.

An idea forms in my head, but I wouldn't know how to accomplish it. I'll talk it over with the others when we're safely out of here.

"I wish to return to the temple pyramid," Henry announces, moving toward the door. "I must complete my mission."

"Mission?" Jack asks. "What are you talking about, Henry? You came with us to see for yourself what the kids are doing."

"You are wrong, Dr. Austin. Viracocha has called me here. I will show you."

Jaina leads the way out to the cavern where the top of the pyramid appears to brush the ceiling. Most of us sit on the lower stairs and wait while Henry climbs one steep step after another, after refusing to allow any of us to accompany him. I'm relieved to have time to think. Murphy and Juliana find a bit of privacy near a fountain we passed, and Jack takes a walk, exploring the nearby buildings and alcoves, careful not to enter any. I'm glad he remembers Jayman's warning about traps.

Dad and Dylan have pulled Jaina aside in an animated conversation, but they speak too quietly for me to hear what they're saying. Jaina mostly listens and nods now and then, while the men map out a plan, using their hands to illustrate. I'm too tired to join them, drifting off until a shout from the pyramid startles me back to full awareness.

"I have found it!" Henry practically dances down the steps a lot faster than he climbed them. He's waving something golden in the air over his head.

When he reaches us, he holds the object in front of him, and we crowd in to see what it is.

The golden disk is the right size to fit into the hole in the door of the Stargate. A face strongly resembling the one on the Sungate stares out at us etched into the gold, surrounded by the same sun symbol on the artifacts.

"The sun disk," Jack says, more somber than I've ever seen him.

"You cannot remove it from here," Jaina says. "Nothing leaves here. You all agreed."

"No. I did not agree, and this belongs to my people. Viracocha sent me to find it. He has promised it to us."

"Henry..." Jack stands a foot taller than the priest, but the little man stares up at him defiantly. "When Queen Meissa paid us a visit, you called her Viracocha. Do you remember Meissa?"

He shakes his head and says, "Not the queen. Viracocha himself came to me. He promised the sacred disk in return for..." His voice trails off, and he glares at me again.

Jaina transforms so quickly, she seems to snap into her Mantoid form. She spreads her serrated arms out and moves toward the cowering Peruvian. She reaches for the sun disk, but he hugs it tightly to his body. The claw moves up to his neck, and he hunches his shoulders up by his ears. I know praying mantis females sometimes eat the heads of their mates. Is she about to snap his head off? I turn away, feeling sick.

Storm slides in between her and Henry, and she backs off.

"Why don't we take this to Jayman," Wolf says, moving to stand next to his nephew. "Would you agree, Jaina? Henry will abide by his decision in the matter, or he'll face all of us."

She nods and turns away, transforming back to human form.

"Jayman will judge."

58

STORM

How could you risk your life like that? Do you have any idea what the mantis could have done to you? Sky's furious panic makes me itch to fight or run.

Yeah, Pax's voice breaks in. *What were you thinking, Ryder?* He sounds angry. His sister's fear is affecting him.

Leave him alone. Jewel comes to my defense. *He's a hero and deserves your gratitude. He saved us all from getting splattered by that creep's blood.*

Wolf is the hero, Jewel. Storm's an idiot. Dang, she's mad.

What do you mean by "creep?" What's wrong, Jewel? Pax usually communicates with her directly, but I'm glad he's using our link. I want to know, too.

Did any of you notice how he glares at me? Did you catch what he was implying when he didn't finish his sentence? He said Viracocha promised the sun disk in exchange for something. For what? For me?

I break in. *Is he talking about Shaula?*

Or someone allied with him, if he's really on that island somewhere else in the universe, Pax says.

I'm thinking Jack and Al may not have tipped the Dracans off about Jewel's whereabouts after all. Jack would have kept in contact with his assistant, wouldn't he? Henry would have known where we were.

I'll bet Henry's the traitor, and not Jack or Al, he says, his thoughts mirroring mine.

Maybe Jayman can get the truth out of him, Sky says. *He's afraid, but also strongly determined and full of hate. I'm sorry, Jewel, but it's directed at you.*

Jack turns around and takes one more look before we leave the City of Gold. I hope he gets a chance to televise an episode when he's allowed to 'discover' it.

Jayman stands at his full height, glaring down at us like a vengeful warrior as we enter the last chamber. His voice thunders and his eyes flash fire.

"One of you has removed something from the city. The whispers of our forefathers reverberate with your crime. The air quivers in rage. Stand forward, thief, and receive your sentence."

Henry hunches over his prize, clutching it close to his chest, staggering as Jaina pushes him forward to stand in front of the giant. He stares at the ground, silent as his employer moves forward to stand next to him. I admire Jack's courage.

He says, "Jayman, you remember. Henry helped you when we found you injured. Please hear him out, then decide what you should do."

Jayman lowers his voice to a rumble and replies, "You were good to me, Jack, but this is a grave offense, punishable by death or banishment. I warned you, but your man ignored me. Normally, I would have sentenced him by now, but for you, I will allow Henry to explain his actions. If I judge him guilty, then I must carry out the sentence."

"Understood," Jack says, bowing his head. He shoves Henry in the side and says, "Speak, or die right now."

Henry's face is granite, and his eyes have the fanatical gleam of a cult member, or an Incan priest, minus the feathers and gold skirt they wear in pictures. I imagine him carrying a bloody machete after lopping off some poor sacrifice's head.

He speaks in his language, and Jaina translates. I didn't know she spoke whatever it is he speaks.

"The Sun Disk was stolen from my people, and I have been charged by Viracocha himself to return it." It takes a moment for Jaina to repeat what he said. Jayman understands him, but for our sake, he waits patiently for her to finish.

"Viracocha?" Jayman roars. "He is gone. You have been speaking to mere men, members of an alien race who wish to bring humanity to an end. You believe Viracocha created mankind and every living thing on Earth. Why would he wish to destroy his creation?" Henry understands English better than he speaks it, so Jaina doesn't bother translating to him.

"You are wrong, giant. He speaks to me. He would never destroy his creation," Henry answers, sucking in his gut and squaring his shoulders in defiance. "His bride has escaped him, and he has given me instructions to bring her back. I will deliver her to him. The return of the Sun Disk to my people is my reward."

Jayman asks, "Are you talking about Jewel?"

Henry nods and turns to glare at her.

"Then you have failed. The one you believe is Viracocha is the Dracan traitor, Shaula. If indeed the Sun Disk was stolen from your people, it will be returned in time, but not now, and not by you. You, Henry, are hereby sentenced to banishment from your people."

I watch the blood drain from Henry's face. I met his family on the floating islands. Sharp pain stabs my gut at the memory of losing my family.

"Terra will not hold you. You will live among the stars, never to set foot on your home world again." Jayman's eyes grow sad. "Because we are merciful, we offer you an alternative. You may choose a quick death over banishment. The choice is yours."

Among the stars? I wonder if they have something like the International Space Station for prisoners, or a wormhole connection to a prison world. Nothing would surprise me at this point.

Henry draws himself up and answers in English, "I have honor with my people. I am a priest. I serve Dr. Austin well. I serve Viracocha. I die." He starts chanting while Jaina transforms into a Mantoid and turns him back toward the City of Gold.

"Wait," Sky calls out. I solidify the air in front of Jaina to stop her. I'm glad I'm not the cause of her pain this time. Jaina whips around and spreads her arms, glaring at me.

Sky turns to Jayman. "He doesn't believe he's serving a liar, but it isn't his fault. This is Shaula's doing. Henry is a victim, and the disk was stolen from his people. Please, Jayman, isn't there another way?"

Jayman hunches his shoulders and turns away from us. He's quiet for a few minutes, and when he turns back, he straightens to his full height and says, "I will speak to Gienika and Queen Jaide. Perhaps we can hold him until the traitor is captured or killed. If Henry is then convinced the Dracan is not his deity, perhaps they will show him mercy and return him to his people."

"Thank you, my friend," Jack says. "I owe you for this."

"Nothing has been decided yet, Jack. The others may not agree, but I will try to convince them. You and Henry saved my life. If they agree, then it will be up to Henry to decide his own fate."

Jaina nods, and I remove the barrier so she can lead her prisoner away.

Dad throws his arm across Jack's shoulders and says, "Jayman, please let us out of here."

In moments, we're outside the Sungate. No one speaks as we walk to the parking lot, where Jack's crew have been waiting for hours. We stand back while he gathers them to tell them about Henry. Their voices rise in anger, but they compose themselves as we approach.

Two of the men glare at Jewel and I wonder how many were in on Henry's scheme to turn her over to the Dracans. We'll have to guard her, even after we get home. While that monster is alive, Jewel is in danger.

Baran and Chara meet us at the compound, ready to summon the ship after we gather our things and say goodbye to Jack.

"I'm sorry for what Henry did," Jack says.

Charles grabs his shoulders and looks him in the eye. "You've been a great help to us, Jack. We're indebted to you. As soon as we get the all-clear from the Allarans and Dracans, you'll have the exclusive story.

"The problem is," Jack says, a wry smile turning up one corner of his mouth, "the world will most likely end before that ever happens."

The ship appears over the courtyard, and we float up into it. I hope Jack doesn't spill the beans early. I'd hate to see what would happen to him if he did.

59

SKY

"How many are up there?" I ask Jewel, who's gently pushing the porch swing back and forth with her foot. I'm curled up against the armrest, watching her watch the sky and enjoying the movement. The weather has finally cleared, after three days of solid rain left the forest dripping and smelling like ozone. Now the air smells of grilling burgers and fry bread.

"Five," she answers, "as I expected. I wish you could see the way the sun glints off them in rainbows."

"Even if the Sentinels were visible, no one would see rainbows the way you do."

I'm wrapped in a contented cocoon, safe for the moment and happy we made it to our eighteenth birthday. Technically, Jewel's isn't until tomorrow, but only because of the difference in time zones.

I reach out, curious if Shaula's influence is still affecting her. Thankfully, her connection to my brother is like a living band of joy between them. Since no one knows how having two marks will affect her, I'm hoping her love for my brother breaks her tie to that snake.

I'm happy for them, but not so much for myself. I thought Storm was finally coming around, but he's thrown up the wall again.

To distract myself, I start counting the cars parked in the driveway and along the road leading to Jewel's house. People mill around the tents set up throughout the meadow, and a group of young kids smacks a ball around with a stick, shouting and chasing each other in a mock game of stickball. The delicious smells are making me hungry. Most of the town must be here. Who knew our birthday would attract so much attention?

The door slams open and Storm announces, "They're ready for us." We get up and follow him inside to be greeted by Pax and our families for a moment of privacy before we join the others in the meadow. Sequoia hugs me, and her baby sends me happy waves.

"I love you, too, Little One," I say to her, snug inside her mother.

"Okay, gather around," Analiese commands. "The four of you get close to the cake." I don't know how she managed to squeeze eighteen candles on the small cake she baked for the family, but when she lights it, and everyone sings the expected Happy Birthday chorus, we blow out the blaze together. Love binds us closer than merely a group of friends with a common purpose. We are family, including our half-Dracan Murphy.

Four sheet cakes, cut into small squares, line the breakfast counter, ready to serve the crowd outside, but Jewel's mom takes the small one into the kitchen to cut into slices. We move into the living room, where Pax, Storm, Jewel, and I share the couch and Murphy and Juliana share one of the recliners. Dad has his arm around Mom by the picture window, and Wolf pulls up a chair next to the other recliner, where Sequoia squirms a little. She's in her seventh month of pregnancy and has trouble getting comfortable. Baby is asleep.

When each of us has some cake, Analiese and my parents take seats, and Charles stands in front of the window, holding a small box in his hand. He clears his throat, and addresses Juliana.

"I've been working on this since we discovered your existence, Juliana. You've been gracious about the others communicating telepathically when you couldn't. Now, I want to officially welcome you to our family as a fully-functioning member with this."

He hands her the box. She's delighted as she opens it and pulls out a fitness monitor set in a cream-colored wristband. Murphy helps her fasten it to her wrist, and she turns to hug Charles.

"Do you know what it's for?" he asks her.

She nods and turns in a circle, holding up her wrist to show it off.

"You won't be able to remove it, and neither will anyone else except for Wolf and Sequoia, who have the code. The kids will show you how to use it. Your personal number is five, and Murphy's is six."

Murphy? Analiese hands her husband a second box, very pleased with herself. Murphy's face speaks volumes. His eyes brim with joyful tears as he reaches for the box.

"Murphy, when your mother and Analiese developed the serum for Jewel and Pax, they discovered a way to bypass the Dracan DNA in you and other hybrids. It made it possible for me to design a wristband for you, too, and, like Jaina's clothing, it will conform to your wrist in whichever form you take. Jewel told me about the colors of your scales, and you'll find the wristband blends in and becomes nearly invisible when you're in your Dracan body."

Murphy takes the box and handles it as if it's a religious relic. He opens it and pulls out a scaled band, like snakeskin, but with light blue scales, each blending into a yellow center. Charles fastens it around his wrist.

"Will it work in my Dracan form?" he asks.

"We won't know until you try it. The others don't work around the D-tech, but yours might since we've incorporated what we've learned."

"D-tech?" Pax asks.

"Dracan technology," Murphy answers. "It's a nickname."

"Analiese and I have the code to yours, Murphy. These wristbands are highly classified. Not even the government knows about them. It's imperative they never find out, so you cannot tell anyone. Is that clear?"

"Clear," Murphy and Juliana say at the same time. Their eyes spark when they glance at each other, and I know Juliana loves and trusts him. That's enough for me.

"Jewel and Sky, please show Juliana how it works. Storm and Pax, you work with Murphy. Remember how it was when you first had yours, and don't overwhelm them."

Jewel and I jump up and hug them both, while the boys hug Storm's sister and slap Murphy on the back. We show them how to open the communal channel, and Juliana sits abruptly.

Can you read my thoughts? she asks, her mental voice sounding a little nervous.

Only what you send, I assure her, and we spend the next half hour practicing and reassuring her.

The smell of multiple grills hits us as soon as we open the door to join the celebration outside. A cheer goes up, and we wave like royalty before running down the steps and into the field. Juliana and Murphy click into and out of our common link. I don't mind. I remember how amazing it was to learn to communicate with our minds.

A group of women head into the house and emerge with trays of cake, which they place on tables. Juliana, Jewel, and I head over to one of the tents and fill our plates with real food. We've had our cake.

The six of us find a tarp someone had dropped on the ground and sit in a semi-circle until the sun sets. My heart aches as I watch Jewel and my brother snuggle close together. They're getting to be as mushy as Juliana and Murphy. Storm goes off somewhere by himself, so I sit cross-legged between the two couples, alone and miserable.

"Stop projecting, Sky. You're bringing everyone down," Storm says as he moves in beside me.

"Where've you been?" I ask, irritation making me sound snarky.

"I got you some lemonade." He hands me a cup of fresh-squeezed juice, with lemon slices floating in it.

"Come here," he says, pulling me close. His arm warms my shoulders, and I squirm closer. He kisses my head but stares straight ahead when I turn my face to him. Dang it.

A loud bang breaks the peace and the sky fills with bursts of color and light. Between explosions, I hear oohs and aahs from the people in the field. If the world is going to end soon, I want the memory of our eighteenth birthday to be my last thought.

60
PAX

ood morning, Juliana's cheery voice jars me out of Jewel's arms in my dream. I don't answer, giving myself a minute to stretch. I'm stiff and can't wait to get back to training. I'll ask Dad how soon we can start.

How is everyone? Murphy asks, sounding every bit as awake as Juliana.

Someone in the link yawns and starts a chain reaction. I didn't know until now a yawn can be contagious when it's mentally projected.

I'm up, Storm says. *Need coffee.*

I hear several echoes of "coffee" and close the link. I'll play with their new toy later. Sky went home with Jewel after the fireworks, and the rest of us went our separate ways. It's just as well. I was asleep before I hit the bed.

After I clean up and get dressed, I hear Murphy in the kitchen, talking to Mom. She's telling him about the day we met the watchers outside the sacred cave while he stares at her intently.

"Hi, Mom. I can take over and tell him the rest. He needs to practice using the wristband."

She hugs me, winks at Murph and heads downstairs to the office.

I open the communal link. *Juliana, you and Murphy never met the watchers, but they explained why the artifacts are dying. Only I don't get it. They said the Dracans had depleted the earth of minerals the tetrahedra need to survive.*

Murphy's indignation comes through loud and clear when he asks, *Did you see how many tetrahedra are scattered throughout the planet? There aren't nearly enough Dracan cities to deplete them of their resources.*

I agree, I say. Then I ask the question stewing at the back of my mind for some time now. *So, if mineral deprivation isn't killing them, then what is? We know love fixes them. Would it be logical to assume hatred is breaking them?*

Are you implying humans are at fault? Jewel sounds indignant, but resignation flows from her. This connection with her is amazing. If every couple had this, I guarantee there would be no divorces.

Not just humans, Sky answers. She must have given this some thought too. *We share the planet with two interplanetary races and at least three other intelligent races native to Terra. People have trouble accepting the differences in our own kind. Can you imagine the scale of conflict if they knew about the others?*

What I'm getting at, I say, *is if there were a way to stop the hatred, maybe the artifacts would repair themselves.*

Impossible, Murphy says. *You believe in Creator, don't you? Wouldn't he have united the races if it were possible? If he can't do it, what makes you think we can?*

The prophecies, I remind him. The more I think about them, the more excited I get. I hope I can convey my optimism to the rest.

Why us? If we're the four mentioned in the Cherokee prophecy, isn't there a chance we'll be successful? And what about the giants' prophecy about Fire Hair? She's the bridge. Do you remember what Meissa said to Sequoia?

Storm pipes in. *She said, "Your child will cross the bridge of hope, built by another to save the nations."* He remembers it word for word, probably because the child in question is his cousin.

There you have it, three prophecies, all pertaining to us. There must be a way to bring the races together and fix all the artifacts.

There may be a way to do it, and we won't have to unite all the races, Jewel says. Everything goes still. *I saw it when Jaina's people overlaid the red dots on the globe with the power grid.*

How? The question spoken through everyone's mind sounds like a shout in my head.

We use the ley lines, she says. *All we need is a way to communicate with all the artifacts at once.*

And how do we do that? Storm asks.

We use the Bridge, Sky answers. A sense of calm flows through the link. I'm afraid it's the calm before the coming storm about to tear the planet apart if we don't stop it.

Thank you, dear Reader, for reading this third book in the Tetrasphere series. If you enjoyed it, please leave a review on Amazon, or where you bought the book. Your positive energy could keep our planet in balance.

By now, you'll want to know whether they've saved the world or not, and if they did, how they did it! Continue the story in **Terra's Anthem, Tetrasphere Book 4**.

Just for you, I've included Chapter One. Read on and enjoy!

TERRA'S ANTHEM

TETRASPHERE – BOOK 4

One - Jewel Amaryllis Adams

I don't know why I'm standing in the meadow. I don't remember getting out of bed, putting on my jeans and sweatshirt, lacing up my sneakers. Nothing. But here I am, staring at the Dracan ship hovering in front of the trees.

My feet move of their own volition, pulled by an unseen force while tears pour down my cheeks unhindered. My gut clenches. Shaula, the Dracan who abducted and imprisoned me, stands in the light of the open portal, muscular arms crossed in front of his chest. His vile eyes gleam yellow.

My arms hang limp, and I can't move to tap on my wristband. I can't open the telepathic link to call out to my friends for help, but my connection with Pax is always open. In my head, I scream his name. *Pax!* I pray he's awake and can hear me. *Pax!*

Jewel, where are you? His love and panic change to rage at the reptilian he sees through my eyes.

Stop! He shouts it in my head, and I do. His pull is stronger than Shaula's, thank God.

Turn around, he says, and I do.

Now run!

I don't look back to check if Shaula is chasing me, but in moments his hold on me breaks. I glance back then and see the empty meadow. He's gone. For now.

Drained of energy, I sink to the ground, double over, and sob, remembering the horror of being Shaula's captive and the pain Pax went through to find and rescue me. Both have a claim on me now, but I only love Pax. It makes no difference to Shaula. He'll kill everyone I love to get to me.

Headlights signal Pax's car racing down the long driveway to my house. He's wasted no time in getting here. I push myself off the ground, meet him in the driveway and fall into his arms.

He holds me close and murmurs in my hair, "I'll kill him. If it takes my last breath, I'll free you from him. He's as good as dead."

My trembling subsides in the strength of his embrace. He kisses me deeply, pouring his love into the kiss.

Let's go inside. You're freezing.

I shake my head and answer, *I'm not cold. I'm afraid...for you.*

Together we walk to the house where I used to feel safe. No longer. Shaula can reach me anywhere.

The smell of baking muffins nauseates me, and I excuse myself to go to my room just as Sky comes out of hers. Pax's twin sister has been staying with us since we returned from the Bahamas, and I couldn't be happier. She's the sister I've always wished for.

She smiles at me, hugs her brother, and the two of them head toward the kitchen. His mental voice comforts me while I close the door behind me.

Get some rest. I'll be here when you need me.

The tears come more often, now. When we first returned from Peru, I was caught up in my new-found connection with Pax and in our birthday celebration. I didn't give Shaula a second thought. Now he's all I think of, even though our other problems are so much more pressing. If we don't solve them, the world will destroy itself, and Shaula won't matter anymore. Nothing will.

I see him in my mind's eye, with his dull scales, razor-sharp teeth, and those yellow eyes. Even the memory of the evil in them makes me shudder. He laughs as if he knows that I will eventually give in to him and lose everything and everyone I love. Pax. I could lose Pax. I'd rather lose my life.

My room is too confining, and I slip outside before anyone notices. The meadow in front of our house, now innocent and empty of threat, beckons me with its spring flowers and thousands of little critters going about their business. I step carefully to avoid harming a single creature, admiring the brightness of each life-force, and drinking in the millions of colors in the grass and flowers. Amid so much life, I'm alone with my thoughts for a brief time.

"Jewel?" Sky's voice calls from the front porch. I turn and wave, knowing it's useless to ignore her. Her flaming aura flows around her in streaks of crimson and yellow, indistinguishable at this distance from the fire of her long red hair. I expect to hear her voice in my mind, but she runs toward me instead of activating the link. As an empath, she must know I need to keep my thoughts to myself.

"May I walk with you?" she asks.

"Of course. I could use the company. Is Pax alright?"

"He's still eating and talking with your Mom," she answers, taking small, careful steps as she walks like I'm doing. She knows I can see much more than she does and respects my love for even the smallest animals, now scurrying away from us.

She sends a pulse of calm and says, "I thought the two of you were in constant mental contact."

"We can turn it off, like the link all of us have through Dad's wrist-bands. I guess I'm reluctant to talk to him right now, and he probably senses it."

"Yeah. For someone with the nose of a bloodhound, he can be sensitive to moods even when he isn't close enough to detect pheromones. I think being my twin has trained him." She laughs, and the mental picture of him with a dog's nose gets me laughing, too.

She taps her wristband, opening our private link. *When we talk like this, I know your mood better. You're deeply bothered. Is it Shaula?*

An involuntary shiver creeps up my spine. *He's close. He came to the meadow this morning but left when Pax broke his power over me. He won't give up, and I'm afraid for Pax and the rest of you if I don't go with him.*

Streaks of dark red shoot through her aura. Her anger is palpable. *We didn't risk our lives to rescue you from that monster just to have you give up and go back to him. How could you even think of doing that to Pax? He'd give his life for you in a heartbeat, and you know it.*

I know. The tears spill over again, and I swipe them away, annoyed at their intrusion. Before all this, I rarely cried about anything.

"Do you think he can hear your thoughts the way Pax can?" she asks aloud. She has stopped walking, and I turn to face her.

"I've been afraid to think about it, frankly," I say, the blood draining from my face. "What if he can hear my conversations with your brother? What if he can hear all of us through me? What if I'm betraying all of you?" A shudder races up my spine.

"It's a mess," I continue. "Not only do we have to figure out a way to fix millions of artifacts before the world blows itself up, but we also have to break Shaula's grip on me before he destroys us all." I can't control the burn of tears, and my gut churns with anger. I can't control anything anymore. Could I ever?

"Let's go inside," she says with a little shiver.

Something more than my problems is bothering her. She's projecting. "What is it, Sky? What's wrong?"

"Storm is troubled, and I think I know why. We need to get over there."

～

~

Don't stop now! Want to know if Pax can save Jewel and if all four can figure out how to save the world? Order your copy of **Terra's Anthem** today!

If you enjoyed **Voice of Viracocha**, please leave a review on Amazon, or where you bought the book. Your positive energy might help fix the millions of artifacts and keep our planet safe.

Visit my website www.ptlperrin.org for this and other books by P.T.L. Perrin. Or pick up **Terra's Anthem: Tetrasphere Book 4** at your favorite online retailer.

I love hearing from you! Please connect with me!

Amazon: www.amazon.com/author/ptlperrin

Facebook author page: www.facebook.com/PTLPerrin

Facebook page: www.facebook.com/AuthorPattyPerrin

Facebook Group: Patty's Book Pals

Email: ptlperrin8@gmail.com

~

ABOUT THE AUTHOR

Patty Perrin, (P.T.L. Perrin), grew up in Europe as a military brat, with no television and a huge imagination. Books were her entertainment and augmented her education in German, Italian and American schools overseas. She speaks several languages and enjoys the diversity of people and cultures.

She wrote the Teen/YA Scifi *TETRASPHERE* series as pure entertainment and to answer some of the unanswerable questions about our amazing universe. Why would the Creator of this vast universe limit intelligent life to one tiny speck of a planet? What if other inhabited planets are interacting with Earth?

Terra's Call, the first book of the tetralogy, was a finalist in the Royal Palm Literary Awards. *Triton's Call*, the second book, won third place.

Patty and her tennis-pro husband Bill are parents and grandparents of a fluid, constantly growing family. Happily married, they live in south Florida where they exercise bragging rights in the winter, and enjoy the long summers, and where Patty is writing books she would have enjoyed reading back when she didn't have television.

ALSO BY P.T.L. PERRIN

∼

TETRASPHERE Series

Terra's Call - Book 1

Triton's Call - Book 2

∼

www.ingramcontent.com/pod-product-compliance
Lightning Source LLC
Chambersburg PA
CBHW060623260626
47161CB00008B/2786